the boy who loved

DURJOY DATTA

Penguin
metro reads

PENGUIN METRO READS

USA | Canada | UK | Ireland | Australia
New Zealand | India | South Africa | China

Penguin Metro Reads is part of the Penguin Random House group of companies
whose addresses can be found at global.penguinrandomhouse.com

Published by Penguin Random House India Pvt. Ltd
7th Floor, Infinity Tower C, DLF Cyber City,
Gurgaon 122 002, Haryana, India

First published in Penguin Metro Reads by Penguin Random House India 2017

ISBN 9780143426578

Typeset in Bembo STD by Manipal Digital Systems, Manipal
Printed at Thomson Press India Ltd, New Delhi

www.penguin.co.in

To Avantika

1 January 1999

Hey Raghu Ganguly (that's me),
I am finally putting pen to paper. The scrunch of the sheets against the fanged nib, the slow absorption of the ink, seeing these unusually curved letters, is definitely satisfying; I'm not sure if writing journal entries to myself like a schizophrenic is the answer I'm looking for. But I have got to try.

My head's dizzy from riding on the sinusoidal wave that has been my life for the last two years. On most days I look for ways to die—the highest building around my house, the sharpest knife in the kitchen, the nearest railway station, a chemist shop that would unquestioningly sell twenty or more sleeping pills to a sixteen-year-old, a packet of rat poison—and on some days I just want to be scolded by Maa–Baba for not acing the mathematics exam, tell Dada how I will beat his IIT score by a mile, or be laughed at for forgetting to take the change from the bania's shop.

I'm Raghu and I have been lying to myself and everyone around me for precisely two years now. Two years since my best friend of four years died, one whose friendship I thought would outlive the two of us, engraved forever in the space–time continuum. But, as I have realized, nothing lasts forever.

Now lying to others is fine, everyone does that and it's healthy and advisable—how else are you going to survive the suffering in this cruel, cruel world? But lying to yourself? That shit's hard, that will change you, and that's why I made the resolution to start writing a journal on the first of this month,

1

what with the start of a new year and all, the last of this century. I must admit I have been dilly-dallying for a while now and not without reason. It's hard to hide things in this house with Maa's sensitive nose never failing to sniff out anything Dada, Baba or I have tried to keep from her. If I were one of those kids who live in palatial houses with staircases and driveways I would have plenty of places to hide this journal, but since I am not, it will have to rest in the loft behind the broken toaster, the defunct Singer sewing machine and the empty suitcases.

So Raghu, let's not lie to ourselves any longer, shall we?

Let's say the truth, the cold, hard truth and nothing else, and see if that helps us to survive the darkness. If this doesn't work and I lose, checking out of this life is not hard. It's just a seven-storey drop from the roof top, a quick slice of the wrist, a slip on the railway track, a playful ingestion of pills or the accidental consumption of rat poison away. But let's try and focus on the good.

Durga. Durga.

12 January 1999

Today was my first day at the new school, just two months before the start of the tenth-standard board exams. Why Maa–Baba chose to change my school in what's said to be one of the most crucial year in anyone's academic life is amusing to say the least—my friendlessness.

'If you don't make friends now, then when will you?' Maa said.

They thought the lack of friends in my life was my school's problem and had nothing to do with the fact that my friend had been mysteriously found dead, his body floating in the still waters of the school swimming pool. He was last seen with me. At least that's what my classmates believe and say.

Only I know the truth.

When Dada woke me up this morning, hair parted and sculpted to perfection with Brylcreem, teeth sparkling, talcum splotches on his neck, he was grinning from ear to ear. Unlike me he doesn't have to pretend to be happy. Isn't smiling too much a sign of madness? He had shown the first symptoms when he picked a private-sector software job over a government position in a Public Sector Undertaking which would have guaranteed a lifetime of unaccountability. Dada may be an IITian but he's not the smarter one of us.

'Are you excited about the new school, Raghu? New uniform, new people, new everything? Of course you're excited! I never quite liked your old school. You will make

3

new friends here,' said Dada with a sense of happiness I didn't feel.

'Sure. If they don't smell the stench of death on me.'

'Oh, stop it. It's been what? Over two years? You know how upset Maa–Baba get,' said Dada. 'Trust me, you will love your new school! And don't talk about Sami at the breakfast table.'

'I was joking, Dada. Of course I am excited!' I said, mimicking his happiness.

Dada falls for these lies easily because he wants to believe them. Like I believed Maa–Baba when they once told me, 'We really liked Sami. He's a nice boy.'

Sami, the dead boy, was never liked by Maa–Baba. For Baba it was enough that his parents had chosen to give the boy a Muslim name. Maa had more valid concerns like his poor academic performance, him getting caught with cigarettes in his bag, and Sami's brother being a school dropout. Despite all the love they showered on me in the first few months after Sami's death, I thought I saw what could only be described as relief that Sami, the bad influence, was no longer around. Now they use his name to their advantage. 'Sami would want you to make new friends,' they would say.

I let Maa feed me in the morning. It started a few days after Sami's death and has stuck ever since.

Maa's love for me on any given day is easily discernible from the size of the morsels she shoves into my mouth. Today the rice balls and mashed potatoes were humungous. She watched me chew like I was living art.

And I ate because I believe the easiest way to fool anyone into not looking inside and finding that throbbing mass of sadness is to ingest food. A person who eats well is not truly sad.

While we ate, Baba lamented the pathetic fielding placement of the Indian team and India's questionable foreign policy simultaneously, 'These bloody Pakistanis! They shoot our soldiers at the border and have the gall to send their cricketers for a friendly cricket series. Terrorists should have bombed the hotel the cricketers were staying in. At least we wouldn't lose cricket matches to these brutes,' said Baba in anger and frustration.

'It's a step in the right direction, Baba. If you have a problem with them, might I remind you that our captain is a Muslim as well?' said Dada.

'That's what I'm saying, Anirban, We were supposed to be a Hindu version of Pakistan, the holy land for all Hindus, and look what we are now! Secular! Bah! A nation of hypocrites. They might be . . .' said Baba, his voice trailing, eating up the abuses that bubbled at the back of his throat. '. . . But they respect and preserve their religious identity unlike us who bow down to the whims of the minorities here. I'm sure they laugh at us!'

'Not again, you two,' Maa interrupted, stuffing Dada's mouth with a comparatively smaller rice ball, cutting off the oft-repeated religiously charged conversation midway.

Baba left to mutter prayers to our Hindu gods, for our floundering cricket team to be led by Saurav Ganguly, a Bengali Hindu brahmin.

'Do well in school,' said Dada before he left.

Maa came to drop me to the bus stop and cried when the bus drove away with her favourite son. I waved to her till the bus turned the corner.

It makes her happy. Maa's obsession and deep love for me is now old news. Maa had no choice in the matter. Dada grew up too early. When I was twelve, Dada went off to the hostel and found friends and happiness outside our family and carved a son-shaped void in Maa's heart. That's when Maa turned to me for succour, the apple of her eye, and loved me with the power of a thousand suns. Even now, she clutches my old clothes and mourns that I'm no longer the child who used to need her for everything.

When I sat back in my seat, the other students in the bus looked at me strangely for they had seen me looking at Maa like a puppy left behind at a shelter. I don't blame them and neither do I care. I will be her best son till the time I can . . . but I also wonder how long that will be.

As Dada told me, I tried to do well in school. Since my shift of school was sudden and unexplained for, a lot of schools had turned me down. My new school isn't as good as the last one; it is lenient, the teachers are a little slow, and the students are rowdier.

I didn't talk to anyone, didn't make any new friends. I picked the empty first bench, sat there alone, stared at the blackboard and waited for the day to end. Just 700-odd days in my new school, 1200 days in whichever college I go to and then some more days and then some more and then some more . . . and then I die. Finally.

One day at a time. Unless I find the courage to . . .

28 January 1999

My plan to hide in plain sight at school lasted till two days ago.

Our class teacher, Amarjeet Kaur, a round-faced, stout and beautiful woman, who had been on leave till then, introduced me to the whole class and asked everyone to say their names out loud. I was prepared to forget every name as soon as possible but one name stuck in my head, entangled in my thoughts like a chewing gum stuck so badly in long hair that it needs to be burnt off.

That name is Brahmi Sharma, the class monitor.

Besides being toweringly tall at 5'7" like every class monitor should be, she is also the march-past incharge and the teacher's pet. From the number of times I have seen other boys throw furtive glances at her I'm fairly certain that she has a long line of secret admirers. I had prepared myself to not join that line the very first time I saw her. I have found an effective strategy to not like someone. All you do is find a flaw in that person and then concentrate all your energies on hating it, fix a magnifying glass to your eye and train it on that flaw. It could be a mole, or a crooked finger; it could be a gender or a religion or a social class too. Slowly, you only see the flaw and not the person. It has worked with everyone other than Maa–Baba and Dada whom I can't hate, no matter how hard I try to focus on their flaws.

I have been searching for something to hate in her. Her hair is long and shiny. It is usually tied into a scruffy, untidy pony, and absolutely un-hateable. Her face is amiable, with an odd pimple here and there. She has a lissome and athletic body, with perfect round mounds, bursting with puberty; she's at the cusp of turning into a young woman. Her uniform is not as orderly as the good kids in class and hence not irritating at all. But then, today, something hit my eyes like a flashlight during load-shedding—her bony wrists. Like a child's drawing, there are cut marks zig-zagging the entire length of her wrist. Then every time I saw her during the day, my eyes rested on her wrists. The little ridges are telltale signs of someone having taken a knife or a paper cutter to those hands. I know because I have pondered on that option, seen it in movies and in magazines. She has been close to death, flirted with it, danced on the razor edge of it, walked on the ledge of a high-rise, watched a train whizz by from inches away, and survived.

Back home, the mood was sombre. Worked for me. I didn't have to put on a smile; I could be sullen just as Baba was, pretending that the Indian cricket team's fortune affected me.

Recurring images of Pakistani men on news channels raising and fluttering their green-and-white flags in Chennai's Chidambaram stadium seemed to cast a funereal gloom on our dinner table, as if the batsmen hadn't lost their wickets but chunks of Kashmir. Baba, having had enough, changed the channel. On this one, the channel flashed a picture of a burnt car. I knew this piece of news. Over the last few days every news channel has been relaying the news of the gruesome murder of a Christian missionary and his two sons by a few Hindu extremists who burnt them alive.

'The sons were just ten and six. I can't even imagine,' gasped Maa.

Baba muttered, 'These Christian missionaries shouldn't be here in the first place. Why do they even come here? We Hindus don't leave our country and distribute pamphlets in the USA or Iran saying our gods are the best, then why do they?'

'They didn't deserve to die,' said Dada.

'But mind you, the funds for all these are being generated abroad. Ultimately it will lead to the erasure of the identity of our country, of our culture.'

'Our culture?' Dada mocked.

Baba, a reckless donor to the community temple and the head of the Durga Puja Committee, slammed his fist on the table. 'You know why you can mock your own religion? Because you're a Hindu. Try mocking your own religion and culture in any other country and see how they pull out your tongue and lash you. Always critical of Hinduism Anirban, respect the religion that gives you this freedom to question it.'

'So there's nothing wrong with burning alive a grown man and two children? Is that what you're saying, Baba? Is that what our religion teaches us?'

While Dada and Baba fought bitterly, I kept squinting at the television to see if they would show the charred bodies of the little Christian children. Did they suffer? Did they scream like Sami had? Did they look at their father hoping he would save them like Sami looked at me that afternoon he drowned? Yes, he looked at me. He begged me to save him. There's no point lying about it now.

What a perfect thought to end the day with. Brilliant.

P.S. Ashiana Apartments. It's a six-storey building about a ten-minute walk from my house. There are no guards at the main gate. Pretty easy to reach the roof. The fall is clean and it will all be over in a matter of seconds. Around here there are hardly any buildings more than three storeys, stupid building laws. I have heard Mumbai is much better, every second building is over six storeys.

Just saying.

29 January 1999

I have turned sixteen. It's my birthday today. Yay. So exciting. Wow. Whatever. Congratulations and celebrations and blah blah blah blah. What's so great about being born? You have no choice or control over the date or the birth. Life's literally forced on you. Where's the fun in celebrating that? At least with death, you have the option to choose, push the eject button when you feel like the cockpit's getting too hot. And a birthday doesn't change anything. Except probably my thirteenth birthday when my throat and my body exploded and, believe you me, it was no reason to celebrate. I grew taller and my voice broke, I was thrown out of the choir and relegated to the back of the line of the march-past.

'You're lucky. Look how tall you are!' said Maa.

Being tall's not lucky, you just run out of places to hide.

Maa gave me the best gift of all, a Parker fountain pen, the one I'm writing this with. She also took a day off and made mutton biryani, kosha mangsho and muri ghonto. Baba made paesh with jaggery and gave me a book, *The God of Small Things*, by Arundhati Roy, wrapped in an old newspaper. He told me the writer, a Bengali, was given 3.5 crore rupees as advance for the book. He was adamant about its greatness though he was a little disappointed in the writer who had chosen to write about Keralite Syrian Christians and not Bengali Hindus. But ah! What coincidence. The book starts with the death of a little child, drowned in a river, left behind by friends. If only Baba had read it.

Unfortunately, my birthday wasn't a secret in school either. My new school had an ancient birthday rule wherein even older students were supposed to break the monotony of uniform and wear anything that was not a part of it—a pair of shoes, a different shirt or miss out the tie. I, of course, was dressed more properly than a Head Boy leading a march. My hideout, the perfect uniform, and my silence, were broken into at lunch.

'Take off your tie and give it to me,' said Brahmi Sharma without missing a beat. She smelt of coconut oil and Pond's Dreamflower talc.

'Why?'

'Happy birthday, Raghu Ganguly. Try to have a good day. Now can I have the tie please?'

I took off my tie.

'How did you know it is my birthday?'

'It's my job to know. I am the class monitor,' she said.

'There's something on your nose,' I said.

'What?'

She touched her nose and soiled her fingers with blood and pus. The pimple at the tip of her nose that had ballooned with white pus last week had finally burst. I touched my tie, which I was holding to give her, to her nose to staunch the flow. She took the tie from me and held it against the nose.

'I will return it to you tomorrow. Don't worry, I will ask Mumma to wash it.'

'You can keep it.'

'Why would I want to keep it?'

'Umm . . . I don't know why I said that. It just felt like a thing to say.'

'It's not a handkerchief,' said Brahmi.

'It's a tie.'

'Yes, it's a tie. Also, the next time you try to hide from your birthday, be less conspicuously dressed. A well-dressed student is an anomaly not the rule,' she said and smiled.

I nodded.

'Enjoy your birthday,' she said as if she knew I wouldn't.

For the rest of the day even though my eyes followed Brahmi Sharma I couldn't see her anywhere during the chemistry double-period practical. If she had bunked the class, she had done it well because no one asked for her. How could people overlook her absence?

Coming back to Dada, he gave me what he thought was a special gift. He told me it was an Apple PowerBook he'd borrowed from his boss. Inside it was a CD with a media file he wanted me to watch and I should have guessed what it was. It was supposedly a rite of passage for every teenager. The media file wasn't just Kate Winslet lying down naked from the movie *Titanic* that came out a couple of years ago whose pirated cassette Dada got hold of. This was much more. Dada was surprised I didn't enjoy the two naked girls touching each other.

'You have to grow up,' said Dada.

'I was kidding, Dada! I loved it!'

I lied and he smiled. I can't have Dada being miffed with me. After all he's my insurance policy against Maa–Baba's grief. God forbid if anything happens to me, self-inflicted or otherwise, there should be someone to hold Maa–Baba's hand. Isn't that the only reason why people have the second kid? To have a spare part if one's broken? In our case the spare's broken.

'I knew it, you bastard. Why do you play these games with me?' asked Dada and slapped my back.

How could I have enjoyed when I knew the two women on screen were play-acting? They weren't enjoying kissing each other or caressing each other's bodies. They weren't in love with each other. I could see that. If they hadn't promised to live their lives together, to die together if they could synchronize it, then how the hell was I supposed to enjoy what they did on screen?

Now that the day has ended, I have successfully fooled Maa–Baba and Dada that I had fun turning seventeen.

But it wasn't all that bad. I have a tendency to focus on the morose and miserable. I am ignoring that Brahmi Sharma, the girl with the bleeding nose, the girl who went missing in the middle of the day, knew exactly how I felt about my birthday.

30 January 1999

There's a rather interesting development to talk about today.

My initial assessment of Brahmi Sharma was deeply flawed. The furtive glances of my classmates weren't because they found her beautiful or smart or like the warm sun on a winter morning but because they thought her to be strange. She sits alone, she eats alone, and she stays quiet until otherwise required, not because she is intimidating but because she has no friends. Like literally no friends, not even one. Isn't that the most wonderful thing? It is the best thing one can do to oneself. I want to congratulate her on that. Why have friends and set them up and yourself for disappointment? Maybe even lead them to flooding their lungs. Didn't Buddha advocate a life devoid of attachments as the only path out of suffering? Brahmi seems to have grasped it well because she glows like a halo's lighting her face up. But what's really getting my goat is where she disappears in the middle of the day, sometimes for consecutive periods. A little sleuthing told me she's a part of a few academic and extracurricular groups, many of which she heads, thus wielding the power to call emergency meetings. Only that she's never in those meetings.

This past week I have been praying to all seven of Baba's gods—Ganesh, Saraswati, Durga, Kali, Kartikeya, Ram, Lakshmi—for a fresh batch of pimples on Brahmi's face so I could be the hero with my handkerchief dabbed in Baba's perfume.

Baba's gods didn't fail me.

Amarjeet Kaur ma'am made me sit with her today. Second bench, third row—that was our seat. Throughout the six periods, I raced her to the solutions of chemistry numericals, maths problems and grammar questions. She won 17–21. She not only had the home-ground advantage she was also blissfully oblivious of the academic battle going on between the two of us.

We will never be friends—I can't afford to have friends and she doesn't seem to want them—but we can be worthy adversaries. The only positive that has come out of the stupid change of schools is that I have new competition. Finally someone who can challenge my ruthless domination of merit lists.

When I got back home, curiosity got the better of me and I dug out Brahmi Sharma's phone number from the telephone directory. It was not an easy task, Sharma being a common surname. Despite not wanting to remember, the number is now imprinted in my memory. I ran my fingers over the buttons on my landline. I want to call her but with calls starts the slippery slope of friendship, love and attachment, and god knows nothing good comes out of it. The last time I dialled anyone's number from the phone was Sami's. He hated long silences. Much to the chagrin of Maa who went (and still goes) through the phone bill at the end of every month with a fine-tooth comb, we used to talk on the phone every day after school. He always had so much to say.

Sami stopped being friends with me in death. Why else would he leave me with what he hated the most? Silence.

It's well-deserved.

P.S. Rajasthali Apartments. It's seven storeys, including the parking stilts. The guards are a little hard to get past but if you are in your school uniform they don't stop you. The roofs of five out of the six buildings are locked and the keys are with the top-floor-flat owners. But getting to the sixth one is a breeze. Only problem? There are almost always children in the flat. But it wouldn't be a problem late at night. A few seconds to touchdown and . . .

Just saying.

31 January 1999

The mystery of my sudden seat change has been solved. It wasn't due to Baba's gods but my guardian angel and the charmer of women—Dada. He had met Amarjeet Kaur ma'am and requested her to make me sit next to Brahmi Sharma because I was still traumatized from the incident in my last school and I needed new, intelligent friends. Amarjeet ma'am would have had to bow down to Dada's panda-like eyes and his brotherly love. Dada's like honey, diamonds and pink colour to women.

'You said she's a class topper, didn't you? Didn't she wish you on your birthday? So what's the problem?'

'You shouldn't have done it.'

'Why?'

'Because it's wrong!'

'What's wrong in it?'

'Because you can't force things to happen.'

'Whatever that means,' said Dada.

'And I don't want anything to happen. She's just—'

'Oh, take a chill pill, Raghu. You can thank me for what I did. Don't think I haven't noticed how you frown, how your voice becomes guarded when you talk about her, like you're hiding something. Aren't you?'

'No, what would I hide?'

'I don't know what goes on in that head of yours.'

'Nothing goes on in this head of mine.'

Dada might not have ever dominated merit lists like I have, but he's sharp. Of all the lies I have told him, he found out about the little seismic shifts in my heartbeats whenever Brahmi's name is taken. I have tried not to define the arrhythmia but now that he has mentioned the word 'like', it's ricocheting in my mind. What are the conditions that need to be fulfilled for saying that X 'likes' Y? For example, one could have liked Brahmi Sharma's face, her fluency in English, her impeccable report card, the smell of coconut in her hair, her handwriting and her long socks.

But for hypothetical purposes if I were to admit I like her, these above-stated reasons mean nothing.

The clincher for me is her being alone and being content with it. She doesn't look wistfully at the other girls talking, laughing, and being with each other, wishing she were with them. She revels in her solitude. I like how she casually leaves the class, goes god knows where, and comes back like nothing has changed. How calmly she marks her missing attendance in the register. I like how her eyes trace the flying patterns of the pigeons outside, how she almost never laughs truly, how she fools everyone with her smiles, and how easily she convinces the teachers that she's like everyone else. Darkness is her friend and her lover. Unlike me I am sure she has decided how she wants to die.

But what if I like her?

Eventually I will have to reveal myself to her along with my darkest secrets and she won't like what she will see. And who knows what she's hiding? It could be much worse. After all, her wrists tell a much gloomier story.

But staying away from her might be easier said than done. Unlike her, my relationship with sadness is fraught with fault lines. My sinusoidal curve today tells me I can do with a little bit of like and hope.

1 February 1999

Baba has been working in a government bank for some twenty years now. In the evenings, he takes Sanskrit and English tuitions for tenth-standard students at a nearby tuition centre. Maa has been a lecturer of mathematics at Shaheed Bhagat Singh College in Delhi University for as long as I have been in this world. In their hands lie the futures of scores of young children who might or might not be the future of our great country. But no matter how important their jobs might be, they will never require them to go on business trips in airplanes like the one Dada went on today, clutching a briefcase and wearing a suit, looking dapper.

'We are so proud of you. Now all I want is to find a nice Bengali girl for you. Don't worry, we won't get you married to the first girl you see. You can pick and choose carefully. Who wouldn't marry my beautiful son?' said Maa.

Once we reached the airport, Maa clung on to Dada's sleeve and wailed for his impending three-day absence, wiping her tears and snot on her *kantha*-stitch saree. It was lovely and sad to watch.

After we dropped Maa home, Baba took me to his bank, probably to show that he was still relevant, despite Dada's newfound economic freedom, his jacketed airline tickets and his office-funded stays in a four-star hotel in Bangalore. Baba has a decent cabin with teetering stacks of smelly files jammed with pages that have yellowed over time and a desktop of his own.

'No matter how senior you are in these private companies, they still make you sit in a cubicle,' said Baba. 'Don't make the mistake your Dada did. Join a government company. Why work for other people when you can work for the country?'

'Of course, Baba,' I said playing the dutiful son.

'You can also take the UPSC after IIT.'

'That's always an option.'

'Are you reading the newspapers every day?'

'Yes, Baba.'

'Who's the defence minister?'

'George Fernandes.'

'Good, very good,' he said.

A few of Baba's colleagues walked in at this point.

While I played Fury 3 on the desktop, piloting a black jet, Baba and his colleagues sat arguing Atal Bihari Vajpayee's decision to start the bus to Pakistan to improve diplomatic relationships. Baba might not have the strongest arguments but he has a heavy baritone which helps him browbeat even the most learned men into submission.

When we got home Maa's bloodshot eyes stared back at us. 'He still hasn't called. What if something happened on the way?'

We huddled around the phone and waited for it to ring. It wasn't the first time Dada simply forgot us, like we didn't exist, like he could live without us. How hard was it for him to understand that Maa–Baba would only be at rest when they know we were safe and well-fed?

Dada called three hours later. Maa broke down again and told Dada he's never going to any business trip again, at which Dada laughed.

'I love you,' he told Maa.

Earlier these words never came easily to Dada. It's only recently that he has picked it up from me. We know these words work like magic on her. Till a couple of years back I used to say it at the drop of a hat—probably another reason why Maa keeps me close to her bosom—but it doesn't come naturally to me any more. Saying those words now seems like a betrayal. Who knows what happens tomorrow? When they read the letter I write them before I go, if I choose to go, will they think I didn't really love them and I was lying all this time?

So now I let Dada say it more often. He may have to take my place some day. Be the favourite son. Be the only son.

Later when Maa–Baba had gone to sleep, Dada called again to say he had something exciting to tell me once he's back. He told me it will be our secret. SECRET. I feel bad for Dada when he thinks I will be his confidante, his brother in blood and soul. Last year I caught him smoking and he told me it was our secret. I made sure Maa–Baba found out about it and emotionally blackmailed him into stopping.

He has to learn to be twice as good a son, make up for my absence. He can't afford to be careless like this.

I will have to take a break from writing this journal for a few days. The board exams start in a couple of weeks and I have got to do well. We need to keep up pretences, don't we? For as long as I can, I will give my best to this role. I will see you in about a month.

7 March 1999

Welcome back.

Today's not a happy day.

It's one of god's cruel games, tempting me with happiness, luring me into a friendship and then splintering my heart. I know god well. He's not kind and benevolent. He's like us, capricious and evil and corrupted by power. How twisted do you have to be to invent birth and death? One moment you're just nothingness, air, vacuum and poof . . . suddenly you're a foetus trapped in a womb, a helpless baby, a confused toddler, an angst-ridden teenager, a depressed young person, a burdened middle-aged person and then you slowly rot to death. Great art never dies but he made us mortal. That's if men are really god's best creation. He loves to play around with us. That's what he did with me. He reminded me of my place, telling me that no matter how hard I try he can fiddle with my fate.

Brahmi Sharma is in my class again.

I thought I had seen the last of her with the tenth standard coming to an end but there she was again. It had been thirty-three painful days since I last saw her. As I am often wont to do, during the first week I lied to myself that I hadn't been looking for her face in others. This, despite the recurring dream I had of the two of us standing at the top of the Statesman House in Connaught Place in the dead of the night with our wrists slashed and fingers intertwined. The dream ended with us endlessly falling, endlessly smiling, endlessly in love.

The second week went by with me reaching and recoiling away from the phone like a drug addict wanting to call her, then not wanting to call her. The third week, and the most painful of all four weeks, was spent imagining an entire fictional relationship between Brahmi and me, at the end of which, we get to know each other so well that we are disgusted with what we have done and we part ways and promise to not see each other ever again. Comparatively, the fourth week was the easiest. I have never had a relationship or a break-up, and I have only seen it in the movies, but I know now how it feels. A bit like your heart's being spit-roasted, turning slowly. On a pain scale of Mom's food to Sami's passing, it was tantalizingly close to the latter. Which makes me feel appalled at my softness and my gall to compare an imagined break-up with his death.

She came and sat next to me. 'Welcome to the eleventh standard. You did well?' she asked. Without waiting for my answer she got back to her crossword. She said a little later, 'Mumma's waiting for the results more than I am. Apart from you, there's no one who can really score more than me so I wanted to know how you did.'

'I might score more than you.'

'No, you won't.'

'I might,' I said.

'Will you? How did your mathematics go? It wasn't easy.'

'Pretty good.'

'Are you lying?' she asked.

'I am actually. I missed a two-mark question. You?'

'I couldn't do the last question. My steps were right, the answer's not. So that's four marks out of the window.'

'My English went really well though,' I said.

'Mine was okay, too.'

'I didn't expect you in this class.'

'Expect?'

'I mean I am just surprised that you're here,' I said. 'So engineering? That's what you want to do?'

She laughed. 'I hope so. Maybe. But my Taiji, aunt, will decide.'

'Why not your Mumma?'

'She doesn't participate in these discussions.'

'Why?' I asked.

'But she supports me all throughout and she tells me to listen to Taiji,' she said and smiled goofily and truly for a change.

'Are we going to sit together every day?' I asked.

'I think so,' she said.

Then we both got back to reading our newspapers.

She said after a while, 'If you don't mind that is.'

'I don't mind,' I said almost too quickly.

'I asked because you look away whenever I talk to you. So I thought maybe you're not comfortable.'

'I don't look away. I can look right at you and talk. See?'

'You're looking away. Your eyes are flitting.'

'You're imagining things,' I said.

'Okay. Now you're not looking away. So I can sit with you?' she asked.

'Yes.'

'Thank you,' she said.

While Brahmi Sharma struggled with the crossword I counted the little ridges on her wrists. Some were deep, straight and longish, others were lighter and half-hearted jabs. They looked like hieroglyphics, like tattoos of the brave.

'Stop looking at my wrists. I fell down on knives,' she said, mocking my interest, pulling her shirt sleeves over her wrists.

'I know you did.'

'None of the knives were sharp enough.'

'Why weren't they sharp?'

'Mumma keeps them blunt. It's because of her,' she said and got back to her crossword.

She filled in three words. 17. Down—BLEED. 21. Across—GRIEF. 15. Across—I. She bleeds grief.

To keep myself from staring at her, I turned my attention towards the treaty between my country and Pakistan. For the rest of the day I tried to beat Brahmi unsuccessfully in all the classes. Unlike some stupid, cantankerous moron she had spent the days before the new session studying. During lunch I followed her as she left the class. Three turns in the basement and I lost her. It took me twenty minutes to find my way back to the class.

Later at home, Baba was in a sullen mood because of the nuclear treaty I was reading about in the morning.

'We should have dropped a bomb while there was still time,' said Baba, in his usual tone of toxic hatred.

Last year Baba had ordered a celebratory dinner from the Chinese restaurant when Atal Bihari Vajpayee had declared us a full-fledged nuclear state, with the capability of obliterating small countries with a mere press of a button. He called Atal Bihari a hero, a patriot, a guiding light for Hindutva in this country. The American chop suey was fabulous.

Baba had waved his fists in the air and said, 'See! Did you see! Didn't I tell you there is no one better than a staunch Hindu to lead the country? To finally make Pakistan pay for all their transgressions! What's the use of an army if you don't utilize them? Ha! It's not a surprise they named the bombs Shakti to signify our goddesses. Raghu! Now see the fun! This country will change! No more of stupid appeasing politics! This is what we deserve! Our country! Jai Mata Di. Jai Shree Ram. Durga. Durga.'

Today, Baba sang a different tune. 'How could a man, an orthodox Hindu, give in to a peace treaty?' He went on to rave and rant about how he felt betrayed.

I listened till I lost interest.

I can't write more today because I have to go prepare for tomorrow's class. I can't have her be better than me at everything.

11 March 1999

Alcohol, drugs and cigarettes are the refuge of the weak, that's what Maa has taught me. Baba toes a different line. They are forbidden in the *shastra*s, he tells me, which I know is a blatant lie. Indra, Varuna and the like drank and ate and got high with impunity. And who can miss Adolf? The eternally, perennially dangerously high one, the god of ganja smokers who renounce everything but their chillums. If we were really bhakts, we too would be living in a happy daze of smoke and soma, still be hunters and gatherers with no EMIs to pay or pollution to worry about. Our only concerns would be if the spear's sharp enough to breach the rhino's thick skin, or whether the mammoth would trample us before it bleeds dry, or if we would live to see another day. Who's to say that's not a better life to have? When death's close and hovering around you, the quality of life improves, doesn't it? That's when we make our bucket lists, try to cram a life full of desires into a few months, live a little in the face of death.

Coming to the point, Dada made a bad day even worse.

Earlier today, our physics teacher took a surprise test. Brahmi caught my furtive glances at her paper and promptly hid her answers. Furious at her assumption that I was cheating, I hid my answers too. We were still playing the game where we wanted to sit with each other but we weren't friends. Maybe polite acquaintances.

When the exam ended, I grumbled, 'I don't need to cheat.'

'Did you prepare for your exam? I saw you struggle in the beginning.'

'That's presumptuous. Skulduggery. That's the word you missed in your crossword today morning.'

'What does that mean?' she asked.

'I can fill the crossword you do every morning and I can do my own physics tests. And from what I saw, I will score more than you.'

'I didn't get anything wrong,' she said.

'Want to take a bet on it?'

'What is at stake?'

'Are you scared you will lose?' I asked.

She spat on her hand and thrust it out. 'I am not scared. Deal.'

'Deal. Do I have to spit on my hand?'

'That's the only way to do it. It's tradition.'

'Are you sure?'

'Absolutely,' she said.

We shook hands and rubbed them clean on our uniforms. Our spit-written bond was struck and the time started to tick. Imagine my consternation when we both tied at 23/25. I waited for the lunch-break bell to ask her what our course of action should be but even before I could close my copy I saw her leaving the class. I wasn't going to let up this time so I rushed after her. Her calm strides took her faster and farther away from me even as I trotted and panted, through the basement, into the abandoned part of the school building, to the exit that was supposed to be sealed. With ease she climbed over the wall and disappeared. I'm no stranger to climbing walls but bunking, yes. I knew if I thought too much I won't do it so I too climbed the wall and jumped. She was waiting on the other side. My voice failed for a bit, struggling for an explanation, and then I said, 'So what do we do? We cancel the bet? You left, so I followed after.'

'Come,' she said. We took a bus to Connaught Place, neither of us bought tickets, and all the way, I tried not to freak out, to ask what happens to our attendance, and would the teachers ask about us, would they suspend us, call our parents and embarrass us, and what happens if the conductor catches us. She, on the other hand, stared outside the window, not a care in the world. When we got down, she said, 'You look like you have lost a litre of blood. When we get back I will tell ma'am we were arranging library books. It's my responsibility.'

'They just let you do that?' I asked.

'I have never come second in this school. They don't doubt my integrity,' she said.

'So this is where you come every day?'

'Not every day. Sometimes when I have saved enough,' she said and pointed to the shop—Keventer's. 'Best milkshake in the city. So you came for the bet, what do you want?'

'Okay. I wanted something but—'

'But?'

'You can choose to refuse but I want to hold your hand. That's what I want,' I said, rather bravely.

Without a thought, she took her hand in mine. I would be lying if I say it didn't feel like I had lost. Her fingers in my palm felt like a calming balm.

'Is that it?' she asked.

I stared at her wrist and gathering courage I ran my index finger on the lightest of the ridges on it. It was haphazard and had healed years ago. 'Explain this.'

'Oh, it's nothing—'

'Don't tell me you fell on a knife.'

'My father's used razor actually. Would you believe that I was scared it would be infected? It should have told me that I wasn't serious about it. I panicked when the blood spouted from my wrists like little beetles.'

'Why did you do it?'

'My first heartbreak. I was thirteen, same age as Juliet. I was drowning and my Romeo was a stray log who came floating to my world. I latched on to him and he stole my stamp collection.'

'That's a frivolous reason to slash one's wrist, is it not? A stamp collection?'

I realized my mistake as soon as I said it.

She laughed, then shook her head dismissively and retracted her hand. 'Is it frivolous to get your heart broken? My reaction might have been stupid, exaggerated but not frivolous.'

'What happened when you let go of him, the log?'

'I learnt to breathe under water,' she said.

'Your turn. Is there something you want to ask? Or want me to do?'

'I know everything about you. Your friend died, you think it's your fault, and you have been sad ever since.'

'That's not all of it,' I said, angry at her oversimplification. How dare she think her grief over a heartbreak is justified and mine isn't? Who died and made her the incharge of grief management? What does she know of the nightmares, of the cold nights, of the searing guilt, of the incapability to feel happiness? What does Brahmi know of the imaginings of alternate realities where I could have saved my best friend? What does she know of the days I stand outside Sami's house hoping I would see his mother smile for a change? What right do I have to return to being normal when Sami's father hasn't gone to work in two years? What does she know of my anger towards Sami's brother who has failed to take care of his parents even after what happened? But even as I was thinking all these things, all I could say to her was, 'So can I buy you a milkshake?'

She nodded and smiled like the sun. I only had money for one so we shared it. By the time we got back to the school we had missed mathematics. Her being the monitor helped, and she manipulated our attendance. Back home I wasn't sure what to feel about the experience which was a little Sami-esque but wholly enjoyable. All the time my heart thumped and throbbed with fear and whatever I felt towards Brahmi. For whom, I couldn't help think, I was like an accessory, like a handbag, or a bracelet, there but not necessary.

I was still ruminating, reminiscing when Dada walked into my room a little while back, hiding miniature alcohol bottles in his pocket.

'What is that?'

'Free alcohol from the hotel minibar. That's what it is!' he squealed.

'You're not going to drink. Do you hear me, Dada?'

'Damn. You sound just like Baba! And why are you walking away from me?'

'Is this your secret, Dada? That you want to slowly poison yourself? Do you have any idea how many deaths are closely connected to substance abuse?'

'God, Raghu. Stop being so dramatic.'

'You're not doing this to Maa–Baba,' I snapped.

'This is not my secret—'

Dada was interrupted by Maa's knock on the door. Dada scrambled to his feet, hid the bottles behind the headboard of the bed and got the door.

'Why was the door locked?' asked Maa.

'I was helping Raghu with his physics homework.'

'Dada was offering me a drink, Maa. He has hid miniature alcohol bottles behind the bed,' I said.

Dada looked at me in horror as Maa searched and fished out the bottles. She left the room, crying, to tell Baba.

'Why the hell would you do this?'

'Because I want you to live! Is that so hard to understand? Do you even know what it will do to Maa if something happens to you!'

Dada left fuming. He would have understood had I told him about New Crescent Public School.

P.S. The security at the school is terrible as I found out today. It's only four storeys but it looks higher. All five roofs are easily accessible. Of course, two of them have bushes and trees in the drop area so that's out. Another one faces a bunch of houses so that's awkward. But there are two roof tops that are totally jump-friendly. I should some day tell Dada about my scouting.

13 March 1999

I met my least favourite person today, my Didimaa, Maa's mother. She's eighty-three and her brain is mush. She took to the bed two decades ago following a massive heart attack. Though she got better, she got used to people fussing over her. She now spends her days lying around on a musty sofa watching television, soiling her diapers—even though she's fully capable of walking around—and rebuking all her five children, especially Maa. Only Mama could afford to be around her. He was the only one of Didimaa's children who was rich enough to hire a full-time nurse and busy enough to not see her often. Didimaa might have been a good woman when she was young but twenty years is a long time to undo all the goodness. Twenty years is enough to overhaul a personality, to shed your old skin, and wear a new one.

Even my earliest memories of Didimaa's are of an emotionally abusive woman, calling Dada and me filthy cockroaches, wishing us to be struck down by polio and smallpox.

'You've come?' Didimaa said as I entered Mama's house. 'Go now, go in the kitchen and eat what your Mama has earned. Go, eat it all and leave us to starve. *Petni* works all day and sends her children here to eat. What does your Baba do? Oh, yes, prays all day to wash away your family's sins. Your Maa's a whore, a *shakchunni*. She goes and sleeps with her colleagues while her mother dies here. Is this why I kept her in my womb for nine months? Gave her my share of the food?

I should have never let her go to college, that ungrateful petni. She will only rest when I die.'

The insults she hurled today were blunt when compared to the things I have heard from her before. Didimaa's the reason why I know how to curse in my mother tongue and why I don't like old people.

Her full-time nurse smiled awkwardly at me.

'If you want to take a break, you can go. I am here,' I said.

The nurse nodded and left us alone.

'She steals,' whispered Didimaa.

'Didimaa, you have nothing left to steal. What can she possibly steal from you?'

Didimaa started to cry. She said, 'My son, your Mama, hits me when no one's there. You know what he does? You know? He wraps little stones in a handkerchief and swings them at me. He sleeps with the nurse when I'm sleeping. People think I don't see things but I see everything, I know everything.'

To her credit, she's a masterful storyteller. But the best stories come pouring out of her when she is asked about the long misshapen scar on her right hand. The story, the context, the characters change every few months.

'But Didimaa, how did you get that scar?'

'Oh, this? You wouldn't believe me even if I tell you.'

'Tell me, Didimaa.'

'World War 2, before your wretched Maa was born. Your brave Dadu had just came back injured from his posting in Egypt. Three bullets, three bullets had hit him! They wanted to amputate his hand at the hospital but he refused! He ran from the hospital with his hand dangling by just a few tendons. It was I who took out the bullets and wrapped his hand with bandages made out of my wedding sarees. And then like Gandhari, you know Gandhari, from the Mahabharata, yes yes, like her, I took a hot knife and cut through my hand and left my wound to fester and fasted till your Dadu was all better!'

She fell silent for dramatic effect, and waited for me to show any sign of having believed this bullshit story. Dadu, sixteen years Didimaa's senior, died in 1962, having fought in both the World Wars and the Kashmir skirmish of 1948. Some say he died of a broken heart after finding out that the Indian Army was decimated by the Chinese in the '62 war.

Didimaa's the only one who knows how I am wholly responsible for Sami's death. Only mad people can keep secrets. No one believes them.

'Are you here to cry again? Tell me how you watched your friend die?'

'I don't know what you're talking about.'

'Do you think I don't remember?! I remember everything! You let him die! You and your mother—both murderers!'

'Whatever, Didimaa. I just came to tell you that I think I like a girl,' I said.

'Ish!' exclaimed Didimaa, suddenly soft. 'You're so young! Why? Who's the prostitute who's trying to snatch my sweet grandson away from me? Who's she? Ish. Who's it? Tell me? I will slap her with my chappal, drag her to the streets and parade her naked.'

'Didimaa, she's a nice girl, very smart and very beautiful,' I said.

'Nice girl, my foot. I will thrash her and then shave her head. I am going to tell your Maa–Baba. I am going to tell them to change your school. Ish! All this because your Maa–Baba are too busy working—'

'Didimaa, who's going to believe you? They will think it's one of your stories,' I said, more calm than I felt.

Then I turned to the TV and put on *The Jetsons*. A little later, without warning, Didimaa relieved herself in her diapers.

'My sweet grandson. Change me?' said she and looked at me, her eyes flickering with hope and tears. I looked away, turned up the volume of the television and waited for the nurse. It was thirty minutes before she came and cleaned Didimaa who levelled the choicest abuses against me, Maa and Baba. 'You will all die poor and unhappy. Worms will eat out your eyes,' she said while I was leaving.

'Thank you, Didimaa.'

We all ate alone today. Maa doesn't eat till Dada gets home and he's rarely home before 11 p.m. Baba can't wait that long but he tries his best and gives up at 10 p.m. I am made to eat early. I wonder what toll this high-pressure job is taking on Dada's heart. I have to remind Maa–Baba to goad him into getting a full-body health check-up.

15 March 1999

Today I went to the Mittals' house to watch an episode of *Hum Paanch* because our TV had stopped working. The Mittals, who live in the flat above ours, and with whom the Gangulys share a rich history of skirmishes big and small. Our car, a ten-year-old Fiat, stands in their parking lot which Baba hijacked a couple of years ago after they sold their scooter. The algae growth on our living-room walls is because the miserly Mittals don't fix their drainage system.

'They have cash and jewellery hidden in their bed boxes! Don't I know these banias? All thieves!' says Baba.

It is unlikely.

Their house smells of poverty and despair. The sofa's old and lumpy, their fans creak, the flooring is cracked and dark in places, the refrigerator doesn't work half the time, and the bed sheets are always stained. Maa says they are saving dowry for their two daughters—Kanika, seventeen, and Richa, sixteen—both of whom study at the Kendriya Vidyalaya. They are both darker than me; the younger one is the colour of my elbow. Last year Richa had accepted me as the love of her life when I had inadvertently walked into the bathroom while she was bathing. She was the first woman I had ever seen naked, and I was the first man who had seen her like that. Ever since that day she shies away from me whenever I'm in the room, blushes excessively when I ask for extra tomatoes or a cup of dahi, steals glances at me till I smile and accept the existence of that secret between us. She's beautiful with her thick black

35

hair melting into her skin and has the body of a grown woman, no doubt about that, but I feel nothing for her. That's unfair. If we were intended to live most of our lives in pairs, why didn't we come with the names of our soulmates imprinted in our hearts? Why do we stumble from one name to another till we make a choice, right or wrong? Why would she fall in love with me when I would never love her back? The checks and balances of love in the world will never settle. It will always be a CA's nightmare.

Coming back to the Mittals.

Despite Maa's affinity for fair skin, she loves both the girls dearly. In them she used to find solace for the void left behind by the daughter, Mina, who left her too early. After Dada, Maa had a baby girl whom she had lovingly named Mina, meaning light. She was born with a heart too small and didn't live past a week. Mina's death severed not one but two mother–daughter relationships. Post Mina's funeral, Didimaa told Maa she had wished for Mina's death, as a punishment for how Maa had ignored Didimaa.

'Now you know what it feels like! Kali has listened to my prayers!' Didimaa had screamed.

Maa, in the grip of fury and grief, had thrown a vase at Didimaa's head.

Mama had found Didimaa after a full hour, lying in a pool of blood; Maa sitting on the couch, watching her. Maa had been there for the entire hour, watching Didimaa plead and bleed and pass out.

Ever since I heard the story, I have searched in Maa's eyes for that streak of insanity which had driven her to let her own mother almost die. What if Didimaa had actually died? Surely our family would have come up with an excuse. Old woman falls from bed, splits her head open. No big deal. To maintain our integrity we would have lied like petty criminals. Our lives would have gone back to normal. The new normal being living with a murderer in our midst. Nothing happened but I can't help thinking, what if. We were an hour away from being a family of abettors to a murder. A family that can hypothetically do this can do anything. It's not a surprise that Maa–Baba–Dada haven't asked me in two years about how exactly Sami died. Neither have they wanted to know why I hadn't called Sami in the four days that Sami was rotting in my school's pool. Had I known he was there? They prefer not to know the answers.

Anyway.

In Mina's mourning or longing, every Sunday Maa used to feed the strictly vegetarian Mittal sisters with her own hands—mustard ilish, muri ghonto and dahi prawns—before the Mittal parents found out. The Mittal sisters are now prohibited from visiting our house, though I can go to theirs.

Today Mittal Aunty served me three chapattis and watered-down daal while we watched the show. When I came back Maa asked, 'Did the girls ask about me?'

'Yes. When Mittal Aunty wasn't around, they told me they miss our food, especially your fish,' I lied.

Maa smiled brightly and told me, 'Now only if you and your Dada grow up quickly, we will have a girl in this house, I will make her everything. But only get a Bengali girl, okay? Who else will know the difference between rui and ilish and katla? In our times, long hair and the ability to pick out the right fish was all that was desired in a girl, and Bengali girls have them both!'

'But even south Indians know their fish.'

Maa was fumbling for a counter, when Baba butted in. 'Those Dravidians are too smart.' I tuned in and out as he ranted about how they did not want to be a part of India and how Vallabhbhai had prevented the country from yet another Partition.

'*Ei, chup koro to* (Just stop it, okay),' said Maa and stopped Baba in his tracks.

'If he doesn't know about our history, where we come from, how we suffered and for how long, how will—'

Maa asked me to go complete my homework when Baba was mid-sentence. I took my registers and my books and sat in the balcony with them. Over the left side of our balcony is the Mittals' and sitting there was Richa, with her books and her registers. Getting up and going inside would have been rude so I just sat there for an hour. I regretted it once I came inside. What if she thinks there's something going on between us? What if she's attached to me? Would she cry when I'm gone? That's sad, though if no one cries when I'm gone, that's even sadder.

My selfishness sometimes baffles me.

P.S. Found a beautiful abandoned building today, a fifteen-minute walk from home. It's seven storeys. No lifts, which means you have to climb all the way up on the crumbling stairs. But it's worth it. It's quiet. And there's no ledge. Which means you don't have to climb awkwardly to jump down. You can just lean into the fall. The only concern is the ragged beams below. Wouldn't want to land on them.

Just saying.

18 March 1999

My fingers tremble as I write this. The serrated military-grade knife Dada's put in my back, in our family's collective back, is slowly twisting, gutting me. What would happen when Maa comes to know? Worse still, when Baba does? How did Dada allow this to happen? Does responsibility mean nothing to him? Didn't the name evoke anything? It wasn't an ambiguous name like Rehyan or Samir. How could he miss that? It's us versus them. It always has been, at least in this house. Didn't Baba's words, his constant brainwashing, have no effect on him? Didn't Maa's warnings mean anything? Dada's words keep ricocheting in my head. They sort of just recklessly bubbled out of him, no guilt, no second thoughts, nothing. Just a glint of madness in his eyes. Maybe having suicidal tendencies runs in the family.

'I love Zubeida Quaze with all my life. I spent every waking moment in Bangalore holding her hand,' he said to me, smiling.

'She's a Musalman,' I said.

'We really love each other.'

'She's a Musalman!'

'You should meet her.'

'She's a Musalman.'

'I told Zubeida about you. She's excited—'

'SHE'S A MUSALMAN! You need to shut up, Dada! You can't say I love her and what not unless you intend to marry her! And you can't marry her, Dada. Maa–Baba would accept anyone but her!'

'Look, we haven't decided if we are going to get married.'

'What do you mean by that? You said that you loved her, didn't you? Why would anyone say that?'

'We need time to think about our relationship.'

'So you think about a relationship after you tell someone you love her? What do those words mean if you are not staying together forever?'

'They are just words—'

'THEY ARE NOT JUST WORDS! And . . . Zubeida Quaze! Did you not think once—'

'No. Please, no. Don't tell me you're going to start crying now. Oh, c'mon, stop being like Maa. Look at you crying!' He laughed.

'Maa has to know.'

'You're not going to tell anyone. When the time's right, I will tell them myself. Okay, Raghu?'

He left the room to answer the ringing telephone. This can't remain hidden from Maa. She will sniff it out anyway, I thought to myself. I will have to tell her before Dada takes this misstep. Missteps. Why would he casually throw around the word love? But more importantly, he can't defy the unconditional love that's supposed to be between Maa–Baba and us. Otherwise what's the point of it? Dada and I are a pursuit of happiness for our parents; of Maa–Baba wanting to have the complete human experience. What are children if not fully interactive, self-learning, sentient toys made of flesh and blood instead of plasticine with multiple difficulty levels designed to engage the players fully? The game of children is addictive and seldom not liked. The job of the toys is to be grateful and love the players back. If Dada were to disappoint our parents, he's defective goods, a video game with a flickering screen, a toy with a loose socket. He's no better than Mina or me. I had been counting on him being perfect. I had been counting on

Dada taking upon himself the care of Maa–Baba, giving them the perfect bride and grandchildren they have always wanted, be the sweet, loving son who makes them happy, the one who celebrates their anniversaries and birthdays, who cuts down on his own expenses for their medicines, who bathes them when they are older, hears the same stories repeatedly from their deteriorating brains thirty years from now, cries for their deaths, lights their pyres. I can't allow Dada to rip this family apart. I can't let Dada make *me* the caring son. I am all but a guest in this family. I might have overstayed my welcome but I have to join Mina sooner or later. I can't let Dada throw a spanner in my plans.

25 March 1999

Dada's secret is corroding my insides. Today we got the results of our first unit test of the year and I embarrassed myself by giving her a ten-mark lead. It wouldn't be a stretch to say my abysmal performance was because of Dada. Brahmi sought me out in the library which was a welcome change. Since our day at Keventer's I have seen her occasionally go missing and have had to physically stop myself from tagging along. Not once has she asked me to accompany her which confirmed my suspicion that I wasn't needed in her secret jaunts outside the school. Our conversations too were strictly academic, carried out in an adversarial tone.

'I was scared you would beat me,' she said.

'Huh?'

'Show me your answer sheet. I want to see how you did,' said Brahmi.

'You beat me. That's all that should matter. I'm not showing my answer sheet,' I said, clutching my pocket where the crumpled answer sheet lay.

'You will have to show me.'

'Why?'

'Because I think I won only because you did badly, not because I did well. Show me your answer sheet now. Quick, quick!'

So I did. The mistakes were silly. The joy of her win slowly drained out of her.

'Do well the next time,' she commanded.

'I will.'

'Whatever you're struggling with, leave that at home when you attempt your question papers.'

'I am not struggling with any—'

'Your lies won't work with me. Don't spoil the only reason why school is fun,' she said.

'Which is to beat me in tests?'

'To be the best at something,' she said as if she was a queen.

'Fine,' I sighed and accepted.

I promised Brahmi a fight in the next session.

'But if I win the next time, do I get to ask you for another story?' I pointed to her wrist.

'Why do you want to know them?'

'No reason. I have never attempted that despite the knives at house being quite sharp. So I'm curious. Moreover I don't think I'm a knife person,' I said.

'What are you then?' she asked.

We were getting into dangerous territory but a sense of abandonment gripped me.

'Buildings, tall buildings. They aren't as ubiquitous as knives or cutters.'

She scrunched her face.

'Why? What's wrong?' I asked.

'I am not comfortable with the disfigurement that comes with it,' she said.

'So no train tracks? Or hanging? Or burning?' I asked.

'No.'

'Sleeping pills?'

'Too risky. Too much time to change your mind and for regret to seep in.'

'But knives? That takes time too.'

'Knives are knives,' she said. 'Should we talk about this with such frivolity?'

'We wouldn't talk about it if not with frivolity,' I said.

We both nodded, surprised at my seemingly intelligent observation.

She sighed and said, 'If there are other factors that determine our choice of you know . . . then I think we are safe. If we were serious about it we would have done it by now, not matter what the means.'

'Not bragging, but I am surprised at how intelligent we are,' I said.

She giggled. Like a real giggle, not the sorts she fakes, if and when she finds herself in a group of girls who don't know she's different. It wasn't annoying at all. Giggles are the best.

'Touchwood. Can I sit here and study now?'

'I don't see why not. Are you not going out today?'

'I have no money and you haven't lost a bet to treat me. Though the next time you do, there's a new burger Nirula's has added to their menu.'

She fetched a book to read and sat next to me. Her invitation was at best dubious but it would do for now. By the time we walked out of the library most of the students were already in class. The corridor was deserted. We had barely walked a few yards when the cooing of a dog drew us to a class long abandoned.

'We will be late for the class,' I said.

'I didn't ask you to follow me,' she said.

'Now that's unfair.'

We jumped over broken desks and props stored from previous annual day functions.

'There,' she said.

In a corner, a pregnant bitch scrambled to her feet seeing us and fell right back. I swear I saw tears.

'Poor thing.'

'Dogs can't cry the way we do. It's some allergy. But she does look like she is in pain,' said Brahmi. She took off her sweater. 'Give me yours.'

'I can't! It's new. Maa–Baba fought tooth and nail for a discount on this.'

Her stare wore me down.

'Fine,' I said and took it off.

She linked our sweaters, arms tied to each other, and draped it on the bitch. Then she cradled her on her lap till she drooled all over her skirt and went to sleep.

'I wash my clothes myself,' she said when I pointed at the mess.

'And the sweater?'

'Mumma won't notice,' she said.

The bitch, visibly comforted, was chewing through our linked sweaters when we left her and her unborn children.

'Maybe she didn't want to live,' I said.

'So?'

'So now you gave her hope. You became her friend. She will now want and expect you to come to see her every day. We should have left her to die.'

'She's Shahrazad.'

'Isn't that an Arabic name?' I scoffed.

'She was a queen.'

'She was in pain. She would have been better off dead,' I said when we got to class.

'Pain's rewarding.'

'That only looks good on posters. How can cutting yourself reward you? What exactly is your reward?'

'Every time I fail I know I would like to live a little more,' she said. 'Moreover Shahrazad is going to be a mother.'

The sweater and Shahrazad, Dada and Zubeida, chemistry and Brahmi—I told Maa nothing when she got home from work. It took Maa an hour to find out about the misplaced sweater, and another two to find where I had hidden the chemistry paper—the letter box of the uninhabited flat 14B.

'Mumma, I . . .'

Maa started to cry.

'In the letter box of all the places! First, you lose your sweater and now this. What am I supposed to do with the two of you? One brother does god knows what in Bangalore and the other one is falling in bad company.'

'I didn't want to spoil your mood, Maa. And my marks might incr—'

'Still lying. Still lying. Where did you learn to lie? What else are you lying about?'

Baba finally butted in. 'There's no point scolding him. He is *boka*, stupid, he will not amount to anything. Five thousand rupees I spent on his material for IIT, five thousand. It's going to come next week. All waste! He would be lucky to get through Stephen's, leave alone IIT.'

Maa–Baba had always been good at worst-case scenarios when it came to their sons. An hour of absence meant kidnapping, a cut on the knee meant tetanus, and running to catch a bus meant crushed skulls. But this time his worst-case scenario didn't even cut close.

'Who's got the highest marks? Tell me! Who got the highest marks?' scoffed Maa.

'Brahmi.'

'How much?' asked Baba.

'Twenty-three.'

'Twenty-three! She has scored ten marks more than you! All this is because of the stupid tramp cards you keep collecting! Where are they? Where have you kept them?'

Maa stormed to my room and got the bunch of cards I had been collecting for the last five years. While Baba held me, Maa burnt a handful of them over the stove.

'Don't do it!' I shouted and cried my fake tears.

Maa threw the rest in the dustbin. Baba took me by my arm and dragged me to the balcony and locked me out. Neither the burning of the trump cards nor being locked outside seemed like a punishment. Trump cards used to be Sami's obsession, not mine.

'That boy is teaching you all the wrong things,' Maa used to shout.

After his death, I pretended to still obsess over Bret Hart, the Hitman, and Hulk Hogan like my other classmates to be, you know, *normal*.

It suddenly fell quiet inside the house. Maa–Baba's voices reduced to distressing whispers. Their sadness seeped through the mosaic of the floor, the fabric of the curtain, the wired mesh of the gate and clawed into me. Maa came to fetch me after an hour, crying and repentant. After dinner Baba came bearing a new set of WWE trump cards. Over dinner, Maa–Baba and I analysed my chemistry question paper and they were as confounded as Brahmi was.

'Don't do silly mistakes the next time,' they both echoed.

'I won't.'

'What do we have other than the two of you?' said Maa.

'I know, Maa.'

After they put me to bed, they took a taxi to the airport to get Dada home. They must have told Dada about today's happenings because he came to me once he was home.

'They expect more out of you. Don't disappoint them, Raghu,' he said.

'And you can go about doing whatever you want to, isn't it?'

'That's unfair, Raghu.'

'Absolutely not! I'm the one who has six scholar medals, thirty-three certificates, and the first row in the annual-day choir. What have you given them, Dada? Just a lousy 1650 rank in IIT JEE? 89 per cent in boards?'

'I didn't get the memo saying we had to do certain things to qualify as being a worthy Ganguly.'

'But you were certainly given plenty of instructions about what they expected you to do.'

'Raghu.'

'And what you weren't expected to do!'

'Oh please, I am too tired for this,' said Dada and left the room like he wasn't so obviously at fault.

These days Dada has a way of making everything worse.

Bad day in all, but right now I'm thinking of Brahmi's and my sweater—twisted and tied and unified.

P.S. That beautiful abandoned building I saw a few days ago? Yes. They are tearing it down or maybe it's just falling apart.

29 March 1999

Dada was born in '78. It was a year of great turbulence, Baba always tells us. The government at the Centre was tottering, the saviour of Bengalis in West Pakistan, Indira—Maa Durga in the words of Atal Bihari Vajpayee—had been re-elected to the Parliament, and two men hijacked a plane with toy guns asking the cases against Indira Gandhi and her younger son Sanjay Gandhi to be dropped.

Ridiculously enough, Baba tells me that both those men became Congress politicians. Of course, Indira and Sanjay Gandhi are both dead now, Dada tells me. Indira Gandhi was shot by her Sikh bodyguards as revenge against her defiling their holiest place of worship, the Golden Temple, and her son Sanjay died in a fiery plane crash.

In stark contrast, 1983, the year I was born, was quiet. Apart from India's historic cricket World Cup win there was nothing to write home about. This tells the story of us too. Dada is the turbulent one, to whom things never cease to happen, sometimes brilliant and sometimes the embarrassingly low-grade drinker of alcohol and maker of friends, finder of lovers from different religions and holder of their hands, doer of a software job, receiver of business trips.

And then there's me, the mama's boy, the more intelligent one, and who has almost never had to hide anything from Maa–Baba. But then Sami died and everything changed.

But Dada still thinks he enjoys a certain immunity because I have been—largely—the mature one.

In a string of his recent stupidities, he has added another one. He has agreed to his company's offer to shift him to Bangalore. They will put him up at a five-star hotel—all expenses paid—for three months. Maa–Baba have vetoed it violently.

'You're not going anywhere! Your Maa didn't feed you, bathe you, and work day and night for you just so you could leave her the minute you grow up. You're not leaving your Maa,' said Baba and left the table mid-dinner.

Maa chose to express her disapproval by maintaining a cold, steely silence.

Later I went to Dada's room.

'You can't just leave them here,' I said.

'Why not?'

'Because you can't.'

Dada frowned. 'Shut up and come here with my office bag. Close the door first. I want to show you something. Get me my office bag. It's in the cupboard.'

From the bag he took out his PowerBook and clicked through to a folder. 'Are you ready?' he asked and clicked on a little icon.

'I'm not ready for anything.'

The screen slowly filled out in a picture.

'What is this?'

It was taken from a digital camera, not like the usual ones with reels. With digital cameras, you get multiple shots at looking happy or sad. But in the picture Dada stood awkwardly next to a girl who was clad from head to toe in black—only her face was visible through her burqa.

'She's Zubeida Quaze, the girl I told you about. Isn't she beautiful? You should meet her. I think both of you will get along like a house on fire. She's quite—'

'She wears a burqa, Dada.'

'Oh yes, she does. So does everyone in her family. It adds so much mystery, doesn't it? I have more pictures of ours if you want to see. She gives me hell when I ask her to—'

I shoved the PowerBook away.

'I don't want to see any more of her pictures! And delete them! I'm going to tell Maa–Baba everything. She's the reason why you're going to Bangalore, isn't it?'

'No?'

'Are you out of your mind—'

Before I could reach the door, Dada held my hand and pulled me away from it.

'Dada, let me—'

Dada struck me. His slap stung my face like a million bees. Before I could register the assault, he had pulled me close and hugged me. 'Look, Raghu, I'm sorry. I didn't want to hit you but you can't tell Maa–Baba anything.'

'Why the hell not?'

'Didn't I tell you? This is our secret. I will tell them when the time is right. Don't spoil it before anything happens, okay? I like Zubeida. I really do. Just the way I like you. She's very important to me.'

Just the way I like you? I freed myself from his grasp.

'I'm your brother, Dada. We are your family; your responsibilities are towards me, towards this family. I won't tell Maa–Baba today but if you don't tell them soon enough, I will. Baba needs to know what you have done. You have to come back.'

I left the room.

6 April 1999

Brahmi's eyes were murderous, fists clenched and she was waiting for me. Without any prelude, she shot out the question that must have been bubbling inside her since last night. 'Did you call on my phone yesterday?'

'Me? No! Why would I? I don't call anyone.'

'Someone called four times at my house yesterday.'

'It wasn't me.'

'There was no voice on the other side!'

'I don't even have your number. Also I have to ask Maa before calling anyone. So it can't be me.'

'Taiji went mad and shouted at me, saying that I must be giving out numbers to boys in my school.'

'That's not right. Why would she say that?'

'Can you do me a favour, Raghu? Can you call home?' she asked.

'Me? Why?'

'Talk to Taiji and tell her you didn't call me? You're the only classmate of mine she knows by name and she thinks you're a rascal.'

'But I'm a not a rascal.'

'Please call and tell her so?'

'But—'

'Please.'

I am the rascal.

Last night it had taken me an hour of staring at the phone to dial her number. I had practised what I would say. *Hi Aunty, may I talk to Brahmi Sharma? It's regarding the notes she took in the physics class today.* The words died in my throat the minute I heard Brahmi's voice. She sounded different on the phone, much older but without her trademark authority. I called her three more times and every subsequent time her voice became mellower but still as lovely. I imagined her in a T-shirt and a skirt, the phone stuck to her ears, saying, *Hello, hello, who's this?* I thought of her not in her uniform but otherwise. It's probably what everyone does. If you're used to not seeing someone in uniform you fantasize about them being in one and vice versa.

'Fine, I will call her. But who do you think called at your place?'

'I don't know. Maybe someone who likes me and is too scared to tell me. A secret admirer? Or someone who just wants me to be in trouble,' she said.

'Probably,' I said.

Excusing ourselves from the class, Brahmi and I went off to call her Taiji from the school phone. I put in the coin and waited for the call to connect.

'Hello . . . ch . . . Taiji. Raghu will talk to you. He is saying he didn't call you. I told you he wouldn't. I'm giving the phone to him.'

'Hello, Aunty,' I said.

'*Sun ladke.* I don't know if you called at my number or not. But if you call in the future I will know. I will come to your house and slap you up in front of your parents. Do you understand, *saali? Rakh ab phone. Saala Bangali.*'

'Okay, Aunty—'

Click.

Brahmi's face flushed pink. 'My Taiji has a bit of a temper,' she said, embarrassed, overhearing some of the abuses.

'This is the first time I have been abused by a grown woman. It sounds strange.'

'She didn't mean to abuse you. She's really nice otherwise. Do you want to sit together at lunch?'

Unlike my lunch which consisted of chapattis (Baba), daal (Maa), paneer (Baba) and raita (Maa), hers was a lone, dry sandwich.

'Mumma keeps really busy. She usually doesn't have time to cook . . .'

'You can have mine. It's too much for one anyway. Half of it goes waste.'

'No, it's fine.'

'I don't eat so much anyway. Maa gets really angry when I waste food. You will be doing me a favour.'

'Thank you,' she said and dug in. 'I haven't had food like this—'

And just then her voice tuned out and something came into focus. Something I had missed all this while because I could only see her wrists and imagine the stories in the ridges. What I had not noticed were the little welts on her upper arms, behind her ears, on her back. They were purple and blue and red and sad. She had been hit at home yesterday. Was it because of the calls I made? If it was, I deserved the abuses from her Taiji and more.

As if she had heard the question in my head, she said, 'I fell down the stairs.'

'Strange stairs.'

'I know. They are stairs I climb every day and yet they . . .'

She hadn't expected me to believe her. She wanted me to stop looking. We shared our lunches and still couldn't finish all the food.

'Pack your lunch and come with me,' she said.

'Where?'

'Shahrazad.'

'That's a slippery slope, Brahmi. Are you sure? Are you really going? I guess you are.'

She didn't share my pessimism which was strange. We went to the abandoned classroom again. Shahrazad had grown even fatter in a week but looked healthier. As if Brahmi's love had healed her, exactly what I was scared about. She came hobbling to see Brahmi, her enormous belly swaying from side to side. Soon she was eating out of Brahmi's hands, wagging her tail gustily.

'Don't be scared. She won't bite,' she said.

'I'm not scared of her biting me.'

'Oh please. Don't overestimate yourself.' Then she talked to Shahrazad in a baby voice. 'Raghu here thinks you will fall in love with him, my little doggy. Who's the cutest doggy in the world! You are!'

'No, I don't think that.'

'Of course he does, Shahrazad. He thinks he's so lovable that people or dogs will miss him so much god forbid he does something to himself.'

'Now you're just mocking me. Also, stop with that baby voice.'

'My fat little doggy, will you tell Raghu bhaiya that it's not so?' she said.

'Brahmi. We are late for class.'

Shahrazad hobbled on to Brahmi's lap, nuzzling her nose into her armpit. Brahmi said, 'Aw, you missed me! Tell Raghu bhaiya that maybe no one, including you, will miss Raghu bhaiya as much as his floating-soul-thing would miss us. Ah! Maybe that's what he's REALLY scared of.'

'Fine, whatever,' I said and patted Shahrazad, whose eyes reduced to little slits.

Brahmi laughed. 'And now pat her with your other hand. See! She likes you. Look at her wagging her tail.'

I did as asked, first to get Brahmi to stop and then because I liked how Shahrazad's warm tongue felt on my hand.

'I know you called, Raghu,' said Brahmi just as we were leaving Shahrazad. 'STAY, STAY,' Brahmi had to tell Shahrazad to keep it from following us.

'I didn't—'

'I know you did. Next time, you can speak. My Taiji thinks something's going on if no one says anything.'

'Did you know this all the time?'

'I knew it the second time the phone rang. I don't have secret admirers or anyone here who would want to trouble me. There's only you.'

Brahmi could have screamed at me, slapped me around like she would have been by her Taiji for my recklessness. She could have paraded her welts and accused me for it. It was incredibly stupid of her to exonerate me in front of her Taiji when she could have blamed me for everything. She didn't have to be nice to me when I didn't deserve it. Why strengthen bonds and make it harder to snap them?

Couldn't Shahrazad not have been cute and cuddly? Couldn't Maa–Baba just be bad people, making it easier for me to leave them and Dada to themselves?

'I'm sorry,' I said as the guilt coursed through me. Maybe Brahmi is right about me. My floating-soul-thing would miss them.

'You don't have to be sorry. You are my friend.'

'Are we friends?' I asked.

'Are we not?'

'Does it mean we have another person to worry about?' I asked.

'That's for you to decide.'

'And you?'

'You ask too many questions,' she said. 'Do you want to go somewhere?'

She hadn't waited for my answer and didn't tell me where we were going.

'Since when have you been doing this?'

'Eighth standard, I was late to school and I wandered around the entire day. One of the happiest days of my life,' she said.

An hour later we were at Nehru Planetarium, our seat reclining, under the stars. I didn't ask why we were here and she didn't tell. What she did tell me was about the compost project she's working on which was our pretext for going missing today. For an hour we travelled around the sun and cruised around constellations and sometimes looked at each other. She pointed and explained to me things she thought I wouldn't get. 'Do you want to be an astronaut?' I asked her on our way back.

'No, I just like to think things beyond this world we see exist,' she said.

In the evening, Maa was happy to see the lunch box licked clean. Right now I am now thinking how alone Shahrazad is.

17 April 1999

From what Maa tells me, Baba was an accomplished playwright and an incredible actor in college. That one time in college he wrote a play in Sanskrit. None of the other actors in the cast could keep up with the words or intonations or Baba's strict instructions. Rather than scrapping the play, he played all the roles himself!

'There were only three girls and two boys in the audience and yet he performed like the world was watching, huffing and puffing around the stage, changing voices, genders, even costumes,' Maa would tell us.

'Then what?' Dada and I would ask, listening to Maa–Baba's love story for the umpteenth time.

'I was so taken by your Baba's performance. It's then that I first thought of getting married to him. He was a force on the stage. He could have been a politician, I have always told your Baba that.'

I have no doubt. Dada and I have seen him in action both as sons and students. Parents all across north and west Delhi, and beyond, seek him out to teach their children Sanskrit and English. He tells stories and fables in his class, holding every child's attention. He was like the Pied Piper before but infinitely more powerful and capable of raising an army of children voicing his opinions, repeating verbatim after him. Age has mellowed him down somewhat. But his very propensity to perform, to enthral, is often an embarrassment like it was today.

'I liked the lady,' grumbled Baba about Jayalalithaa, the charismatic chief minister of Tamil Nadu, pointing at the television, veins popping in his neck. 'But look what she has done!'

'Ishh, turn the volume down,' said Maa, nudging Baba.

'Turn the volume down? The country's government just fell and you want me to sip tea and eat mutton chops! Is that what you want me to do?'

'I want you to stop discussing politics with our guests,' said Maa.

In the audience were our new neighbours, B.B. Bhattacharya, his wife, Shanta Bhattacharya, and their daughter, Arundhati Bhattacharya. They had shifted into the flat next to ours just a day before. They are a lovely family—arrogant yet humble, rich but understated, beautiful but unassuming. We on the other hand were a bunch of people with megaphones strapped to our mouths.

'We are so lucky they are Bengalis,' Maa had chimed yesterday when the loaders unloaded their furniture. 'I will call tomorrow.'

And so, here they were. While Bhattacharya Uncle and Baba argued about Jayalalithaa, I stole glances at Arundhati, who had carried a thick book with her. Maa's eyes had lit up seeing Arundhati when she walked in. She is a studious-looking, bite-sized, feet-touching, nice Bengali girl—a Bengali mother's prize.

'Dada, you tell me?' Baba continued, addressing Mr Bhattacharya. 'Does it make any sense? If only Atalji had one more vote, we wouldn't have elections again. Does Jayalalithaa not know how much it costs the country to hold elections again? What a leader! Bringing a no-confidence motion against the government when the country is already so weak.'

Bhattacharya Aunty butted in, 'She topped the tenth board examinations in Tamil Nadu. So—'

'I know, Boudi. But what did she do with it? She went into the movies!'

'She was a big hit,' Aunty said.

'I know! That only shows how much these politicians want fame and money!'

'Take Arundhati inside. Show her your books,' said Maa to me and her. 'Go, now! Don't be shy.'

'I'm not being shy,' I said. 'I just . . . Do you want to?'

'Okay,' said Arundhati and smiled.

Maa–Baba have the knack of making the most mundane things awkward. Do they not sense our shame or our consent? No, Maa, I don't want to recite a poem to these strangers. No, I don't want to dance in front of them. Don't you know they are not interested? Why are you so obsessed with your sons, Maa?

Arundhati Bhattacharya put her book aside and followed me to my room.

'These are the books,' I said, pointing at them.

'Hmm. I thought there will be more.' She flipped through the books, opening them, going through them and then telling me, 'I have them all.'

'Do you have *The God of Small Things*? The author shares—'

'I know. She's the best, isn't she? Like me,' said Arundhati with a bright smile. 'You can borrow a few books from me if you want. I have a nice collection. But do return them and don't dog-ear them.'

'I have my course books to finish. Baba ordered the IIT material so I need to do that too in my free time.'

'IIT material, already? Isn't that a little early?'

'The exam is in two years. They think there is not much time.'

'Is that what you want to do? Engineering?' she asked.

'No one will approve of what I really want to do.'

'And what's that?'

Yeah, right. As if I could tell her.

'I am not sure if I want to do what I really want to do. So I think engineering it is for now.'

'My parents would love to adopt you and your brother. They were devastated when I took humanities. They think I am ruining my life. But I won't know until I try, will I?'

'Which school have you joined?'

'Model School. I have not seen the school yet. What's the school like? Is it good? Are there cute boys there?'

From what I have heard, it's a school of geniuses or children who find drugs rather easily. Our conversation was cut short when Uncle entered and told Arundhati that it was time to leave.

'It was nice to meet you.' She shook my hand firmly, smiled warmly and left.

I polished off the samosas and the namkeen left behind by our guests. By now Maa's opinion of her had changed. There was no longer a glint in her eyes. I chose not to tell her about Arundhati's query about cute boys.

'She was beautiful, wasn't she?' she asked me.

'She was okay.'

'She must be bad in studies though. She's taken humanities like Paula Aunty's son. Remember Paula Aunty? Her son did English honours and is now working in advertising for 5000 rupees. He's twenty-eight. *Chee chee.* And look at your Dada, already doing so well.'

'Maa?'

'Yes, *shona*?'

'Nothing.'

'Is there something you want to tell me, Raghu?'

'No, Maa.'

As I write this, I am thinking if I am eligible to be a cute boy. Does Brahmi think so? But what if I am really a cute boy? How long can you stare at a cute boy?

26 April 1999

Today was simultaneously the happiest and the saddest day of my entire life.

During the lunch break, it took me everything to coax out the words from a crying, shattered Brahmi.

'She is d . . . dying. She's . . . just lying . . . lying there . . . Shahrazad. She is dying . . . she i . . . is . . .'

Seeing her cry, face smeared with tears and lips trembling in fear, a strange overwhelming sense of heroism gripped me. Which was weird because the last time death was around me, I had run like a coward and held my silence for four days. Back then I was hoping that shutting my eyes and lips hard enough would make what had happened not real.

I held Brahmi's hand and ran to the classroom. My sense of heroism and bravery fizzled out in a loud gasp when I saw Shahrazad, our friend and lunch-sharer from the last few days. Her big brown eyes were trained at us as if asking why we were so late. Her two pups nuzzled their noses into her belly, trying to go back to their safe place. There was more blood than I could stomach. Brahmi and I tiptoed towards her. Neither asked whether we could run to the principal, take her to the vet, save her life. We knew her death was certain. It hung around in the basement, waiting to whisk her away. I recognize the presence of death because I have felt it around Brahmi and had not known what it was until today. For the past few weeks I wasn't sure why I was waking up anxious every morning. Now I know. Because somewhere in my subconscious a flash forward played in a loop. *Just another morning. Tuesday maybe. I am my usual moping self, standing at the end of the line in the morning assembly, searching for Brahmi in the girl's line. The principal tells us the reason of the emergency assembly. 'Our beloved student, Brahmi Sharma, passed away last night. Let's all pray for her and observe a minute of silence.' Two more brush strokes of red on the art on her wrists.*

We rested Shahrazad's head on our sweaters. While I ran my hand over her head, Brahmi sang a lullaby in her ears. Shahrazad matched the lullaby with her soft moans. Half an hour later, she fell asleep with her eyes open, still looking at us.

Two pups, eyes closed, tiny as my fist, now writhed aggressively in their mother's blood, mewing at their dead mother, nudging her, willing her to wake up. Shahrazad, one who had shared our lunches and our sweaters, was now just flesh and bones, much like Sami.

'We need to bury her,' I said. 'I will pick her up. We can go to the football ground.'

'I will do it.'

'Brahmi, you pick—'

'I said I will do it!' snapped Brahmi.

The tears had given way to a sense of purpose.

I picked the puppies up, cleaned them with scraps of newspaper, put them in a little cardboard box and punched holes in it. Brahmi wrapped our queen in the old soaked sweaters and lifted her up. She looked sad now that she had stopped crying. Carrying Shahrazad and the whimpering puppies, we walked to the far end of the football field. While I dug a shallow ditch, Brahmi used dead leaves to clean Shahrazad. Then she took the puppies out of the box who rushed to lick their mother's face. We buried her and said prayers on her grave.

In her death we gave her a religion.

We were called to Amarjeet ma'am's room when news got around that we had missed our class.

'Where were you two—'

'Ma'am.'

'God! What happened to you, Brahmi? All this blood! Are you hurt? What happened— '

'It's not mine,' said Brahmi and told Ma'am about Shahrazad and her pups.

'The school can't take responsibility for the puppies. You should have come to us when you found her. This was highly careless of you two. What if the dog bit you?'

'It was our friend. It wouldn't have,' said Brahmi.

'You would have turned it out to the streets. We had no choice,' I said.

'How long were you two feeding her?'

'A couple of weeks I think,' I said.

'I won't report it to the principal. I will write in the attendance register that both of you were in the sick bay because of food poisoning. If someone asks, you will have to tell them the same, okay?'

'Okay, ma'am.'

'I will try calling a few adoption agencies. Till that time you will have to take care of the puppies. Is that clear?'

'Yes, ma'am,' we echoed.

After school, Brahmi and I emptied our school bags and put in one puppy each inside. We took a Blueline bus home, the rickety fleet of buses driven by overworked drivers with expired licences who routinely have to wash the blood of passengers off the tyres.

Brahmi was quiet so I spoke.

'Shahrazad must be in a happy place right now,' I said.

'Hmm.'

'It was the best way for her to go. By the time her puppies grow up, they wouldn't remember their mother. And as for Shahrazad the last thing she saw in the world was something beautiful. Her puppies.'

'She also saw us. Her friends. You made that possible,' she said and looked at me.

'Hmm.'

'You did well today, Raghu. We both did. I think we were . . .'

'Brave?'

She smiled like she meant it. In that split second I was tempted to tell her everything. I wanted to break down in her arms and tell her what really happened in that pool with Sami and me. But we hit a road bump and the moment passed. It was for the best.

Also, I didn't think Shahrazad was in a happy place or that the last thing she saw was beautiful. What she saw was that she was abandoning her newborn puppies, entrusting them in the hands of two little humans, and that's not a happy thought to die with.

My heroism at school and delay in reaching home was met with a tight slap by Maa. She was home from work already and had panicked when she didn't find me at home.

'Where were you? I went to the bus stop. Everyone had got down but not you! The conductor said you hadn't taken the bus! Where had you gone? I was going mad here! I called your school and they said you had left!'

'I took a Blueline bus.'

'What! Why? You have started smoking? Is that why you're late?'

'No, Maa. I was—'

'Ishh! You have you started smoking. Show me your lips!'

'No, Maa. I was—'

She snatched my bag to look for a cigarette box or matches. As if on cue, the pup started to mew. Stunned, she dropped the bag and the little puppy crawled out. She sat down and picked up the little one, and ran her fingers on its tiny head. Her eyes flooded with instinctive maternal love. She looked at me for an explanation. When I told her, she patted my head.

'*Khul bhalo korechhis. Ki darun!* You did a good thing! He's so sweet! Look at it sucking on my finger. I should get some milk for it. Look up the Yellow Pages. We need to go to a vet to get it checked. Quickly!' she said and disappeared into the ·kitchen, cradling the puppy with one hand.

Maa named the puppy Mina.

When Dada came home, we all went to the veterinarian. We bought a little bed, a blanket and a collar for her. When we got home with our new family member being passed from one set of hands to another, a special delivery awaited us—a 25-inch state-of-the-art Videocon television. It was probably another attempt from Dada to make up for his betrayal.

'We will watch the World Cup here,' Dada announced as it flickered to life. Baba was impressed.

'You don't like it, Raghu?' asked Maa.

'We didn't need a new TV,' I said obstinately.

'What's going on between the two of you?' asked Baba.

'Nothing,' said Dada.

A little later, Bhattacharya Uncle and Aunty dropped in and saw the new TV. The picture quality was crisp and unlike the last TV, the screen was flat. It looked like NASA had built it. Arundhati came too but not once did she look at the television. She brought books for me to read instead and didn't let anyone take Mina from her hands. She pestered her parents to get her one too but they shot her down.

'This is just like *A Game of Thrones*,' she said to me. 'She's so ADORABLE! I LOVE HER!'

'What's *A Game of Thrones*?'

'A book in what's supposed to be a series. No one I know knows about the book and I don't think the writer will come around to finishing it. But anyway the story starts with a group of princes finding the exact same number of dire wolf puppies as there were siblings.'

'Brahmi and I are not siblings,' I said.

She laughed. 'Of course, you're not. But nice name—Brahmi. All this while she was "that girl". Is she cute?'

'Maybe.'

What's with Arundhati and people being cute?

1 May 1999

There's a common wall between the Bhattacharyas' flat and ours. Arundhati has taken the room on the other side of the wall, and now every morning I wake up listening to Arundhati's renditions of English pop songs I have never heard before. Both our rooms are illegal encroachments, two-bedroom flats turned to three. My room was almost broken down twice by the Municipal Corporation of Delhi; Maa–Baba have no doubt that it was the Mittals who had complained about the extra room we had constructed. It took the greasing of quite some palms before the authorities turned a deaf ear towards the complaints. Mina likes Arundhati's songs. She whines and scratches at the common wall whenever Arundhati sings. I don't mind them either. Mina's tiny paws and Arundhati's songs help me with my morning anxiety.

Arundhati stops by every morning to play with Mina and that hasn't gone down well with Richa Mittal who's forbidden to touch the puppy—the Mittals think it's being brought up on raw meat.

'*Ram jaane* what they feed the dog,' Mittal Uncle had shouted at the weekly residents' welfare meeting. 'I'm warning all the members of the society that she will grow up to be a menace. What if she bites my daughters? Your sons? Who will pay for the injections, haan? Bolo Datta saab.'

But there was no beating the theatrics of Maa–Baba. Baba shouted, screamed, gesticulated wildly and even went as far as saying Mina was his dead daughter incarnate. At which Maa started to cry and so did a few other women. What works is not Maa–Baba's actions but how genuine they are in what they do, no matter how implausible their cause.

The Mittals were soundly humiliated.

Now every time Richa sees Mina, Arundhati and I, her eyes burn with an anger I thought she was incapable of. She doesn't blink till the time she walks out of sight. As the love of her life, I had broken her heart by not stopping Baba from demeaning her father publicly.

Just as I was leaving for school in the morning, Bhattacharya Aunty came to Maa to enquire if there was a temple nearby and if I could accompany Arundhati to one after school. 'Arundhati used to go to a Hanuman temple every Tuesday,' Bhattacharya Aunty told Maa.

So in the afternoon after school I rang their bell. Arundhati locked her house and followed after me. She was still in her school uniform, her shirt carelessly untucked, socks bunched up at her ankles and her shoes muddy. Her school seemed even more lax than mine.

'Don't your teachers say anything to you?' I said, pointing to the shoes.

'Everyone in my school dresses like this. There are seven hundred students in my batch so no one cares. Many of them come wearing sneakers. Back in Kolkata they used to slap our knuckles with wooden scales,' she said.

At the temple she sat down on her knees, folded her hands and said silent prayers to Hanuman's idol. She knew none of the Sanskrit chants Baba had taught me. She talked to her god in English.

'Teach me a chant!' she exclaimed when the pundit told Arundhati that I was one of the learned bhakts.

While we distributed our prasad to the beggars outside, Arundhati chanted the verse I taught her. Sounded much better coming from her.

'*Manojavam Maruta Tulya Vegam, Jitendriyam Buddhi Mataam Varishtham, Vaataatmajam Vaanara Yooth Mukhyam, Shree Raama Dootam Sharnam Prapadye.* I got it right this time, didn't I? What does this mean by the way?'

'Let me pray to the one who is swift as thought, the one who is more powerful than the wind, the one who has conquered his senses, the supreme among all intelligent beings, the son of the wind-god, the commander of the army of forest creatures, give me refuge, the messenger of Lord Ram, the incomparable Lord Hanuman. Please accept me and my prayers at your feet.'

'That's so cool!' squealed Arundhati.

'Is it?'

'You use it to impress the girls in your class, don't you? This is how you made Brahmi like you? Isn't it?' asked Arundhati.

'She doesn't like me.'

'If you say so. What did she name her puppy?'

'Adolf.'

'Nice!'

She made me chant some more and clapped like a little child every time. To thank me she gave me a mixtape of her All Time Favourites English songs. When the cassette player gave up, I had to eat my pride and ask Dada for his Walkman.

'That's it? You don't want to tell me why you need it?' asked Dada.

'I will tell you when there's need to tell you.'

'Raghu? Zubeida is coming to Delhi tomorrow. Would you want to meet her? I told her you would,' he said.

'I would rather cut off my tongue. Why would I want to meet that Musalman—'

'Raghu! That's really—'

I stormed out. Back in the room I listened to the songs whose words remained a mystery to me. Maa made biryani today but it tasted like ash.

'You don't like it?' asked Maa.

'Why don't you ask Dada if he likes it? He seems to have developed a taste for biryani, haven't you, Dada?'

'Shut up, Raghu.'

'Yes, you seem to be pretty good at shutting up these days.'

'Whatever it is between the two of you,' interrupted Maa, 'don't get it to my dinner table.'

P.S. Have noticed a building from the bus back from school. It is a good twenty minutes away by a bus or car from home. I intend to check it out soon. It must be at least twelve-storeys high. It's also new so I am thinking the security might be a little bit of an issue. But let's see.

Just saying.

3 May 1999

Aren't there times so sad even crying doesn't cut it? Like on a pain scale, what you're feeling is immeasurable? That's what Dada and Brahmi made me feel today.

Brahmi had been lying to me all this time. She had called me a friend. Why did she have to throw the word around casually if it didn't mean anything to her? I didn't ask her to label what we were. She chose the word and sullied it. Maybe I deserve it. Damn it. Adolf is dead. Mina's brother is dead, gone, lost. And Brahmi's wholly to blame for it. Brahmi's parents hadn't allowed the puppy home so she had kept the puppy outside, feeding him, wrapping him in blankets, smuggling him home in the nights after everyone was asleep. She never thought to mention it when we discussed Mina and Adolf, or even ask if I wanted to take him home.

'How could you do this to me?'

'Your family had accepted it and mine hadn't. I couldn't find it in my heart to tell you,' she said.

'So you would just lie?'

'I didn't—'

'I didn't what! You didn't think that he would get lost? He was a puppy! What else did you expect from him?'

'We can find him.'

'Of course we will find him. We will find him dead! DEAD!'

'Don't say that,' she said.

'Why didn't you tell your mother to keep him inside?! Didn't she have sense? Or is she as stupid as you are?'

'Raghu—'

'Just shut up!'

Brahmi started crying and I stormed off. A part of me wanted to apologize for what I had said about her mother, the other was still furious. A little later she found me in the basement.

'You should have told me,' I said when I saw her approach.

'I'm sorry.'

'We will search for him after school.'

'Are you still angry?'

'No.'

'I know you are.'

'I'm sorry for what I said about your mother,' I said.

After school we spent two hours scouring every lane and road near Brahmi's home, screaming his name till we lost our voices and didn't find Adolf. She thought he would come running to us. I knew we would find his bloodied body at the side of the road. I wondered if his end was painless. I was even jealous that he got out of suffering so early in his life and I am still here, living one day after another.

Adolf was gone.

'I should go back home,' I said.

'We will look for him tomorrow,' she said.

'Sure.'

I boarded the bus. She waved me goodbye. As the bus rolled out of the bus stop, I heard Brahmi scream out Adolf's name again. I ran to the back of the bus and peered out from the window. Brahmi was still looking for Adolf. Soon her shouts were reduced to a whisper and the bus turned at the corner.

It's all her fault. If we hadn't saved the pregnant Shahrazad that day nothing would have happened. At least we wouldn't have been in the middle of this. Two of the three lives we supposedly saved are now lost. What was the point of it all?

If our friendship was a living, breathing organism, it was born the day the bitch gave birth to Adolf and Mina, and she let it die. But unlike Dada she was at least repentant. She apologized every twenty minutes, if that's any consolation.

I couldn't share what happened with Maa–Baba, or Arundhati—they would think less of Brahmi if they knew, and I wasn't ready for it. I whispered in little Mina's ears the news of her brother's death but she was more interested in chewing my little finger. I waited for Dada to come home which was not until 3 in the morning.

'Where were you, Dada? Don't tell me you were at the office like you told Maa. I called and they said you had left at 9. So where were you?' I asked.

'Why are you still up?'

'Where had you gone, Dada?'

'God, what's with you? You're worse than Maa. I was with Zubeida. Happy?'

'Zubeida? Where? How? Till 3?'

'I was in her hotel,' he said.

'Like in the lobby of the hotel?'

'In her room,' said Dada.

'In her room? Just the two of you?'

'Yes? Why?' he asked. 'Why do you look like you're going to faint?'

Fighting tears, fingers clenching-unclenching, I told Dada I needed to meet Zubeida.

'Why?' Dada asked.

'You spend the night at a girl's hotel room and you don't think I should meet her?'

'No, of course you should meet her. I am just asking because the last time I had asked you to meet her you had flipped—'

'BUT THIS time you were in her room, Dada! It's different,' I added with emphasis in my voice.

'How the hell is it different?' he said, shrugging as if it wasn't a big deal.

'Dada, are you in love with her?'

Dada shrugged. 'Yes, so?'

'Are you just in a relationship, like you like her, or are you in love?'

'I'm in love for sure,' he chuckled.

'SO WHY THE HELL DON'T YOU TELL ME IF YOU WILL GET MARRIED TO HER OR NOT!'

'Is it so important?'

I didn't deem it necessary to answer Dada's stupid question. How stupid is Dada to think he can spend a night with a girl he loves in a hotel room and not get married to her? Of course, he's getting married to her. I'm not an idiot to think that staying a night together could mean a pregnancy but there are certain moral obligations that come when you say you're in love. Maa–Baba didn't throw the word 'love' around so frivolously and neither did they teach us that. Maa–Baba never said we-were-figuring-out-what-we-wanted-to-do after they professed their love. Quite unlike Dada who tells her he loves her, stays in her room, and then behaves as if he's not going to get married. Is he lying to Zubeida and me about his love for her just like Brahmi had lied to me about Adolf?

Is nothing sacred any more?

7 May 1999

RECKLESS. That's what we all are. ABSOLUTELY RECKLESS. Why don't we think twice before doing something? What could possibly be going through the heads of those girls when they played this little prank? Let me tell you what happened.

When I entered class with Brahmi after the PT period I saw a few girls, fighting and giggling, sitting on our desk. They walked away as we approached, smiles pasted on their faces. Their happiness was like spiders on my skin. But what would they know of Adolf's death? The past week had been harder on Brahmi than on me. I had run through my cycle of denial, anger, bargaining, depression and acceptance.

Brahmi still harboured hope that one day Adolf would come back to nap at her feet. And isn't hope just the worst thing?

'Adolf's not coming back,' I told her.

'He might. We can't lose hope.'

'This is not hope, it's delusion.'

'He will come back.'

'No, he won't.'

'He will. You can choose not to wait but I will. He will come back. I can't lose hope,' she said and scratched her wrist involuntarily. 'What else is left if not hope?'

I looked at the scars and assumed every time she lost hope she reached for a knife or a blade, so I said nothing.

'Fine. Let's hope he comes back.'

Brahmi was like the mad woman from the movie *Karan Arjun* who kept repeating that her sons will be back. That's what hope/delusion does to you. Brahmi's keeping the pain of Adolf's death at arm's length and harbouring hope and that's much worse.

It wasn't until the next period that we discovered a bunch of badly scribbled papers in the desk left behind by the girls. On every note there was a single message: *BRAHMI LOVES SAHIL.*

'There's no need to complain, Raghu. It's just a prank.'

'So?'

'The teachers would think Sahil was in on it as well. Let it go,' said Brahmi.

'What they did was stupid. Today it's these notes, tomorrow they will take decisions that will hurt their entire family,' I scoffed. 'I'm telling the vice principal. She will decide what to do. A minimum three-day suspension I want for them. Not one day less!'

'Why are you so angry?'

'Because . . . it's . . . it's just wrong!'

'If you want to get them suspended, do it. But I won't talk to you for as long as their suspension lasts.'

She stormed out of the class. I sat there, the notes in my hands, the reason for my anger staring right at my face. It was plain and simple. I wanted my name where Sahil's was. Even if it was a prank. Have I not felt like putting the word love between our names? Of course I have. But neither am I one of those stupid girls nor my reckless brother. Saying something like that is a bond of a lifetime.

'I didn't complain but if they do it the next time, I would tell the teachers.'

'They left the same papers with Sahil Ahuja as well. He came to apologize and assure me that he had no part to play in it.'

'He came and talked to you?'

'Yes, he did.'

I had never seen Sahil Ahuja talk to anyone except the teachers whom he terrorized. He always took the last seat of the class which was a vantage point for audacious behaviour. From there he routinely threw good and crude jokes alike at the teachers, little paper bullets from rubber slings at us, and frequently got expelled from the class. Though now he ranks middle in class, he had failed twice in the fifth standard. Being two years older than all of us gives him three extra inches of height, making him the only person in the class who's not shorter than Brahmi. Sahil smiled when he caught my eye. I turned to Brahmi to find her smiling back at him too. And I could be overthinking here but I saw Sahil Ahuja looking at us through the day. I kept leaning forward and backward in my seat to block his view of Brahmi's hair.

It was only later while we were in the Blueline bus and away from Sahil Ahuja's imposing presence and his devilish smile that I remembered what I had been meaning to ask Brahmi.

'My Dada stayed out the entire night. The girl he is in love with was in Delhi and they were in the same room,' I said.

'My cousin too had a love marriage. So when are they getting married?' she asked.

It was the first time I smiled today. Brahmi knew what being in love means. Isn't it just wonderful when you can sleep and wish to wake up the next day? I don't feel like killing myself today and it feels absolutely awesome.

15 May 1999

Today was the first day of our summer vacations.

While our classmates celebrated the time off from school Brahmi and I opted for extra assignments for the time. She didn't say anything explicitly but she opted for them after I did. But then again hope is a bad thing. Maybe she didn't do it for me but for the same ulterior motives I had. Our school was renovating the physics and biology labs during the summer vacations and we could be the first ones to try out some of the equipment. Since we are both non-medical students the summer vacations were the only time we could go to the lab and cut open some frogs like our classmates in the biology section.

'They might ban dissecting animals soon,' Brahmi complained.

'That's sad. Are you sure about handling knives?'

'It will give me practice,' she said and chuckled.

'That's not a laughing matter.'

'Is it not?'

Today we didn't meet to cut open a frog. I had to meet Zubeida Quaze and I asked Brahmi to tag along. I needed someone on my team. I had maintained a demeanour of equanimity but Brahmi had seen through it and suggested bunking school. 'Don't worry, the auditions for the debating society are today,' she had said. We both went first, fumbled, got rejected and then sneaked out. Where, I had asked, and she brought me to Lodhi Gardens, where we picked flowers and got chased by watchmen.

'Are you sure you want to do this?'

'I have no choice,' I said.

'You look nervous,' she said and gave me her water bottle to drink from.

'I am not nervous.'

'But why do you want to meet her? You can be with your Maa–Baba on this and ask Dada not to get married to her.'

'I can't do that to Dada. Dada is in love. You know what heartbreak feels like.'

We were to meet Dada and Boudi, wasn't she to be my sister-in-law, at United Coffee House.

'Shouldn't they be here yet?'

'He's being cool. Being late is cool for him.'

'What?'

'His definition of being cool is warped. As you can see. In love and not sure if he's going to get married! How nonsensical is that?'

Brahmi laughed. 'True.'

'Can I ask you a question, Brahmi?'

She nodded.

'Did you think you will marry the boy you cut your wrists for?'

'Both of them.'

'You cut yourself twice for love?'

'Isn't love death by a thousand cuts? I'm glad I am through with two. Why are you looking at me like that?'

'What did the second boy do?'

'I didn't cut myself for him but for how stupid I was to keep lying to myself that he will change, that he really loved me, to believe in every lie he told me. I was punishing myself.'

What I felt at that moment was a lot of jealousy mixed with a feeling of incompetence. I was a relationship novice and had no advice to share or similar anecdotes to bond over.

The only girl I have ever liked—before Brahmi—never knew I liked her and that was five years ago.

Once they arrived and we settled down, Dada leant away from us and towards the man on the other table who was listening to the commentary of the first World Cup match. England–Sri Lanka.

Next to Dada, Zubeida sat in her distracting and flowing black burqa. Only her round face was visible through it, like it had been framed.

It looked suffocating but her smile betrayed no such emotion. She looked at Brahmi and me, still smiling warmly, her brown eyes devoid of any malice. Her burqa screamed '*Them! Those people!*' but her eyes said '*Us. We.*'

'You're so beautiful,' said Brahmi.

'That's so sweet of you. You're very cute yourself,' said Zubeida and touched Brahmi's hand lightly.

'Thank you,' said Brahmi and smiled.

'You're so quiet, Raghu. You wanted to see me. Your Dada told me you have some questions for me. Don't you?'

'I have three questions,' I said.

'Raghu? I can't believe you're going to do this—' Dada started to say.

Zubeida interrupted him. 'Let him ask.'

'How did you meet my brother?' I asked.

'Oh. I thought you had some tough ones for me. This one is easy. Your brother and I were in IIT Delhi. Though we never talked in college. It was when we started going to the same office that we started to talk. So I met him way before I first talked to him. Phew. What is the next one?' she asked and looked at Brahmi who smiled back.

'Why did you fall in love with him?'

'Raghu? That's rude,' said Dada and kicked me under the table.

'It's not, Anirban. It's only fair he has questions,' she said and looked at me. Not even a single hair peeked out of her burqa. She continued, 'Umm . . . well . . . your Dada is the most intelligent, kind man I have ever met. The choice, if you put it like that, was obvious. I understand your reservations, Raghu. My family would react the same way if they come to know. Before Dada I hadn't even been friends with a boy. Love was never an option for me.'

'My last question. Why didn't you fall in love with someone from your own community? A Musalman boy? We could have avoided all of this.'

'You can't choose whom you love. Did you choose to be friends with your gorgeous friend here?' said Zubeida.

'Of course I did. She was the most intelligent girl in my class. The choice was obvious, unlike yours. Weren't there Musalman boys in IIT or at your office?' I asked irritably.

Zubeida laughed. 'There were but I never talked to them.'

'Then why did the two of you do this when you knew how your parents would react? It's just wrong, isn't it, that you should decide to hurt them like this? When you had choices, why didn't you choose otherwise? It's not as if you wouldn't have found anyone else! They are billions of Hindus and Muslims alike. Then why?'

'Raghu. You shouldn't talk to her like this,' Dada said angrily.

'Your Dada is right,' echoed Brahmi.

'I'm sorry.'

'You don't have to apologize,' said Zubeida. 'Is anyone of you hungry? Do you want a milkshake? I have heard they have the best milkshakes here!'

'I don't want a milkshake.'

'You can keep asking me questions, Raghu. I'm here for you,' she said, smiling softly at me.

I tried refusing the milkshake, I tried hard not to drink it, and I wanted to hate it when it swished around in my mouth. I failed on all three counts. I failed at hating Zubeida Quaze.

'What should I call you?'

'Call her Didi,' said Dada.

'I will think about it.'

'You can call me anything,' said Zubeida.

'I can't call you Didi because what if you two get married.'

'Raghu!' interrupted Dada.

'Dada, I'm not talking to you. I just remembered I had one more question. Sorry? Can I ask that too?'

'Please go ahead, Raghu.'

'Are you getting married to Dada? And don't tell me you haven't decided on that because why would you be in love if you don't intend to get married? Am I right, Brahmi?'

'Absolutely!' said Brahmi.

'You are so cute,' she said to both of us.

'That's not the answer to my question.'

'I might but your Dada has to agree to it,' said Zubeida and looked at Dada lovingly.

'Dada? Do you agree?' I asked.

Dada nodded half-heartedly, still leaning to hear the commentary of the ongoing match.

Later, Brahmi told me on our way back to school, 'She's so sweet.'

'Is she sweet enough for Maa–Baba not to notice the burqa?'

Baba came back home early for India's first match in the World Cup. Imagine the gloom in the Ganguly household when despite Ganguly's valiant 97, India lost its first World Cup match. Dada and Baba refused to eat the malai prawn curry Maa had made in anticipation of an Indian win.

'It's because of you we lost,' said Baba. 'You celebrated too early. Next time I will lock the kitchen till the time India wins!'

'But—'

'Baba is right. You jinxed our win,' Dada concurred.

'That's unfair!' I protested.

Dada and Baba left the dinner table and walked to the balcony. They closed the door behind them. Dada was first invited to stand outside with Baba when he cleared IIT. He had smoked his first cigarette that day and had vomited promptly. Maa–Baba had a huge shouting match while Maa cleaned up the half-digested Chinese food we had eaten earlier that day. I peeped in through the window and found the two of them lighting their cigarettes. Mina nipped at my toes. I ate their portion too. The results of the board exams will be announced next week and I have better things to do than mourn our cricket team's losses.

P.S. Saw many tall buildings today. That's why Connaught Place is my favourite place. Right there on Barakhamba Road, there are two buildings, each quite tall but each quite hard to get into. Two watchmen outside each building but I'm guessing they must go off to sleep late at night.

21 May 1999

More than the strong-jawed, long-limbed devil Sahil Ahuja, I hate myself for what I'm feeling today. Today was our first dissection. The twelfth grade biology teacher had promised us that. But I reached the biology lab twenty minutes late and saw Brahmi's scalpel hovering over a pinned frog. On her side was Sahil Ahuja smiling his satanic smile. Brahmi lowered her scalpel and cut through the frog with the dexterity of a surgeon. The teacher and Sahil stood by her side and encouraged her. The teacher then made Sahil finish what Brahmi had started. Once they were done, they both accepted the pats with wide smiles.

I hid from them.

From the laboratory, they went to the canteen and had two Gold Spot cold drinks. Not once did Brahmi look over her shoulder to see if I had come. They were in the canteen for an hour. My blood boiled. Sahil Ahuja was a liar. It was all a plan, I could see that now. He would have orchestrated the chits, rendered a fake, charming apology to claw into Brahmi's good books. I followed them to the bus they took home. Sahil had the gall to get down at her stop—he had insisted—and then take another bus home. What was this if not a shameless attempt to woo her? And why was Brahmi encouraging this wanton behaviour?

What made me angrier was what happened before I saw Sahil's wicked plan in action.

The tyre of the first bus I took in the morning had burst and in the few seconds that the bus was out of control I saw my own death. I literally thought I would die. I was happy for a brief bit—like I am always when I picture myself dying—but then I didn't want to.

I wanted to live!

You know why?

Because I had to get to school and share a scalpel and cut open a frog with Brahmi. For the first time in the longest while I wanted to live on, not because I didn't want to disappoint anyone but because I wanted to stay alive for myself! In those few seconds—that seemed to last a lifetime—I didn't see Maa– Baba or Dada, I saw her. I saw my future as clearly as day. In the future that flipped in front of my eyes like a graphic novel I saw myself clearing IIT, scoring much higher in the entrance test than Dada had, and then I saw myself graduating from IIT, then calling Brahmi's mom, and informing them of my existence. I saw them liking me, and then in two more years I saw myself slipping into the possibility, quite randomly in a conversation with Brahmi, of us getting married, and then I saw her take it to her family and them agreeing to the union on grounds of my loyalty and success.

And the first thing I saw after this wonderful possibility of love and life was Sahil's stupid face.

I called up at Brahmi's house.

'Raghu? Why didn't you come to school today?' asked Brahmi.

'I was a little sick. So what did you do in biology today?'

'You wouldn't believe it! We dissected a frog. Oh, by we I mean Sahil Ahuja and I.'

'Sahil was there?'

'The frog had such a tiny heart! We saw it stop beating. It was sad and beautiful. Wait? Did you not come because you were scared?'

'I wasn't scared.'

'The teacher might let us cut another one next week. Will you come? Sahil Ahuja is coming too.'

'I will,' I said.

'Okay, fine. I will have to cut the call now. Taiji is coming! Okay? Now, bye—'

She seemed happy and I couldn't be happy for her. Once again, my selfishness and envious nature confounds me.

I was the frog. Pinned to the dissection table, my tiny heart beating in full view of Sahil Ahuja and Brahmi, them nudging my little heart with their bloody scalpels and bright smiles, laughing, and then watching it beat its last beat. Lup-dup. Lup-dup. Dead. A flat line.

22 May 1999

Here are the board exam results.

Raghu Ganguly: 91.2 per cent
Brahmi Sharma: 91.2 per cent

Like I'm being mocked.

Sahil Ahuja scored a 62 per cent. I walked out of the school before Brahmi could spot me. She seemed happy high-fiving Sahil Ahuja and laughing with him like she was the only one who scored that high.

The mood at the Ganguly household was upbeat through the day.

'I knew you would score more than me,' said Dada, smiling. 'But not by this margin.'

'You have always been a little slow, Dada.'

'Wow. Maa–Baba never really taught you modesty, did they?' he said and ruffled my hair which was irritating because I'm not a three-year-old any more.

In the evening there was a party at home to celebrate my No.1 position in my school. SO MUCH FUN. LIKE SO MUCH FUN. I'm being sarcastic, of course. Sounds much better when you say it out loud rather than write and read it.

No one cared to mention to the attendees of the Gangulys' Son's Board Exam Result Celebration Party that I shared the top spot with Brahmi Sharma, the breaker and breakee of hearts. Countless Bengali families including the Bhattacharyas were home eating Maa's mutton chops. Despite their daughter Arundhati's rather dismal performance, it was hard to spot the disappointment on their faces.

'She got a 100 in English!' squealed Bhattacharya Aunty.

'So nice,' said Maa.

The women and the men skilfully concealed their envy and congratulated me and showered love on me like I was their own son. Richa Mittal on the other hand scored a 43 per cent and there was considerable gloom in her house. I know because they complained of the noise we were making and they made Richa make that call.

'Hello?'

'Richa?'

'Can you please ask your guests to stop making noise? Or my father will complain to the residents' welfare association next week. We don't say anything doesn't mean we will keep bearing this,' she said in a voice that seemed to have churned from an ocean of limitless sadness. This was also the longest string of words I had heard from her. Her parents would have made her mug up the sentence I think.

'Okay, I will tell Baba.'

'Congratulations, Raghu.'

'You too.'

I don't know why I said that.

'Is Arundhati there too? I know she is. She's so beautiful, isn't she? She is. She is very beautiful. And intelligent. She lives right across you and gets to go to the temple with you. Very nice.'

'Yes, she has come with her parents,' I said.

She disconnected the call.

After the dinner, the men and the women were inside drinking and talking about politics and sarees and marriages; and the younger ones were sent outside to the balcony and busied themselves with Mina. Mina revelled in the attention and let all of them be her masters and licked them equally.

'You don't seem to be happy? What did you expect? A 95?' asked Arundhati.

'No. 92 per cent. Just half a per cent more than Brahmi. I could have got it. I still don't see how I could only score 92 in mathematics.'

'You both scored the same? Like you are soulmates! That's so sweet.'

'There's nothing sweet about that!'

'Of course it is. And why are you so grumpy? Beat her in the next boards. Big deal. No one will ask us about these marks when we grow up anyway.'

'Please don't talk to me right now.'

'Fine, grumpy head.'

She sat next to me and stayed quiet.

'I'm sorry,' I said.

'It's okay.'

'Tell me something, Arundhati. Like you only scored 62, don't you feel you're letting down your parents?'

'Why would I? They were expecting lesser. If anything, they are impressed!'

'But they would still want you to score as much as, say, I did, wouldn't they?'

'They would love it. But they know I'm not smart enough—'

'Oh please! Not that intelligence crutch again. Everyone can score. It's just about putting in the hours. I'm not gifted, I just work harder. And you don't work hard enough for your parents' happiness.'

'That's not very nice of you to say.'

'No, I am saying that's good. Like how do you do it? Like how do you ignore your parents' wishes just like that?'

'By doing what I want! It's pretty simple. You should try it out sometime,' she said and giggled.

25 May 1999

A deathly silence has descended over the Ganguly household. The three men had each vowed wars—the father against a religion, the elder son against an ideology, and I against love. The mother looked like she would have a stroke any moment. Let's start with the eldest—Baba—whose worst fears have come true. In what's being said to be one of the biggest intelligence gaffes, 800 Pakistani infiltrators have been found occupying 25 kilometres of Indian Territory in Kargil and Drass.

'IT'S A WAR!' said Baba, waving his fists. 'Look at the betrayal. Our government sends buses to them and they send us dead bodies of our soldiers. See, Raghu, didn't I tell you? We Hindus are too soft! We gave them a country and yet they want more! You think the Musalmans who live in Hindustan are loyal to the country? Thoo!' Baba spat on the ground and stomped on it. 'If they are so loyal, let them fight on the front lines, let them fight their co-religionists, spill their blood!'

'Baba, you're overreacting. Why do you think the Muslims chose to stay back? Because we promised them a secular state. Their allegiance lies with us. Our country was built on these principles,' grumbled Dada.

'Bullshit! Secularism, my foot! What will we get out of secularism, haan? Tell me?' he shouted. 'It's because of people like you that we are treated like second-class citizens in our own country. Always with the appeasing of the minorities. You think they will be brothers, no they won't, they find you sleeping and they . . . ' Like always, Baba put forward a chilling scenario of an impending massacre. Gruesome stories with gruesome endings come easily to Baba. Strange that he and Didimaa don't get along.

'Ei!' Maa shrieked to stop Baba but the words had flown out of his mouth.

'I'm saying nothing wrong. Just wait and see what happens to us. We should all band together before it's too late and . . .'

Midway through Baba's rather hilariously impractical but cruel plan, Dada had left. Baba turned his attention to me. He said, 'Do you have any Musalman friends?'

'No, but—'

'Good. Good. Never make a Musalman your friend. We are not the same, remember that!'

Maa asked me to go to my room. I was happy to oblige. Pakistan's betrayal of the olive leaf that the Indian government had extended to them was nothing compared to what Brahmi and Sahil Ahuja had done to me. Today's lesson wasn't about an arch nemesis's betrayal, but that of a friend's.

Earlier today I was intentionally late for school. I had given Brahmi the chance to wait for me but she went about her day like I didn't exist. I had followed their trail . . . the dead frog with the still heart in the dustbin, the crumbs of wafers in the canteen, the lingering echoes of Sahil's laughter in the empty corridors. I found Sahil and her sitting with their legs dipped in the swimming pool, their hands within touching distance.

Of all the places—the swimming pool—where it had all begun.

They must have sneaked in like Sami and I had, feeling brave, feeling adventurous. Unlike the swimming pool here, the one in my older school had new diving boards, the ones Sami and I were the first ones to test. They were dismantled soon after Sami plunged to his death. I didn't want to enter the swimming-pool area but Sahil's laughs drew me in. And in the water, I saw Sami. He was right there, struggling, looking at me, taking my name and begging me to save him.

Their smiles, their little murmurs shook me out of my reverie and broke something inside me, like Sami himself was reminding me what I had done to him. It could have been a minute or an hour that I stood there, watching. The pain spread through my body like a plague. The anxiety gave way to despair, the despair to anger, the anger to pain, and the pain fuelled an urge to avenge myself. I woke up the watchman and told on the two of them. The watchman hurried inside and caught them by their ears. I came back home and waited for her call. None came. Now I'm thinking of ways to lay waste their love story before it begins.

I will have my war.

I was still weighing my strategies when Dada stumbled into my room. It was only then that I noticed the scraggy beard and the overcast eyes of a heartbroken lover. I know because I have looked into the mirror and I look a bit like him. Two brothers with doomed love stories.

'Her parents know,' he said, slowly and painfully, as if the words were carving their way out of his throat. 'They have locked her in. Her brothers said they would strangle me if they found me near her ever again. They are planning to get her married to someone else.'

'Dada.'

'Can you imagine what she must be going through?' he asked, his eyes glazed over.

'You should have been ready for this. You should have never fallen in love, held her hand, gone on dates. What good has ever come of falling in love? Didn't you tell me you weren't sure?'

'I need to talk to her parents,' he said with a sense of urgency. Like he wasn't listening to me.

'Won't you make it worse by talking to her parents? Just let it be. Slowly everyone will forget everything,' I said, despite knowing that if his love story meets this abrupt end, it will break his heart and he might not love ever again. We aren't on a merry-go-round; love doesn't keep happening to us. It's one moment, one person, one life.

'I don't want to forget her. I want to get married to her.'

Poor, naive Dada. He doesn't know how much love can hurt.

'Dada, but this is an escape hatch. You can get away from this toxic relationship. Even Maa–Baba will be happy. Take this opportunity, please. I know you love her but—'

'That's bullshit. I don't care what her parents or Maa–Baba think. I'm looking out for my own happiness,' argued Dada.

'But she's a M—'

'One more time you say that and I will smack you. When did you become so bigoted?'

'Dada, I'm not. Like I'm okay with them.'

'Them? When did they become THEM?'

'I mean, Dada. I don't mind at all. I like Zubeida Didi. But Maa–Baba. They want—'

'SHUT UP,' he screamed and got up.

'Bu—'

He strode out.

How quickly things fall apart.

I feel feverish.

I can see Sami looking at me. He's saying, we will jump at the same time, Raghu, on my count, one, two, three, you jump at the same time, okay, I can't swim but you can, okay, so jump. I promise him that I will jump. I can see him jumping. I have not jumped. I am still there. It's too high, it's too high. And suddenly, he's drowning, he's calling out my name. He's calling out for me. A minute passes, then another. There's time, there's a lot of time. I can climb down. But blood, the water, the splashing around. It's too high, it's too high. My feet are bolted to the ground. I can't move. It's too late. His voice is fainter, his eyes are looking at me, and now his body is limp. I should have done something. I can do something. He's floating lifeless, right there. I have to run, run from the swimming pool, go out and say nothing to anyone. I'm too scared.

Sami rotted.

I feel sleepy.

27 May 1999

There are rumours about Sahil Ahuja. I hadn't thought much of him or the rumours around him because he or his supposed charm with girls older or the same age hadn't had a bearing on my life. Now it does. After all, he made the dissection of a frog into a romantic activity. He's a threat and so are Brahmi's smiles. I will not be abandoned and be wrested of my will to live.

If I had to wage a war against them I had to take the rumours surrounding Sahil Ahuja seriously. It is said that last year a girl two years older to him was found in a manner of undress with Sahil Ahuja. This was the worst of all the urban legends that surround the boy who is talked about in whispers on the last benches across all sections. While I was alternatively chalking out plans to drive a wedge between them and sulking, the bell of my house rang.

I peeped through the peephole and she shouted from the other side. 'It's me! ARUNDHATI. I wondered if you would want to join me for a game of carrom. I can give you a head start if you want one. I'm really BORED!'

'I have homework to do,' I said as I opened the door.

'You can come when you finish, can't you? There's leftover kadhi-chawal too if you like that?'

'I am quite full.'

'Don't be a spoilsport now.'

'I am not being anything,' I said.

'Just one game? Come, no? It's not as if your IIT will run away if you don't study today.'

And then it struck me. I stood there smiling stupidly at Arundhati, the gears in my mind clicking into position, the domino effect of what I would do from here visible clearly in quick cuts and montages in my head.

'What? What are you thinking?' she asked.

'Nothing. I will come and play with you. Of course I will,' I said.

She led me into her house and arranged the carrom table swiftly. There was a corner dedicated to it, complete with an extra set of coins and a lamp hanging overhead. I committed her house to memory just in case. If I had to have a pretend girlfriend, I had to make it sound as plausible as possible. Every detail should fall into place if I had to make Brahmi believe in the tragic, heartbreaking love story of Arundhati and me.

'Why didn't you go to school today? Are you not well?'

'I had a little fever but I'm fine now. I'm playing after a really long time. I might be really bad at it.'

'Should I break or should you?'

'You break, it will give you a little advantage.'

Mindful of not cutting a sorry figure, I flicked the striker with all the might of my fingers. Not one coin found a pocket. The striker skipped the board and rolled under the sofa. She crouched and pulled it out with a broom.

'You're such easy pickings!' she said and promptly cleared half the carrom table.

Four more turns and the game was over.

'Don't feel bad. I have not lost a single game in years and I'm talking about people who take this game seriously.'

'Did you call me over so you could beat me?'

'We can move to Scrabble if you want. Or ludo? Or snakes and ladders,' she said.

'We will play another game of carrom. But this time something should be on stake.'

'I just wiped off the board, Raghu. How do you—'

'Let's play,' I said and arranged the carrom coins. 'If I win you will have to do something that I ask you to do and vice versa. Shouldn't be a problem since you're good at this, right?'

'You have a deal,' she said.

I spat on my hand, and thrust it out.

'We need to shake hands?' she asked.

'That's the way I have been taught. It's tradition,' I told her. We shook on it.

I should admit I wasn't sure of my victory. At best I would have given myself a 40 per cent chance.

Little did she know that three years ago, I had fractured two fingers on my right hand when Dada had inadvertently closed the door on them. After the fractures healed my physiotherapist suggested playing carrom to regain mobility in those fingers. For three months I had played day and night and night and day, trying to outdo myself. My obsession ground to a halt when Maa–Baba decided that Sami was a bad influence and his coming home every day for a game of carrom was slowing my academic progress.

Unbeknownst to me, the carrom board was kept out in the rain and sun for a week. The wood rotted and with it my flights of fancy of being the best carrom player humanity had ever seen.

'That was amazing!' she exclaimed as I cleaned up the board.

'I didn't know I still had it in me.'

'You're a liar. You led me to believe that you don't play well. And that begs the question, what is it that you want from me?'

I told her what needed to be done. She didn't think twice before agreeing. I had given myself a much slimmer chance on that. We got back to our carrom. The rest of the games were keenly contested. She won the overall tally, I think.

Even though Ganguly had earlier hit a sublime 183 against Sri Lanka, his highest score ever, neither Dada nor Baba showed any joy. Pakistan had shot down two Indian pilots, one dead, another captured. Baba looked like something had broken inside him.

'One of you should have been in the army, killing these fanatics. What do you think they would do to the poor pilot, Nachiketa? Raghu, tomorrow I will find out what the process of going to the NDA is—'

'*Ei ki bolchho*, what are you saying? No one is going to the army from my house,' Maa snapped.

'I don't mind,' I said.

Maa looked at me in horror and said, 'If you even think about going to the army you will see my dead body. Touch me and swear you will not go.'

'So what should we do?'

'I should join the army,' I said again.

'No!' squealed Maa.

'So we should sit around and do nothing while these fundamentalists destroy our country? You can't give one son for the country,' scoffed Baba.

Give? I wasn't his to give away like a paper cup or a torn blanket. Why should I be given away? But in those short moments I imagined joining a fast-track enlistment, a rapid-fire training, a quick cargo flight to the front lines, an oversized helmet on my head, an AK-47 assault rifle in my hands, and me charging into enemy barracks, shooting indiscriminately, and getting shot at twenty times before I drop dead with the name of the country and the girl I love. India. Brahmi. That should teach Brahmi a lesson. To ignore such a goddam war hero for Sahil Ahuja!

'Even if I had a hundred sons I wouldn't give up one,' said Maa.

'And look what happened to the hundred sons of Gandhari. You're as blind as she is!'

'*Ish. Chup koro to*, keep quiet. Nothing will happen to my sons,' said Maa and kissed us both, pushing our faces into her bosom.

'It's all you Bengali mothers' fault. Coddle your boys so much they turn into meek women!' ridiculed Baba.

'Ei Raghu, come to your room,' she commanded. She led me to the room and locked the door behind us. Baba shouted like a madman at the door, 'Go now and sleep soundly! Don't regret it when Musharraf sweeps like a tide over our country, burns our temples, loots us and bathes our holy land with Hindu blood. Raghu? Are you listening?'

'Go, sleep,' Maa shouted.

Baba continued to shout. 'Ask your Maa to tell you how Mahmud Ghazni raided our beloved Somnath temple. Raghu, are you listening? He raided and killed thousands of us, broke away pieces of the lingam we worship and embedded them in the steps of his mosque. Anirban, tell them!'

I heard Dada say, 'I have to go to Bangalore tonight.'

Baba, with his exalted talks of sending me to the border to die, immediately softened and asked Dada if everything was okay. 'This private sector will work you to death. It's not too late. You will get another job,' Baba said.

We all went to drop Dada at the airport.

Maa–Baba were worried about Dada losing hair and weight alarmingly under the strain of the job. It was only I who knew of Dada's shocking betrayal.

I knew he was going to fight for Zubeida.

'What are you going to do?' I asked him.

'I will get her home,' he said.

The days of peace in our house are now numbered.

P.S. I didn't spot any new buildings. All I am thinking of is the high diving board and an empty swimming pool.

28 May 1999

I was set for my suicide mission. Not like a real suicide mission but metaphorically. You can't tell with me so I thought I will clear that out. Sahil Ahuja and Brahmi were fiddling with the new pendulum set when I walked into the physics lab. They stood up straight like thieves caught red-handed.

'Finally. Where were you all these days?' asked Brahmi.

'Sahil Ahuja,' said Sahil and shook my hand. His fledging beard looked even more bushy and rather warrior-like up close. I wanted to strap him to a chair and pluck the hairs out one by one.

'Something came up. I don't want to talk about it.'

'Do you want to join us in the experiment?' asked Sahil.

'I came yesterday though and finished the pendulum experiment. It was a tricky one but I have the observations with me if you want to cross-check,' I said and handed over the diary to them.

Neatly tucked in between the pages was the pretend-heartbreak-letter my pretend-ex-girlfriend had written to me. It was written on the backside of a picture of the two of us— get this—holding hands, smiling at the camera.

I continued nonchalantly, 'I will go cut some frogs. Pendulums are boring.'

I waited outside, read reports of Indian helicopters being shot down by Pakistan, and waited for the photograph-cum-letter to drop out of the diary. And when it did, Brahmi and Sahil passed the piece of paper between each other, disbelief writ large on their face. The letter, I should reveal now, told of a passionate love story between Arundhati and me. It started with Arundhati and me being accidental pen pals, and then being lovers. We had kissed not once but multiple times. Our love transcended all boundaries. But now it was breaking down. I had shattered her heart because we were too young to be in love, too naive, there was a world left to explore, and because I felt we were limiting ourselves. The letter was her lament against me, her anger with herself for falling in love with a charming boy like me, and her failure to hate me. In the letter, I was the heartbreaker.

'How could you do this to Arundhati?' asked Brahmi in he canteen.

'Do what? I didn't get you.'

'We found a letter in the diary. We know everything. Did you not think what Arundhati would go through?'

'I seriously don't know what you're talking about,' I said.

'Please stop lying. How could you hold your brother responsible for anything when you're like this? You're a hypocrite, Raghu,' said Brahmi.

'Listen—'

'No, you listen, Raghu. You kissed that girl and now you're leaving her? Weren't you the one who was all up in arms against your brother because he was behaving in a similar way?'

'I know it seems wrong but you have to listen to me,' I said.

'What possible explanation can you have, Raghu?'

I leant back and affected a learned pose. I said, 'I did this for her and not me. Was it easy? No, it wasn't. But rather than it happening later, it happened now. We are both too young to take this decision of being together. I wouldn't recommend it to anyone younger than twenty-two. I agree I made a mistake but I'm now correcting it. Sahil, you would know, right? I have heard a lot of things about you. You must have been in love with girls, right? Broken their hearts? Left them to cry as you left them behind?'

Brahmi looked at me with disappointment dripping from her eyes.

Sahil sighed. 'Yeah, that happens sometimes.'

'Yeah,' I said, chewing the word lazily and spitting it out like I was cool.

Brahmi looked at both of us. 'I thought both of you were better than this. If both of you can't grasp the simple concept of love, there's no point in us being friends.' She then picked up her bag and left. I watched her leave the canteen. Now that my task of splintering their relationship was done, I got up too.

'Where are you going now?' asked Sahil.

'I'm going home, genius.'

'I have nothing to do back home. Would you fancy a game of basketball?'

'Would you fancy a memory game with the periodic table?' I scoffed and left the physics lab.

Later in the evening, I found Maa giggling on the phone for a good ten minutes before handing it over to me. 'It's a friend of yours from school. Sahil Ahuja. He's a charming young boy, isn't he?' She smiled.

I took the receiver. 'Hello?'

'Hello, friend!'

'Sahil?'

'Yes, Sahil!'

'Where did you get this number from?'

'Telephone directory. Hey, listen, I'm sorry for the basketball thing. I just assumed you played the game too since Brahmi did. I didn't mean to offend you.'

'I wasn't offended. I just think it's a stupid game loaded in favour of taller people like Brahmi and you. It has nothing to do with skill.'

'I never looked at it like that. But hey, there's something I also wanted to talk to you about. I don't know how to say it but I will just say it. I know you like Brahmi.'

'What are you talking about? I don't—'

'I have seen you following us in school, Raghu. Unless there's any other reason for why you were peeping in from the lab windows for the last couple of weeks. I know the letter was fake too. You're not dating Arundhati, you never did.'

'Of course I did!'

'You played the entire charade to keep Brahmi away from me, didn't you? Am I correct?'

I slammed the phone down. Blood rushed to my face. I closed my eyes, forced them shut, willed time to turn back. Having failed, I picked up the phone again. He hadn't cut the call.

'Hi again,' he said. 'I am not going to tell any of this to Brahmi.'

'What do want in return?'

'Nothing really,' he said and laughed.

'If you want I will never talk to Brahmi again.'

'I don't like Brahmi. I just want to be friends with you two. And if you want to know a secret of mine then I'll tell you that I did orchestrate the chits in her desk to be friends with her. But you already know that, don't you?'

'Why would you want to be friends with us?'

'Why wouldn't I? I like both of you. Who else comes to school during holidays and finds joy in boring things? Now that's admirable, isn't it?'

'Umm.'

'But I don't know how you will get Brahmi to talk to us again. She seemed pretty angry,' he said. 'Anyway, come to school next week, okay? I will see you then. And loosen up, I won't tell her. I am a man of my word. You can trust me.'

Click.

'Raghu?' I turned to see Maa. There was that look on her face. When she digs a secret out and gives the secret-keeper a chance to confess.

She asked, 'Is there something you want to tell me?'

'Maa, what are you talking about?'

This was it. I thought I would have to tell her about Brahmi, about Sahil, about everything.

Maa sat near me, took my hand into hers, rubbed it gently, stared at me, and said, 'You're my shona baba, the apple of my eyes, and I know you will never lie to me. So tell me, is there something you're hiding?'

'Umm . . . n . . . no . . . Maa. Why would I hide anything?'

'Are you sure?'

'Yes, Maa.'

'Remember the first day of school?'

'Yes, Maa.'

'You were dragged away from me and put in a room with other children. Your teacher told me you kept asking every other kid in the class where I was, whether I had abandoned you. For Baba it was embarrassing but I found joy in you clinging to me, loving me unconditionally. But you have grown up now. You don't love me like you used to. You don't need me like you used to. Remember how you used to beat your fists at the door when I used to leave you with your brother? *Where are you, mumma, where are you, mumma?* You would cry for hours. Your Dada never did that. You always loved me more.'

'I remember all that.'

'So your Dada hasn't told you anything?'

'Dada?'

'He looks so tense these days. I don't know if it's work or something else. He hasn't been eating and has lost so much weight. You will tell me if something is bothering him, right?'

'Of course, Maa.'

And then out of nowhere she asked me, 'Does your Dada have a girlfriend? Like, does he love someone?'

'What? No! Why are you asking?'

'I just checked the telephone bill from the last month . . . there was a number he has called from the phone. It's a Bangalore number.'

'Oh, must be the office number, no?' I said.

'I checked the area code. It's not around his office. I called the number too. It was someone's house, a girl's,' she said.

'Must be a colleague?'

'Zubeida. Have you heard of that name? You will tell me if you know something?' she asked, her face twisting as the Muslim name rolled off her tongue.

'Of course.'

'You kids are growing up so fast,' she said wistfully. She let go to my hand and left.

I can't sleep now. Things are going to change. They have already been set in motion and I fear the worst. I have already lost Brahmi who believes I think as shallowly about love as the others, I just lied to Maa about Dada, and Dada's gone to get his to-be Musalman wife.

I feel like the mutineers of 1857 who were strapped to canons to be blown to pieces. What must have gone through their heads in their last moment? When they smelt the gunpowder and the match being struck. That. I feel exactly that.

P.S. 250 home owners got possession of an apartment building near my house. It's nine-storeys high. Just saying.

1 June 1999

It has been three days since Maa sniffed out Dada's secret and hasn't left the house since then. I wanted to warn Dada before Maa caught him in his lie. Dada came back today afternoon looking worse. Before I could tell him, he stared dead straight at me and said, 'I'm telling them about Zubeida.'

'Maa knows,' I said.

'What do you mean?'

'Maa asked me if I knew about any girl named Zubeida in Bangalore. She saw the STD number on the bill. Why would you call from the house phone? You could have called from the market.'

'That doesn't matter any more. I'm telling Maa–Baba that I want to get married to her.'

'What if they don't agree?'

'They will have to. I will tell them I love her and that I can't live without her. I shouldn't have to make this choice. And if I have to make one, I will pick Zubeida. As you said before, I held her hand, I told her I loved her. And what kind of a man would I be if I went back on that? I'm getting married to her. I am telling them tomorrow.'

He locked himself in the room. I wished I could call Brahmi but that option was thrown out of the window.

2 June 1999

It's all coming to an end.

The Gangulys will never be the same.

Dada's betrayal of the Gangulys will rank over Mir Jafar's selling our beloved Bengal and, in consequence, India to the British, over Judas' poison kiss to Jesus, over Brutus' knife, and over the hunchback Ephialtes' betrayal of the band of brothers at the battle of Thermopylae.

Years of unconditional love laid waste.

Zubeida Quaze was our Cyril Radcliffe, the man who fashioned two countries, India and Pakistan, out of one. And on hearing the news the Gangulys crumbled like pre-Partition India did—in disbelief, tears, disappointment and then violence. Zubeida Quaze, like a pebble flying at a high velocity, smashed against us, once a strong windshield with a clear future, leaving behind spiderweb-like cracks and a cloudy way ahead.

Only a few sentences had been exchanged when I was sent to my room. I had my ears pinned to the door and occasionally peeped through the doors. I could only hear little snippets of the conversation that fractured our family in a matter of minutes.

'What's the problem if I get married to her? I love her! There's no other way,' Dada was saying.

Maa was crying, her voice like a dying animal. She said, 'We strictly told you. No Musalmans! Chhee chhee! I won't let a Musalman girl step into this house! Over my dead body! Is she ready to convert? Will she be a Hindu like us?'

'Why will she do that Maa? Maa, I will die without her, and she without me. We can't live without each other. We can't even imagine such a life. Why don't you understand that, Maa?'

I saw Baba step forward through the space in the doors and it looked like he would hit Dada. 'Look at him talk! Bloody roadside Romeo! Who are you? Govinda? Where did you learn to talk like this? And what about your Maa? Haan? Look at him. He's already calling the girl and himself as us. And why would you die? Kill us instead! You would be happy with that, wouldn't you? First a stupid rank in IIT, then this mindless job, and now this!'

Baba swung at Dada. Maybe. I'm not sure, I couldn't see properly. But had he slapped Dada, Dada would have taken it boldly like an indignant satyagrahi. Always the pacifist, Dada, the Gandhian. But Baba is also Godse, and he would have slapped Dada again. Once. Twice. Thrice. Till the blows would have been dull and powerless, till the violence would have stopped making sense, till Baba would have realized you can't hurt someone who's inviting hurt, even embracing it and celebrating it. He would not have flinched. Tears would have sprung to Dada's eyes but he would be standing tall, clutching on to his mast of love. Baba would have thrown something at him. Dada wouldn't have ducked. Instead, he would have worn the oozing blood as a trophy. And then, Maa, the crying mother, always the one left behind in wars like these, would have begged for the violence to stop.

I remember wishing it to stop too. Dada was burning his bridges. That meant I would have to bear not only the sadness within me but also Maa–Baba's share of it. I know I'm not strong enough to do that. I couldn't possibly drag on much longer. I remember thinking that what happened with Sami had robbed me of being able to be happy but it had not stopped me from experiencing hurt. How unfair is that?

'We are getting married, Baba. There's no other option,' said Dada.

'Is she pregnant?' screamed Maa.

Baba butted in, 'What if she is? She can get an abortion. I will pay for it. That will solve the problem of commitment. You're not getting married to her, and that's final. You're not going to Bangalore any more.'

'I am, Baba. I was informing you, not asking for permission. I would really like it if you would happy with my decision,' said Dada.

'What did we do wrong to see this day?' screamed Maa.

'WHAT ABOUT HER PARENTS? HOW COULD THEY LET HER BE SUCH A LOOSE CHARACTER?' screamed Baba.

'Baba! Don't—'

'Don't you dare raise your voice at me! I didn't pay for your education for you to do this to us! What did we not do for you? We put every paisa we had into your education! We gave you everything you wanted, for this? So that you could get married to a Musalman? Why! What face will we show in the society!'

'How does it matter?'

Maa ran to Dada and rained slaps on him. 'It matters to us! I will talk to her parents! Are they putting pressure on you? I will tell them that this is not going to happen.'

'Maa! Stop! Her parents don't agree to this as well. They have thrown her out of the house. She has nowhere to go.'

'See, shona! See, my love! Then why are you being so obstinate? We will give her money. You don't have to get married to her. You're only twenty-one! What is love? You know nothing about love! It's all infatuation. You will get over it. I beg you, shona! I beg you! Don't do this.'

'Maa, I won't—'

Maa slumped on to the ground. Dada went to help her but Baba shouted, 'Don't touch her!'

Maa muttered as Baba helped her to the sofa, 'I hope she dies! I curse her! I hope she dies! I hope she rots!'

'Maa . . .'

'Don't call me that! Your Maa is dead! She was dead the day you touched that woman.'

At this, Dada started to cry as well. About time, I would say.

'Our decision is final. Either you have us in your life or that girl,' said Baba.

There was a brief silence and then I heard the doors slam. Dada would have walked out of the house. I'm crying now. I am crying for Dada to come back. But I'm also crying for Maa–Baba who don't deserve this, especially Maa. Baba has always had his prejudices against Muslims and Christians and Jews and anyone with a Holy Book but Maa had often made an earnest request to both of us. To let her choose our wives. Often she would call us to the living room and point to a Bengali actress on screen and say, 'This is how your wives should look.'

We would both roll our eyes.

This is Maa–Baba's worst nightmare come true. And mine.

All I can think about is going up the stairs of the tall building on Barakhamba Road, or even Ashiana Apartments, or Rajasthali, or any of the buildings I have scouted. How easy would it be to let it all end? Just one step and . . . poof.

Game over.

4 June 1999

It's been two days since Dada stormed out and Maa hasn't
stopped crying. With every passing hour, her cries sound less
human. I have been made to call all his friends and classmates,
Zubeida Quaze's house, his office, and there's no news of him.
Maa slapped Baba repeatedly, her hands barely reaching Baba's
face, and told him she wouldn't forgive him if Baba had driven
Dada to do something to himself.

She said she would throw herself in front of a train. *Did
this suicidal streak run in the family and I had not known of it
before?*

After Maa was done with Baba, she turned her attention
towards me.

'You knew about the Musalman girl.'

'Maa.'

'Why didn't you tell me? Why did you lie to me? Of the
two I knew you would never lie to me about something like
this. Did you not think about your Maa even once?'

Maa beat her fists on my back. I couldn't answer. I could
only cry.

'Dada will come back. He wouldn't do anything stupid,
Maa,' I said.

'He won't come back. I saw it in his eyes. He won't come
back, I know. My heart says he won't.'

'Maa.'

Maa's voice softened a little as she said, 'You won't do
anything like this na, shona? Hurt us like your Dada did? But

how do I believe you? You will lie to me as well. You will do the same as what your brother did. Leave me to die alone.'

Maa left the room. Later tonight we watched the news silently at the dinner table. The news anchor reported the handing over of the prisoner of war, the pilot Nachiketa, tortured but alive. Unlike earlier, Baba didn't exhort me to join the armed forces.

In bed, I thought about Nachiketa and his wingman, Ajay Ahuja. From what I have seen in movies, wingmen are thicker than thieves; they are like brothers. When Nachiketa was shot down by Pakistani forces, his wingman, his brother-like friend, was sent out to look for him. He, too, was shot down but unlike Nachiketa he was killed, taking a bullet through the heart, martyred. As I saw Nachiketa's images on the screen, I felt a deep sadness for him. How would he ever face the family of his wingman, Ajay? Ajay died heroically but it is Nachiketa, his brother, who would have to live with the consequences. What if Dada doesn't come back? He would marry for love, for the girl Zubeida, he will be a hero, a martyr. *But what about me?*

I wonder if Nachiketa would ever wish that he hadn't survived the ordeal. Even Mina's sweet licks aren't making things better. I miss Brahmi. I wonder how she is doing.

The phone just rang outside. It was Dada. He asked us not to try and contact him.

6 June 1999

The funereal silence that had been hanging over the Ganguly residence lifted early today morning. Dada returned. His beard grown, hair ruffled, and wearing the same shirt he had on the day he left us. He looked like a man. Mina jumped at his feet. She yelped in delight. I took her away and locked her in my room.

Maa rained blows on him, slapped him and hit him with her fists; the glass bangles on her wrists shattered like a new widow's. But she also hugged him and cried and kissed him on his arms, while he stood unmoved.

Baba stood there stone-faced, looking at him as if he'd seen him for the first time, with happiness and bewilderment and distilled hatred.

Outside, Arundhati was staring at the tamasha.

Baba asked me to close the door. Maa asked me to go to my room, they needed to talk to Dada in private. Dada interrupted Maa.

'Let him stay. He needs to hear this too.'

'Yes, I do.'

Maa–Baba and I sat on one sofa. He sat on the one in front of us as if he were a guest. Baba spoke first, 'Where had you gone?'

'I was with a friend.'

'Zubeida?' asked Maa.

'No. But she came yesterday. She's staying there too now.'

'What kind of a girl—'

'I told you her parents won't take her in. She had no place to go. I came to tell you that I'm getting married next week. We have taken a date from the registrar's office. You can come if you want to.'

Shock coursed through Maa's body like lightning. She shrieked and covered her mouth.

'When you can decide everything on your own why do you need us?' asked Baba.

'Because I want you to be there. She will be a part of *our* family.'

Maa looked at Baba. 'Look at what he's saying.'

Dada's words felt strange, as if out of a movie. How could he say things like these? Where did he get the courage?

'No Musalman will ever be a part of my family,' said Baba.

'Tell him he can't get married. Tell him I will kill myself if he does that,' said Maa to Baba.

'No, Maa, you won't do that. Don't talk like that. No one will do anything. I want to be married to her. I have to spend a life with her, not you. Maa, I have decided.'

'Then, so have we,' said Baba. 'If you won't listen to us, we don't have anything to say to you. You can go get married to any whore you want to. But we will never talk to you. We will be dead to you.'

Maa started to cry.

Dada said, 'Maa, Baba is over—'

Maa got up and ran to her room, crying. Dada got up too, running after her but Maa slammed the door on his face. She shouted, 'GET OUT, ANIRBAN! GET OUT! I DON'T WANT TO SEE YOU! YOU'RE NOT MY SON!'

Dada turned to look at us. Baba said, 'You heard your mother. Get out of this house. We don't want to see you till you come to your senses and leave that Muslim girl. If you can't respect all that we had done for you, there's no meaning for this relationship to carry on.'

There's a certain power in things that are said in a calm, impassioned voice.

Baba strode towards Dada, held him with the force of a much younger man, and led him outside the house. For the first time this morning, Dada looked weak. His body loosened as if betraying his mind, wanting to stay back. Baba shoved him out and locked the iron grill door we only locked at night while sleeping to keep the thieves out. Dada rang the bell for a good half an hour after which I was asked to take the batteries out. I don't know for how much longer he stayed out there. I was asked not to peep through the eyehole.

Later I was instructed to fill two suitcases with all of Dada's clothes and leave them outside the door. Maa protested feebly. Baba stood his ground. I filled the suitcases up. I realized how sparse or monotonous Dada's clothes were—white shirts, blue denims, a few check shirts, and a few grey T-shirts. When I was dragging the suitcases out, Maa stopped me. In the side pockets, she stuffed two of Baba's handkerchiefs filled with jewellery she had acquired over the last two decades for Dada's future wife and her first daughter-in-law, the daughter-in-law she had often vowed to treat like her own daughter, whose nickname she had decided long ago—Mina, after the daughter she had lost.

Just before I took this journal out, I saw Maa staring at Dada's empty cupboard.

Sahil called in the evening.

I am not proud of it but I told him everything. I had to or I would have exploded. What I hate even more is that Sahil's charm worked on me as well. Those ten minutes were the calmest of the day.

14 June 1999

Maa–Baba, who had stopped talking to me for keeping Dada's secret, thought it was best I started going to school again to divert my attention. I know they sent me so they could mourn in peace. The thin walls of our house can barely contain Maa's wails.

Back in school, Brahmi and Sahil enthusiastically welcomed me. No one mentioned how Brahmi walked out on both of us a few days ago. Sahil must have told her about the situation at my home. She was being extra sweet, which was highly uncharacteristic and slightly irritating.

Sahil and Brahmi were much better friends now, a fact that I would have been envious of earlier. Brahmi was supposed to dissect the rat because it was she who caught it in a trap outside her house but Sahil ironically named the gigantic rat Chhotu, the little one, as soon as he saw it. Brahmi couldn't kill it after that since it had been baptized.

'Why would you name it!' she complained.

'Why wouldn't I?' he argued. 'If you're killing something the least you can do is give it a name.'

'Do you name the mosquitoes before you burn a coil?'

'Apple, and oranges. Might I introduce you to malaria and dengue?' said Sahil.

'And might I introduce you to the plague?'

'Fine, you win,' said Sahil.

While I pinned the drugged rat on the dissection table, Brahmi and Sahil argued about India's position on the Kargil matter.

'Bombing Pakistan out of existence is not the solution to get the US and other Western powers on our side in the future. A lot of people will die unnecessarily,' asserted Brahmi.

'But soldiers are dying anyway, aren't they? Who cares if a few Pakistani civilians die? It's the public who elected a fascist, authoritarian government. It's not a great loss if they die instead of Indian soldiers.'

'It's not the same!' said Brahmi. 'Every person in the armed forces must know that this day could come. That he or she could possibly die, no? But civilians dying is just . . . collateral damage.'

'So you would have more of our soldiers dying than a few civilians of theirs.'

'Of course.'

'You're a traitor. I hope you know that,' said Sahil.

The scalpel in my hand slipped and cut through the heart of the poor, furry bastard, Chhotu.

'No!' echoed Brahmi, seeing the blood spurt out as if from a little water gun.

'I think Chhotu is dead,' said Sahil, chuckling.

The collateral damage of the three of us trying to make the best of our summer vacations was lying dead on the table. Ironic, considering Maa–Baba and I, we were all . . . collateral damage of Dada's love story.

Coming back to the rat, Brahmi insisted we bury it instead of throwing it away like the unnamed frogs. Sahil played no part in it. We dug a ditch near Shahrazad's grave.

'How are you doing?' asked Brahmi.

'I have counted seventeen buildings in a three-kilometre radius which are perfect.'

'So not so good?'

'Then again Maa–Baba need me right now,' I said. 'Also I'm a coward.'

'I would disagree.'

'Hmm.'

'You never told me why your Baba is so against, you know . . .'

'It's a long story.'

'We have time,' she said.

'It's depressing.'

'We are no strangers to that.'

'Okay, so where should we start. Umm . . . would it surprise you if I tell you that Baba was not really born an Indian, he's a Pakistani by birth?'

'What?'

'Well, Bangladesh, but it was Pakistan or East Pakistan to be specific in '54, so yeah,' I said. 'I have heard the story in snippets over the years from everyone else but Baba. The adoption of his national identity is a story no one tells in the family. I'm not sure even the little stories I have heard are true or not—'

'Tell them anyway.'

'Okay but what's true is that Baba was the second youngest of three siblings and that he came to India a couple of years before the East Pakistan genocide of 1971.'

'Was he there?'

'No but his entire family was. Technically my family too but you get it. So—'

'So what happened? Did they all die?'

'You're a bad listener, aren't you?'

'Okay, sorry, go on.'

'He was sent to study at the Bishop Cotton School in Shimla, away from the madness and the uncertainty in Dhaka. And in the middle of the madness of my grandfather, Shukumar Ganguly. I will show you a picture some day. He's more handsome than any of the Ganguly men. He was a double doctorate in Bengali and Urdu, and it was for his love for Bengali that he died. East Pakistan was almost all Bengalis so my grandfather, along with others, fought for Bengali to be recognized as an official language.'

'So they killed him?'

'Not exactly. Once that happened, the Urdu-speaking elite in West Pakistan already had a bone to pick with what to them were "backward Bengalis". So when a Bengali-speaking man won Pakistan's first general election, their President Yahya Khan ordered the wiping out of the Bengalis in East Pakistan, Musalman or not. Out of the hundreds of thousands who were exterminated was Baba's family. My Dadu was one of the first ones to die. The Pakistani Army systematically hunted down the intellectuals. Phew. I am surprised I remember all this.'

'And your Baba was in school during all this time?'

'Yes. Probably taking his exams while my pishi, father's sister, Rupi Ganguly, was picked up from the university and carried off to a military camp where she was repeatedly raped and killed when she got pregnant. His eldest brother, Hemendu Ganguly, was bayoneted through both eyes till his brain dribbled out of the sockets in the corridor of Dhaka University, where he was completing his master's in mathematics. It wasn't until the Indian Army was sent that the madness stopped.'

'That's horrible!'

'From what I have heard, Baba had spent twelve months in post-war Bangladesh, looking for their graves. He must have been my age,' I said.

Like I so often have, she must have spent the next five minutes adding visuals to the story.

We buried Chhotu and loitered around aimlessly in school.

I stayed out of the house for as long as possible.

Back home, Baba sat glued to the television. Pakistan returned the bodies of six soldiers of the Jat Regiment. The soldiers had been tortured—their genitals were cut off, their eyes punctured, teeth removed, and they had been burnt with cigarette butts. Maa asked Baba to switch the television off.

'Let him see,' said Baba, his eyes clouding over.

So I saw and let the violence wash over me. Just like he would have in 1971.

I looked at the names of the soldiers on the screen. I wondered what if they were my brothers. How long would I harbour the hatred against the perpetrators? Baba's family was killed by the army of the country he thought was his own, the anthem of which he sang, the flag that he saluted. How deep would that hurt be? I wonder if Baba had been taught to hate India growing up, like I have been taught to hate Pakistan. And how would it have felt when it was the Indian Army that had helped put a stop to the atrocities? Was his love for India, his change of heart, instantaneous?

I blurred my eyes and imagined an alternate headline.

'Captain Anirban Ganguly and five others tortured and killed.'

I can still feel anger course through my veins like molten lava. But I like Zubeida Quaze. She had no part in this.

Why can't Baba see it like that?

Maybe because he was there.

12 July 1999

The summer vacations ended today and I was back in school, sitting next to Brahmi, taking mental images of her to make up for all the time I had not seen her.

'Are my pimples bleeding?' asked Brahmi, dabbing her face with a tissue.

'Why would you say that?'

'Because you're staring,' she said.

'I . . .'

All I wanted to do was to shrink in size, crawl into her lap, and cry my heart out, and also slip in a little confession of my love while I was at it. Instead when she asked me what I had been doing in the last one month, I told her and Sahil that we had taken a little holiday.

'Tell me later,' she whispered, catching my lie.

I got out my newspaper and started reading it. INDIA WINS BACK TIGER HILL FROM PAKISTAN. Deaths avenged, enemies vanquished, a nation saved. What could this victory mean to anyone? It's a piece of land, a pile of rocks, stained with the blood and guts of innocent soldiers, an obsession of politicians. What's the meaning of such all-consuming love and hatred? Of land and of people? And what kind of people? What kind of society? One that turns Maa–Baba into people I can barely recognize?

Sahil has shifted from the last desk to the one behind Brahmi and mine. On his previous seat now sits a new boy whom Amarjeet ma'am introduced as Rishab Batra, a transfer from G.D. Parekar School, a school for children who can't live without central air conditioning. The class was asked to introduce itself to him. We did so, like nursery students, standing up one by one and telling him our names.

When Sahil's turn came, he stood up and acted like a class clown should, 'Hi. I'm Sahil Ahuja. G.D. Parekar is a much better school, isn't it?'

'Of course it is,' said Rishab.

'Then why are you here?' asked Sahil.

The class giggled and Amarjeet ma'am shushed them.

Rishab Batra smiled and said, 'I was asked to leave.'

'For having too many girlfriends?' asked Sahil and the class laughed.

Rishab smiled. He was handsome, like boyish handsome, like a movie star, and I saw Brahmi also looking at him like that. It shrank my heart. He looked like the kind of boy who would hold a girl's hand and tell her she is beautiful the first time he meets her and make her fall in love with him.

'I used to drive to school and might have influenced a few classmates to drive their parents' car to school as well. The parents complained and here I am,' said Rishab, continuing to smile.

'Which car do you drive?' asked Sahil.

'Sahil! One more word and you're out of the class!' shouted ma'am.

'It's either a Peugeot or the Lancer,' said Rishab. 'I like the Lancer.'

'We can be friends if you teach *me* how to drive.'

The class laughed and Sahil was thrown out of the class. It was now that I looked at Rishab again closely to ascertain if he was a threat to my embryonic, one-sided love story with Brahmi. Rishab Batra wore a watch with a metallic band, his hair was a well-made puff and his posture was that of a rich, spoilt kid. By the time school ended, Sahil and Rishab were laughing and backslapping each other like long-lost friends, which irritated me to no end. Rishab shifted to the second bench and laughed at everything the three of us had to say. Sahil was disappointed that Rishab didn't have and never had had a girlfriend, didn't smoke, hadn't ever been to a club, hadn't stayed overnights at a friend's place, hadn't travelled abroad or had a passport even, or banged his car into a hawker, all things Sahil expected rich kids to do.

It was clear our group had swelled to four people, which was exactly what I was wary about. There was only a minuscule possibility that Rishab, or even Sahil, could ever affect me— they didn't have the power to—but after Maa–Baba's swift and cruel change in behaviour I couldn't really trust anyone, not even myself. Because wasn't I in all my wisdom obsessing over what might happen to Maa–Baba if I die? How swiftly had I changed from a benevolent son to a love-struck boy who only wanted one more day, and then one more day with Brahmi.

We didn't take the school bus or a Blueline home. Rishab insisted that his driver drop us home, and Brahmi insisted that she be dropped off near my house.

'So where were you all these days? We missed you,' she said as we waved Rishab and Sahil goodbye.

I wanted to ask her if *we* included Sahil or the biology teacher, or was it just her, too embarrassed to accept that it was only she who'd missed me?

As I narrated the sequence of events that had transpired at home, how my parents refused to let me out of their sight, lest I turned out like Dada, in the past few days, I felt sorry for myself. Surprisingly, there was no shock on Brahmi's face.

'They sound just like my Tauji–Taiji.'

'Do they talk like that to you? Don't your Mumma–Papa say anything?'

'They are elder by ten years and my Mumma–Papa are the quiet, peace-loving sort. They stay away from arguments.'

'But these aren't arguments. It's just them spewing venom all the time. It's so hard to take the constant abuses and the disturbing things they say about Dada and Boudi.'

'But Raghu, you shouldn't have hidden anything from them. That was on you,' she said slowly.

'So what? As if you haven't ever lied to your Maa–Baba.'

'I have never lied to my Mumma. That's the point of having parents, Raghu. They are the only people who will forgive you for everything,' she said.

'For everything? Even the boys you loved and these cut marks on your wrists?' I asked.

'They know about everything. They don't judge me. Mumma holds my hand every time I do something and talks to me about what's going on with me.'

'Hmm. I am surprised they don't slap you for it.'

'Raghu, I won't hear a word against my parents,' she said.

'Fine, I'm sorry. Unfortunately I do have to rely on lies. There's sometimes no way out of it,' I said.

We were close to my house.

'I should go now,' she said. 'Who's that girl, by the way? She has been looking at us for a while.'

I turned to where she pointed. On the balcony, Richa had been staring at us. She saw me and disappeared inside the house.

'A neighbour.'

'I will see you tomorrow?' she said.

'Brahmi? There's something I wanted to ask you.'

'What?'

'What do your parents do?'

'Is that important for you to know?'

'Me? Not really,' I said and realized how stupid it must have sounded. 'Maa asked me a few days ago. Never mind. I will see you tomorrow.'

'They are both engineers,' she said.

Today was a quieter day. I wasn't cursed and neither were Dada and Boudi. They maintained a steely silence and apart from being chided for leaving the light on in the bathroom, no words were exchanged between Maa–Baba and me.

16 July 1999

Maa–Baba were home when I got back and like the past few days, they ignored my presence. I coughed lightly. I have taken to coughing quiet frequently now, hoping Maa would show some concern, maybe think that I'm suffering from a mild strain of tuberculosis, realize the folly of her ways and apologize for the treatment that's been meted out. Either way, she has to do something because their behaviour is tellingly hypocritical. Because if they hated their sons so much then why were they still obsessing over Dada's marriage?

Today both of them hovered nervously around the telephone expecting a call. An hour later the phone rang and Maa put it on loudspeaker.

'Mr Chatterjee! We were waiting for your call. How are you?'

An old, cracked voice answered from the other side, 'I'm good, I'm good. I studied your son and daughter-in-law's *kundli*s. I am afraid I have some bad news.'

'What?' asked Baba.

The man sighed on the other end. 'Anirban will have a troublesome marriage. I don't see it lasting long. You can do a puja to remedy it but the girl—'

Maa cheered up and interrupted. 'Anything else?'

'I don't know if I should tell you,' the old man croaked with the air of an oracle.

'Please tell us,' said Baba.

'I see another problem.'

127

'What kind of problem?' asked Maa.

'If they choose to have a child, it might not survive the first two years,' the man said. 'You couldn't give me the exact time of birth of the girl so I could be wrong.'

Maa–Baba asked me to leave the room.

Later Maa came to my room to give out a single-line instruction.

'Ask Dada not to bring a child into this world.'

17 July 1999

Maa is one of the most beautiful women I have ever seen. I'm not saying that because I'm her son. Even till a couple of years back she used to be mistaken for Dada's gorgeous elder sister. Both Dada and I used to be proud and embarrassed about that. In PTA meetings, not only was Maa the most beautiful mother, she was also always the smartest, her confidence and poise unmatched. Her spoken English and Hindi, between which she switches comfortably, is better than mine or Dada's.

But today morning, she looked like a ghost, her skin pale, fingers gangly and her hair sparse. She sat beside the landline, waiting for it to ring. It was Maa's birthday today. Every year, no matter how hard I tried, it was Dada who wished her first. I peeped out from my room for half an hour, hopelessly willing the landline to ring. For a large part of the past few weeks, Maa–Baba kept the phone unhooked to avoid Dada's calls, who called us often despite Baba's reprimands.

The phone didn't ring.

'Happy Birthday, Maa,' I said.

'Stop this acting. I know you don't love us, shona,' said Maa and got up. Her voice was ice, her eyes angry.

'But—'

'They say when children grow up, they love their friends more than their own parents. But you—'

'What about me?'

'That's why you don't have friends, shona. Because you couldn't stand by them when they needed you, just like you did with us. You only think about yourself. Don't I know you well, shona? How you're constantly hiding behind the diary you write.'

'Maa. I have friends—'

'And are you a good friend? Were you? To Sami?'

'I was!'

'I should have known. If you can lie to Sami's parents about him then you can lie to anyone. He was your best friend after all.'

She walked to her room and closed the door behind her. Happy Birthday, Maa. Thank you for the wonderful return gift.

To celebrate Maa's birthday and her impression of me, I wandered out of the house when no one was looking.

An hour later I was at Sami's house. I hadn't been there in months, which corroborates Maa's statements about me being selfish and what not. The door was locked, spiderwebs on the windows, yellowed newspapers outside their door. Sami's parents had moved. It's hard not to feel guilty about that. For the few months after Sami had died I used to go to their house, watch them cope, partake in their grief from a distance. Then I stopped.

I loitered around, Maa's jagged words still reverberating inside me like shurikens, shredding my heart till I found myself inexplicably outside Brahmi's house. I sat on the pavement facing her window. I saw a silhouette in the window which I'm not sure was her. It was stupid what I did and I knew it sitting there but I couldn't make myself get up and leave. I felt myself heal, the auricles and ventricles found their place again, the tendons snapped back, the blood flowed in my veins once more. Then I got up and came back home.

Maa–Baba hadn't missed my absence.

19 July 1999

A piece of advice to you, future Raghu, if you're reading this: First, don't bother with secrets, you're horrible at it.

You get to keep only one big secret in life. Second, never underestimate the scorn of a woman you have seen naked. Richa Mittal hadn't yet had her revenge. Her cunning was baffling.

Today morning Sahil called me and told me what had transpired over the last couple of days.

'Sorry, Raghu. I couldn't lie. Brahmi made me swear on my mother and I could not lie about anything after that,' said Sahil.

'What happened?'

'Brahmi knows about the fake picture, the letter, and why you did it.'

From here on, my memory of the conversation that followed is hazy. I couldn't hear or process it properly over the sound of my shattering heart.

'Some girl in your colony followed her.'

'Richa?'

'I don't know her name. She told her that Arundhati and you were new friends, and not pen pals, not lovers, not anything.'

'But how could she—'

'Maybe Arundhati told her?'

Could that be? How could she have wheedled it out of Arundhati?

'I need to talk to Brahmi.'

'Raghu, I—'

'What?'

'That's why I'm calling you. She asked me to tell you to not talk to her. She told me she's sorry about what's happened but she can't talk to you any more.'

'She said that?'

'Yes and neither can I or Rishab. Both of us can't get stuck between the two of you and so I chose her. So did Rishab.'

'Why exactly would it matter to me who Rishab chooses?' I asked.

'We were a group.'

'WE WERE NOT A GROUP! Brahmi and I were friends and you two just butted in. So yes, I don't care what you choose to do. DO YOU GET THAT?' I said, and I must have regretted saying it but I don't remember it now.

'Glad to know what you think of us.'

I slammed the phone down and gaped at the gall of Richa Mittal, that mute girl who suddenly found in her a wickedness till now unknown. I strode to the Mittal house; they didn't open their door.

When I asked Arundhati, she said, 'Richa told me you were best friends with her. I didn't see any reason to hide it. Why? Something happened?'

I shook my head and came back home.

I took my journal and went to the roof of Ashiana Apartments. I was writing and I was looking down. No, I was not going to do it and I know that and I knew it when I was leaving the house to come here. Despite everything that has happened in the last few weeks, I am the farthest I have ever been to doing anything stupid. I feel I'm tethered to Brahmi like a stupid lovelorn goat. I can go round and round her, close or far, but I can't disentangle myself from her. I want to see her again, talk to her, know her stories if she would tell me, and just be around her. So in true goat fashion, I left Ashiana Apartments for Brahmi's place. Had it been a movie,

I would have barged in, given a credible explanation for how I found her address, and then got on my knee and told her that she meant quite a bit to me. But since it's not, I hovered around awkwardly, came back home and got an earful from Maa, who gave me the staple 'Is-this-house-a-guest-house-for-you!' line.

20 July 1999

For the first two periods, I sat alone in class.

Brahmi had changed her seat and sat with Shrikant Gupta, a dour-faced, unimpressive fellow, in another row. Sahil and Rishab were sitting on the seat behind her. Conciliatory smiles were exchanged. I might be in the wrong but that did nothing to blanch the fury that ran through my veins like molten lava. The sadness of my love story ending before it had even started was manifesting itself in anger.

During the lunch break, Rishab and Sahil, who talked to and laughed with Brahmi, were at the basketball court playing football with a Cosco cricket ball. I followed them and volunteered for the opposite team. Brahmi watched from the sidelines, frowning, hurt flowing in abundance from her eyes. The match started and an inhuman strength grew within me, it churned in my stomach and flew through my limbs, and I ran and shoved and bumped and kicked and jumped like a Russian soldier on steroids. Gasps surrounded me as half a dozen players suffered injuries and humiliation, including Rishab and Sahil. None of the boys cowed down to my domination because like Brahmi there were other girls watching the proceedings. The only plausible reason for my behaviour was some ancient genes controlling mating practices among gorillas kicking into action within me—beat your fellow mates to get the girl.

Five minutes from the lunch-break bell, the other team took me out in a well-planned and perfectly executed

134

manoeuvre. A shove and a trip, a sharp nudge and a punch, and I was on the ground, bleeding from my mouth and my head. Two of the boys from my team took me to the medical room, ignoring my protests. I walked past my three ex-friends, head held high, lips pursed, blood dripping from my head.

Later I was told that my team, short by three boys, lost by two goals.

The rebukes from the medical teacher and the spilt blood drained the anger from me. I was mended and bandaged and was free to go. The painkiller made my brain swim, my limbs numb and my tongue loose. Floating in my head and stumbling through reality, I left the medical room.

Outside, Sahil, Rishab and Brahmi were waiting for me. Brahmi dismissed Rishab and Sahil like lowly courtiers.

They nodded at me and left. Brahmi patted the concrete stairs she was sitting on. I went over and sat next to her.

'That was a stupid stunt,' she said.

'It seemed like a fun game to me.'

'You didn't have to lie to me. Why did you?'

Lup-dup. My little frog heart beat again. Lup-dup. A little blip on the heart monitor. I wouldn't have said what I did but I had no control over my tongue. The chemicals from the painkiller gave me an unforeseen courage to accept the consequences of what I was about to say.

'I didn't know Sahil well. I had heard frightening things about him and when the two of you started getting close I was terrified. I have grown to be possessive of you even though I have no business to. It was a misstep trying to control what you feel. I felt helpless and angry. There was nothing between Arundhati and me, or for that matter anyone else. You're the first girl I have grown to like.' I said without stopping for breath.

'You should have told me that.'

I stared at my fingers which could have been any number from ten to fourteen, too scared to look up.

'But don't worry, I won't talk to you from now on. I'm sorry for what I did on the field today. I wanted to hurt Sahil and Rishab,' I said.

'And you did,' said Brahmi. I felt her hand hover near my head. She adjusted the bandage. 'So you like me?'

My voice failed me for a bit. The words came out in a stutter. Is the painkiller wearing off? Her smile only made it worse. I said, 'I have never had a girl for a friend so . . . also, you're so much like me. So I think I just . . . I don't know. I spoilt everything, didn't I?'

'You were right about something. You're just like me.'

'Am I?'

'Richa could reach out to me easily because that day wasn't the first day I was near your house. I have been there before, multiple times, just like you have been to mine.'

'But . . . but—'

'It shouldn't be surprising to you since I know you have done the same. But if you want to know why I was there, I'll tell you that I wanted to see Mina. It assuaged some of my guilt over losing Adolf. After a few days I realized I was looking at you, not Mina.'

'Why would you look at me, Brahmi?'

'Why would you look at me, Raghu?'

LUP-DUP.

'I have talked to my Mumma too about you.'

LUP-DUP.

'Did you tell her I scored as much as you did in the boards? Because you should tell her I scored as much as you did.'

'I might have missed that,' she said.

'Why would you not tell her that?'

'It's entirely my decision,' she said.

'And what is your decision?'

'Raghu. If we are to decide to like each other more than we like others then there is a minefield of ground rules to follow.'

'I will never lie again.'

'That's the least of our worries, don't you think? What if tomorrow I wake up to an assembly announcement of your suicide? What will it do to me?' asked Brahmi.

'Do you get these dreams too?' She didn't answer. I continued, 'But I will have you know that I haven't felt suicidal for a very long time. The little voice inside of me has quietened. So much so that I feel almost selfish for having moved on from Sami's death,' I said.

'Raghu.'

'Let's decide we won't do it then? Let's promise to live. Let's save each other,' I said.

'This is exactly what I am afraid of, Raghu. I can't promise you that and you can't promise me that even. You know nothing about me.'

'Why don't you tell me?'

'I don't know how to,' she said.

'You parents clearly know, why can't I?'

'Because you can't,' she said.

'So us liking each other is off the table? Is that what you're saying?'

'It's not off the table. But I don't want to be a reason for more sorrow.'

'How's that even possible?'

'Didn't you think that about your parents?' she asked. 'But fine.'

'Fine, what?'

'Let's decide to like each other. I have a question though,' she said. 'Are we using the word "like" because love is too scary to use?'

'I love you.'

I heard my heart stop and jerk back to life as if jolted with a thunderbolt.

'I love you too.'

'Can I know all your stories now?' I said.

'Was all this a trap to juice me out of my stories?'

I shook my head.

She laughed, and that was the most beautiful thing.

'I can tell you about this one,' she said pointing to a jab rather than a slit. 'By god, how stupid was I two years ago?'

I had to concur after she told me why she had jabbed her wrist with a compass. A couple of boys had drawn a lewd picture of hers, Xeroxed it and stuck it on noticeboards as revenge for her before-time submission of an assignment. I wanted names, addresses and a handgun to hunt the boys down, paint the world red with their blood. Later we decided to say the words, I, love, and you in different combinations and wondered how if only spoken in the correct order these innocuous words turn powerful and all-consuming. We backed it up with physiological evidence when she placed her hand on my chest and felt it thump. We decided we would give each other three short missed calls in the evening just in case we missed hearing it from each other.

We bunked the last period and went to the planetarium. The universe witnessed our first date.

24 July 1999

My somewhat stellar mood of the past four days was reduced to ashes when I found Dada waiting for me outside the school. I followed Dada to the hired taxi. Zubeida was waiting in the car and smiled widely on seeing me. I could have smiled back at her since now I know the wondrous world of being in love—the missed calls, the stolen glances and the electric awareness of an accidental touch. But I didn't because Dada's abandonment and Maa–Baba's misplaced anger towards me still rankled deep. I noticed Dada's facial hair growth—an ominous small tuft was growing on his chin and fired my first salvo.

'You're growing your beard. What name have you chosen? Aslam?' I asked him.

'Raghu, let that be the last time you mock her faith,' Dada spoke gruffly.

'Let him,' said Zubeida. 'I'm sure he's going through a lot. It's okay for him to vent.'

'By venting, do you mean I can tell him that he has destroyed our family and left me behind to deal with the consequences? If only you had tried harder to convince them, Dada, I wouldn't be in this shit.'

'How am I supposed to try when they refuse to talk to me? It's they who need to accept that the situation is not going to change. That's the idea behind marriage.'

'Had you not told me I wouldn't have known, Dada. Thank you for your limitless wisdom.'

'Raghu, I didn't come here to fight. Zubeida and I got something for you and I wanted to give it you. That's all,' said Dada.

'I don't want anything from you.'

Zubeida Boudi took out a slim rectangular box from a huge polybag and gave it to me.

'Open it. Zubeida Boudi bought it for you.'

I ripped the box open. It was a brand-new PowerBook.

'I don't want it,' I said, my voice betraying the import of my words. Inside the box was another little box. They were CDs of five games. Race, Arcade, Combat and two more. 'Why are you giving me this?'

'There's something we need to tell you,' said Zubeida.

'Zubeida is pregnant,' said Dada.

'She's having a baby?'

'We are having a baby. That's what being pregnant means,' said Dada.

'I can't believe it, Dada.'

'What is so hard to believe?' asked Dada, smiling.

'You don't look happy,' said Zubeida.

'But the astrologer—'

'What astrologer?'

'Maa–Baba consulted one. He told them your marriage wouldn't last long and that there would be a problem with your child if you choose to have one. He or she wouldn't survive the first two years. They asked me to tell you to hold off having the child. They are planning to do a havan at the house to make things all right.'

'Oh, fuck off!' snapped Dada. 'Did they? You can't be serious? God!'

'What do you mean make things all right?' he asked after a pause.

'Dada, you know. To make the Gangulys whole again? For your marriage problem to go away. They—'

A look of horror passed over his face.

'They will be praying for my marriage to break?' fumed Dada. He paced around the car, holding his head. His face flushed red. 'You go home and tell him, tell Baba that he's dead to me now. Tell him that he has nothing to do with me any more. You know what . . . You know what . . . tell him that I will convert! I will fucking convert to Islam and then I will see how his ridiculous religion with a thousand gods and contradictory logic and stupid rituals touch me or my wife! TELL HIM THAT, OKAY! ASK HIM TO DO AS MANY PUJAS HE WANTS TO DO. ASK HIM—'

Dada's voice broke and tears splashed out of his eyes. I rubbed Dada's back. He coughed and phlegm splattered outside from his nose. He used my handkerchief. The words dried up between us. He leant away from me as if I would infect him with Maa–Baba's insidious plans against his wife.

'I'm sorry, Dada. I'm sorry, Boudi.'

Boudi patted my back. 'It's not your fault.' She looked at Dada and said, 'Don't worry. My Allah will protect me.'

It seemed funny at the moment. Gods being summoned like Power Rangers.

They left soon after. But on my way home, the PowerBook kept getting heavier for me to carry. It was as if the guilt of betraying Maa–Baba even further seeped into the box and morphed into lead. I called Sahil from a PCO. He couldn't believe his luck—and neither could I—when I told him I would give him the PowerBook and the CDs for safekeeping. We met outside his house and he asked me if he could use it and was grinning when I told him he could. I told him it's not his, and he would only keep it if Brahmi refuses.

Maybe Sahil is playing with it as I write this.

I have chosen not to tell Maa–Baba of Boudi's pregnancy right now. Today I'm going to revel in the imagined future of a little kid calling me Kaku and seeing me as his or her hero. And since we are going that way, he/she's going to call Brahmi Kaki, and he/she's going to love spending time with us rather than his/her stupid, stuck-up parents.

In my imagined future, Dada and Boudi are scraping past their expenses while Brahmi and I are the power couple but with a lot of time on our hands to live a fulfilling life.

Today's not the day to tell Maa–Baba.

25 July 1999

Rishab and Brahmi lost their minds when I told them about Boudi's pregnancy. Sahil was less enthusiastic.

'They are potty-producing machines. I see no reason why anyone would go through nine months of pregnancy and three years of potty-training a half-wit when you can easily adopt a trained one,' said Sahil.

'Hey! My uncle's a big doctor,' butted in Rishab. 'He handles deliveries of even film stars. If you need any help, just tell me. I will set you up.'

Rishab and Sahil engaged in a no-holds-barred argument about whether kids are a waste of time and resources. Brahmi and I excused ourselves since we were in love now and we could do that. The school has caught on to our relationship as well. Their reaction has mostly been of shock—since we are the only couple in our standard. The shock was tempered only because we are seen as two of a kind. Outcastes and weird, like our rules didn't apply to them.

'Are you excited?' she asked.

'I think I am.'

'I am guessing you haven't told your parents yet!'

'No, I haven't. I want to savour the news before they spoil it all. You should have seen how happy Dada and Boudi were.'

'You're calling her Boudi now?'

'These days she seems more a part of my family than Maa–Baba do.'

'I know it feels terrible when your own family treats you like this,' she said. 'My Tauji–Taiji . . .' Her voice broke and failed her. A rarity.

'What about them?' I asked.

She looked at me, as if appraising whether she loved me enough to tell me. I conjured up the sincerest expression I could manage and told her she could trust me; what would be the point of being in love, otherwise?

'Every time they hit me, I wonder if I too would grow up to be a person like them. Earlier I used to rationalize their violence, think that I deserved it somehow. Now I know I don't. We are children and we deserve better.'

'Your Mumma–Papa? Don't they stop your Tauji-Taiji?'

'They travel a lot. Being engineers, they keep busy. I'm glad you're happy though,' she said.

'On our way back home, she asked me, 'Can you come see me tonight?'

'Where?'

'Outside my window. If it's not—'

'Wait for me.'

'I will.'

I waited for Maa–Baba to hit me with their routine taunts, discuss their misery and ruined life, and then slip into deep sleep worrying what the world thinks of them.

I stole from Baba's wallet, sneaked out, took an auto to Brahmi's house, and stood under the street light beneath her window. A little while later, the lights of her room went out. A candle flickered behind the frosted-glass window. The window opened with a groan and creak. She poured wax from the lit candle on to the ledge and fixed two more candles and lit them. The flames burnt yellow and blue and she smiled at me under their pale glow.

She mouthed, her eyes lowered in shame and shyness and things I have never associated with her, 'Now what?'

On the pavement, I drew in bold letters with the chalk I had taken from school. 'I see you.'

She let her fingers linger around the flame and smiled. She scribbled in the air—I see you. We spent the next hour writing messages to each other on the pavement and in thin air. Then she rested her chin on the ledge and I sat on the pavement and we stared at each other. The candles were about to blow out when she said—tomorrow. The flames died and it was dark again. The window closed.

I came back home looking forward to tomorrow.

27 July 1999

'The later you tell them the worse it will be,' Brahmi had told me, and so I didn't think it wise to wait any longer. In the light of recent developments, there's no one else I would trust more with my life decisions than Brahmi.

When I told Maa–Baba about Boudi's pregnancy, Maa started to beat her chest, cry and laugh in a mad frenzy and Baba cursed Zubeida like the crazed *kar sevak*s who had brought down the masjid in '92.

'You shouldn't have gone to the astrologer,' I said. 'If anything happens then—'

'GO TO YOU ROOM, YOU RAT!' shouted Baba.

I stood there, looking at him, in the eye, challenging him to make me budge. Which he responded to. He slapped me on my shoulder and bellowed his instruction again. Tears pooled in my eyes, my lips quivered but I didn't take my disapproving eyes off him.

'DIDN'T YOU HEAR ME?' he shouted. He took my hand and shoved me inside my room, slamming the door on my face. Soon after that the bell rang and I peeped out of the balcony. It was Bhattacharya Uncle and Aunty. Maa–Baba lifted the embargo on the Gangulys' relationships with the neighbours and let them in. After suitable condolences were offered, hearts were opened, and tea was drunk. Maa cried into Bhattacharya Aunty's arms. Aunty said, 'Of course that Muslim woman would do that. Ensnare him and then make sure he doesn't leave. All the modesty is really a tool for seduction.'

146

'We are ruined,' wailed Maa. 'Our lives are over. Is this why we carry our children in our wombs? So they spit on our faces when we are old?'

Baba nodded and drank the whiskey Bhattacharya Uncle had got him.

Then the Bhattacharyas left, leaving Baba with the bottle. Baba was up till late, drinking which was at odds with my plan to see Brahmi again tonight, try our new communication channel. When I got up in the middle of the night to check on him, Baba scrambled to his feet, eyes bloodshot and teary, smiling like a lunatic.

'Did you hear, you son of a whore?' he pointed at me. 'You didn't, did you? We will kick those Pakistani troops out of our country. We won the war. We won't allow them inside this country or this house. Go to Pakistan with them!'

He slumped back into the sofa, cradling the bottle like a child, smiling and crying. I waited for him to slip into a daze. I sneaked out to see Brahmi. By the time I got there, she had slept with her head resting on the window ledge. I waited. What if she woke up looking for me and finds me gone? What precedent would that set for our love story? She woke up after an hour. We tried what she had taught me over the past week—Morse code. Together we memorized the little dashes and dots for every alphabet. I learnt the words I LOVE YOU rather quickly.

. _.. .. _ _ _ . . . _ .

_ . _ _ _ _ _ . . _

'So for every dot you flick your torch once and for a dash, twice without pause,' she had explained.

Little flashes of light for every letter in the alphabet. Every phrase we said to each other during the night took a painstakingly long time to execute and decipher which meant we were really careful in picking what to say. Which I think is the only way to have a conversation. The flickering of the light carried our messages between us through the night. But no matter how many different ways I tell her I love her it always seems inadequate. I could use up all the words in the dictionary but I still wouldn't be able to aptly say how I felt about her. She felt like a part of me.

28 July 1999

Rishab, Sahil and I hung out at the terrace of Rishab's rather aristocratic house, sitting, talking about the girls in the class. Rishab and Sahil were at ease talking about skirt lengths, the imagined boyfriends of our classmates, and their projections of the peak breast sizes, all of which made me uncomfortable because others might be discussing about Brahmi and me too. Rishab told us stories from his last school, about his legendary seniors who had dated each other and sometimes college-going women, and in some cases—teachers (though those seem more like myths). Sahil, at one point, got bored and said, 'Are we going to do what we are here for?'

'What are we here for?' I asked.

Rishab scrambled to the terrace door and locked it. Sahil took out a cigarette pack from his back pocket and dangled it in front of me. He said, 'And for the record I don't smoke. But there's always a first time, isn't there? So who's going first?'

I didn't believe a word he said. The way he held the cigarette gave him away. Had it been his first time he would have held it like Rishab, who was holding his like a knife. Which is ironical because it is after all life-altering in a permanent sort of way.

Every few months, either Maa or Baba would launch into a rant about someone whom they found smoking. 'Look at Bannerjee's son,' Maa would say. 'Smoked and died at thirty-five of a flooded lung. Tragic.'

The names would change but every story ended with death. I believed Maa–Baba's stories till Dada told me we were subjects of systematic story-based brainwashing. Stories of men dying of smoking, in motorcycle accidents, through bad marriages, were fictional.

So yes, I decided to smoke.

Sahil lit the cigarette in his second attempt.

Sahil said, 'I think you two are my best friends. If I don't take my first drag with you, then what's the point of being friends?'

Sahil took the first drag and coughed. He took three more drags. It didn't get better.

'Damn,' he said before thrusting it out towards us.

I took it.

'Are you sure?'

'Never been surer.'

For the next half an hour, we smoked and coughed and our lungs and cigarettes burned. We ran through a pack in no time. How much worse could the cigarette smoke be than agarbattis, the incense sticks which Maa–Baba lit a lot to drive away the evil influence from their lives? Three pundits had spent four hours at our place to ensure the well-being of the Ganguly family. They told Maa–Baba that the havan would remove the *buri nazar*, the evil eye that had befallen us. How much further were they from making a voodoo doll of Boudi and pricking its stomach?

Sahil and I had lunch with Rishab's parents, his two elder sisters and a younger brother. They all talked and laughed loudly. Envy wrapped around me like a creeper and bled me of any joy I had left inside.

29 July 1999

Brahmi called me tonight which was new. We had strict rules about calling each other. Maa took the call and her revulsion was clear on her face when she heard a girl on the other side.

'Five minutes,' said Maa and handed over the receiver to me.

We pretended to talk about homework while Maa hovered around. When Maa finally disappeared into the kitchen, and I told Brahmi that, she said, 'It's my birthday tomorrow.'

The school register had another date; I had checked.

'My real birthday is tomorrow, the official is on a later date. Will you call me at twelve? I have permission to stay up late,' she said.

'Am I the only person you're calling to ask that or are Sahil and Rishab calling too?'

'Why is that even a question?' she asked.

'So it's just me?'

'Just you, Raghu. Just you.'

At 11.50 p.m., I checked on Maa–Baba. Then I tiptoed to the drawing room and called her. She picked up midway through the first ring.

'Happy birthday in advance! May you have the best year possible,' I whispered into the receiver.

There was silence.

'Are you crying?'

'Why would I cry? It's my birthday,' she said.

'So happy birthday!'

'Thank you,' she whispered back.

'There are still three minutes to go.'

'Can I cut the call after a minute? Will you call again? I don't want Tauji–Taiji to think it's a long call,' she whispered.

I cut and called her again. She called me Naina this time and thanked me for calling her.

'You sound sad. Why is that?'

'I have been wished for the first time in ten years. Mumma–Papa are never home on my birthdays.'

'Where are they now?'

'Bombay.'

'But they will surely call?'

'I should cut the call now. Can you call again?'

There were fifteen more calls after that one that I made to her. Every time I was a different girl. At 12.30 a.m., I heard Taiji scream for her to disconnect the call. Before I could ask her if I should come see her, the line was cut. At 2 a.m., I was below her house waiting for light to come on in her room. The window stayed shut but on the glass was a paper with a note scribbled in black sketch pen. THANK YOU. I waited for three hours for her and came back. She had told me to not worry if something like this happened.

I came back cursing her parents for skimping on STD calls. When I sneaked in, I saw Maa on the sofa, staring dead straight at me. She didn't even bother with an entire sentence.

'Brahmi?'

I nodded.

'You won't go from tomorrow. I don't want people seeing my son sneak out in the middle of the night to meet a girl. If you have to live in this house, there are certain rules you have to follow. There's plenty of time in school. There's no need to go in the night to meet her. And what kind of parents does she have who allow this?'

Maa didn't wait for an answer. She got up and left.

There's no way I'm not sneaking out tomorrow. I have inherited my self-preservation streak from Maa.

2 August 1999

Dada and I had been on the receiving end of quite a few beatings, he more than me. Being the academically weaker one, he was the one who was often chastised for low marks, suspensions and unfinished practical files. Though I detested it, I am for the parents' and teachers' right to slap a child. Though, sometimes there comes along a teacher like Raman Verma; he teaches mathematics to eleventh and twelfth graders. He is the weapon of choice our principal uses to rein in students and dole out disciplinary beatings. He pulls guys by their belts and smacks them right across their faces. I have borne the brunt of it once for unpolished shoes.

It hurt for two days.

Brahmi's bruises were more severe and Raman sir wasn't the perpetrator.

'Volleyball match,' she explained to Rishab and Sahil.

In the next period Brahmi slipped me a piece of paper.

Will your parents be home today?

No, I wrote back.

Can I come, she wrote.

Of course, I said.

Through the rest of the day at school, I alternated between being furious at the cause of the bruises, and being confused as to why she would want to come to my house when no one was around. I didn't ask her out of nervousness for what her answer might be.

'Raghu?' she asked as we entered my house, which was more dishevelled than usual. 'Where's you room?'

I lead her to my room. She drew the curtains shut.

'Do you have a first-aid kit?' she asked.

'Yes.'

'Can you get it?'

'Of course I can but—'

'Can you close the door on your way out?'

I nodded and ran to get it from the bathroom cupboard. When I came back, she was tucked inside a blanket, only her bare back showing, her face away from me. My heart thumped in fear and excitement and embarrassment.

'I'm sorry. I didn't mean to look,' I said and turned away.

'Come here,' she said.

Unsure, I walked up to her, my eyes glued to her back. A part of me was thinking of Richa and how uncomfortable I was seeing her but how natural this seemed.

She was still wearing her bra but the straps lay limp on her upper arm.

'Are you here?'

I moved quickly. It was then that I noticed the bloodcurdling welts on her back. There were three huge gashes, blood clotting around them, inflicted with a belt. Two Band-aids were stuck on them clumsily.

'Take the Band-aids off.'

I did as instructed. Her back quivered as I ripped them off even though I tried to be gentle.

'Now do as we were told in the first-aid class,' she said, her voice resolute, unshaking. 'First Dettol.'

My fingers trembled as I dampened a little piece of cotton with Dettol.

'Are you sure?'

'Do it,' she said, biting into my pillow.

I cleaned her wounds. She muffled her cries. The more I cleaned a wound, the bigger and deeper it seemed to get.

More and more raw flesh stared at me. I bit my tongue twice and tasted iron. I put a piece of cotton and stuck the gauze to it with medical tape.

'Will they stay?' she asked.

'Yes.'

'Double tape it?'

'Okay.'

'Thank you,' she said.

I packed up the kit and left. She came to the living room once she had dressed.

'Sorry, you had to do that. There was no place I could have gone,' she said.

'Tauji did this to you?'

She nodded.

'Why did he hit you? Please don't evade my question. I want an answer. I love you, we have established that. So I need to know.'

She fought away her tears. 'I made a few STD calls to Mumma–Papa. They caught me.'

'Can't you tell your parents about this?'

'What would they do? They are away and I don't want to trouble them,' she said.

'But—'

Her eyes flooded with tears and she put her arms around me. And soon I was crying, and crying more than her and it was she who had to quieten me, 'Oh, Raghu, you're so stupid! Why are you crying, stupid, stupid boy, shh, shh, I'm fine, Raghu, look, I'm fine now, stop crying now, such a stupid boy. What am I going to do with you? Just look at you, you baby.'

Weren't parents supposed to be our saviours? This can't be repeated. She can't be another Sami. I won't watch on helplessly this time.

'Do you want to watch television?' she asked.

I nodded vigorously and she had to ask me if I was okay. We watched TV for what seemed like hours. She thanked me when it was time for her to leave. We had just stepped out of the house when we bumped into Arundhati. I introduced them.

'Ah! So you're the famous Brahmi? Hi! I'm Arundhati! I played the role of Raghu's pretend girlfriend for his master—'

'I know,' said Brahmi.

'You're cuter than I imagined,' gushed Arundhati.

'She has a thing for cuteness,' I said.

'We should make her meet Sahil then. He too has a thing for cute people,' said Brahmi.

'Is he cute?' asked Arundhati.

'Is he cute?' I asked.

'Maybe,' Brahmi said and the girls laughed.

When Maa came back from work, she saw the soiled bandages in the dustbin and didn't even ask me the wheres and hows, or if I had hurt myself. Her apathy had only begun to hurt when she came to me with an instruction.

'If she comes one more time inside my house, I will throw you out.'

Little does she know that she will come back, in a few years' time, as her daughter-in-law. Yes, I have imagined that. And why not?

7 August 1999

Brahmi deals with pain much better than I do.

I had dodged Brahmi's outstretched fingers for a good thirty seconds before the Dettol-drenched cotton ball found the open gash on my forehead. I ground my teeth while she cleaned and dressed up my wounds.

'You're so stupid.'

'Your Tauji needed to be taught a lesson.'

'If I wanted him to be beaten up I could have done that myself. I'm stronger, taller and fitter than you,' she said.

Fair point but where's the heroism in that?

Redemption was in my reconnaissance and strike mission against her tyrant Tauji that I had planned and that had failed splendidly. Today morning I charged at her Tauji with a steel rod when he drove past me in his Bajaj Chetak. I had counted on him losing balance and being pinned beneath the scooter. I would have then beat the shit out of him, aiming at soft tissue and legs, and asked him to not lay a finger on Brahmi from there on. I'm not stupid, I had covered my face with a crêpe bandage. Her Tauji was bigger, smarter and quicker than I had anticipated. He swayed out of the first blow and it all swiftly went downhill from there. He shouted a war cry, parked his scooter with surprising deftness, scrambled for a rod which he found readily and charged at me. I was prepared for a fight unto death but people had heard Tauji's hoarse screams. I turned and ran and fell. Her Tauji caught up and got two blows in till I managed to run away, the crêpe bandage coming off my face, soaked in blood.

'What were you trying to achieve?' she asked.

'I hadn't thought long-term.'

'Raghu, if I need help I will ask,' she said.

'But you can't live there any longer.'

'You say the most obvious things sometimes,' she said.

'Can't you tell your Mumma–Papa to shift elsewhere?'

'Tauji is like a father to Papa. Papa owes everything to him. Moving out would be partitioning the house. And for what? Me?'

'Why not you?'

'You're sweet,' she said. 'I'm trying to find a way to leave the house.'

"How?' I said, wondering what she meant by find-a-way-to-leave.

'There's a cousin who lives in Gurgaon, Vedant. He might take me in.'

'That sounds far away.'

'I'm hoping it works out,' she said.

'Why didn't you do it before?'

'There was no reason to.'

'What reason do you have now?'

'Don't you miss the most obvious things too? You, of course,' she said.

Between then and now, I have rewound and replayed the conversation in my head a *bajillion* times. The more I did the worse I felt about not being the knight in shining armour for her. I was more like a jester in bandages.

In continuance of the dramatic events of today, Maa noticed the sullied bandage on my head. And just like that, the wall of her indifference crumbled and she forced me to see a doctor, and held my hand in the auto, in front of waiting patients, and the doctor, and while my bandages were changed, and on the way back, and when I ate dinner.

Baba maintained his cold indifference.

12 August 1999

Brahmi hasn't been coming to school since the day she bandaged me. For the first two days I called her phone and it was constantly engaged. Ma was keeping strict vigil so I could not sneak out at night either. By the third day I thought I would lose my mind so I went to her house during school hours. I walked around the house, passing it every ten minutes, hoping to catch a glimpse of her. I made several such rounds. I managed to spot her a couple of times but could not make eye contact. She came to the balcony around 11.30 a.m. to wring and put clothes on the clothes line, and then again at 3.00 p.m. to take the clothes off. She seemed fine, which only begged the question, why hadn't she been coming to school. Yesterday I knocked on the flat above and below hers, pretending to sell tickets, and asked the people at the door questions about the people staying below/above them. They would look at me strangely and slam the door on my face. Today, to my relief, she was sent to drop clothes at the dry-cleaners' and I caught up with her. We walked a few yards away from each other to not raise eyebrows in her neighbourhood.

'You should be in school,' she said.

'So should you.'

'Taiji has gone to her mother's. I had to cook. Were you worried?' she asked.

'Why would I be worried?'

'Is that why you were outside for the last few days?'

'I was absolutely not here. I hope you can sense the sarcasm in my voice.'

'From a mile away,' she said and asked me to wait till she dropped off the clothes. We found a secluded spot where her neighbours couldn't spot us. 'I called Vedant. He told me he might find me a job. I will leave this house and never look back!' she said and clutched my hand.

'Your parents? School?'

'Mummy–Papa will have to understand. I will see when it comes to that,' she said, eyes brimming with hope and recklessness.

'Can't you ask for money from them?'

'Tauji–Taiji won't allow it. If I ask for help, they will drag me by my hair back to the house. I don't want to depend on them for my happiness. They should have helped me when there was still time,' she said, and for the first time I noticed a tinge of disappointment in her voice for her parents whom I absolutely hated.

'You have thought this through?' I asked, my cowardice bubbling forth. Would I be willing to leave the security of a household—no matter how abusive—and venture out alone in the world? Find a job? Earn to eat, to survive, to stare at a future which is hardly so? Every class I had attended till now, every test I had taken had been geared towards success not survival. Jobs were a means to a career not sustenance. And here she was, talking in a language so brave that it was scary.

'Hmmm.'

'You're frowning.'

'You won't be in school. You can't expect me to be 100 per cent happy.'

'But I will finally be able to leave this house.'

'And that's why I'm about 80 per cent happy. How's this Vedant person? I want to meet him,' I said.

She laughed and said, 'What are you going to do exactly? Charge at him with a rod?'

'This time I won't miss.'

'You're sweet,' she said. 'Now go back home and start going to school. Both of us can't be illiterate, can we?'

'So has the school seen the last of you?'

'Believe you me, it's only you who will miss me.'

I came back home to find Maa–Baba shouting at each other, their voices carrying to the ground floor. I was asked to go to my room and I couldn't make out what they were saying but it went on for an hour. Baba left for his tuition centre in the evening and Maa started packing her bags.

'Maa? Where are you going?'

'To see Dada. I can't keep up with your Baba's madness. If he wants to keep away from his son, it's his choice, but I won't!'

'It was your choice too, Maa.'

'But I'm a mother. How long does he expect me to stay away from him?'

'So?'

'I can't stay away from my son,' she said. 'Get out of my way. I'm going to miss my train to Bangalore.'

I was sitting on a pile of Maa's clothes, a little dazed to be honest, to see Maa's quivering lips, trembling fingers, and her sudden change of heart.

She said, 'What happened has happened. Your Dada broke our hearts but what kind of parents will we be if we don't forgive him?'

'Are you going to get him back?'

It was I who wanted to squeal with joy. In that split second, I imagined a future—like I always do—of Dada, Boudi, that little kid, and Brahmi, who in my version chooses to shift to our house rather than Vedant's.

'Stop asking questions! I'm late! Move!' She slapped me on the back. Before I could react, she pulled me close. She held my face and apologized.

'Will you let Boudi come here too?'

'I don't know if Baba will ever allow him in this house but how long can a mother stay away from her son? But till the time I'm not here you need to listen to Baba, okay? You need to do everything that he tells you. Now help me close this suitcase. Yes, like that. I will be back soon.'

I revelled in seeing Baba's stricken face when I told him that Maa had left. He stood there dumbstruck, like the cat got his tongue. He disappeared inside the kitchen and cooked dinner for himself and for me. We ate early, after which Bhattacharya Uncle came over. They both drank from the bottle Bhattacharya Uncle had got. Later Baba slept on the couch, quite restless without his partner in crime.

14 August 1999

Brahmi was back in school but not for long if her plan was to work out. I could tell she was getting a little put off by my incessant questions about Vedant when she seemed to be in a jolly mood. Brahmi and I had stayed back in the school and were waiting for Vedant. He was already an hour late which tells a lot about a person. He could be Mother Teresa and I would still hate him for wresting away from me the opportunity to be her hero.

'He ran away from his house a year ago,' she explained about Vedant. 'He has not been in touch with his family ever since. He now lives alone.'

We had been waiting for him at the reception for an hour when he walked in. Brahmi smiled brightly when she saw him. He scooped Brahmi up in his arms with a flourish and kissed her on the cheek. There was something overwhelmingly positive about him.

'Who's he?' asked Vedant the second he saw me.

'Raghu. We are in the same class,' explained Brahmi.

He sized me up. I didn't hold his interest for long. He turned back to her and said, 'How have you been? Sorry, I couldn't be in touch. I wanted to but you know how it has been . . .'

'I know,' said Brahmi.

'It's been a year since I have seen anyone from my family. It's so good to see you. And how tall you've grown. Look at you!' Vedant said and held her hand. He looked at me and told me what I already knew. 'I failed my twelfth grade and Papa would have wanted me to sit at his stupid little paint shop. Who wants to do that shit, right?'

Vedant, with his nice shirt and shiny sunglasses, would have been a misfit in any paint shop, little or big, stupid or not. *Who wants to do that shit, right?* There was a way he said it, with a sense of danger and style. I can still hear it my ears; I am murmuring it right now. He said it with the slight accent of someone who only talks in English.

'I'm working at a call centre in Gurgaon. It's a shit place to live in but the job is good, pays me Rs 8000. They pick me up in a cab at night and drop me home in the morning. I sell insurance to the Americans. It's an easy job. Once you've sold an extra litre of paint to a Marwari businessman, there's nothing you can't sell. It's the next big thing.' He lit a cigarette. The guard asked him to put it out. He continued, 'I got in early. I could be a lead soon. I will show my stupid family what I can do. They didn't even ask me for my tenth certificate. I'm going to be really big.'

Brahmi and I stared at him, dumbfounded, a little appalled at his optimism.

'They train you for a month. You will be as good as me,' he told Brahmi.

We sat and listened attentively to his stories of achievement, debauchery and how he was successfully beating the system. Seeing him, the years of engineering seemed pointless.

'Keep your bags ready,' he said before leaving.

Brahmi hugged him and her eyes were little pools of tears.

'It's a good plan,' I told her later, not wanting to dull her smile. 'But your parents?'

'They will understand,' she said.

With that, I gave up that line of questioning her escape plan.

Baba came back home with a big ilish fish.

'I used to cut fish myself when I was your age. That's the key to how it tastes later. Come, I will teach you. It will be the best fish you have ever tasted,' said Baba.

I had about ten comebacks for him, each more biting than the last, making up for all they had made me endure in the past few weeks.

Instead I instantly forgave him and prepared the fish with him. Every once in a while he would call out Maa's name. The empty echoes would remind him of Maa's absence and he would turn pale. The fish preparation turned out to be bland, nothing like what he had initially bragged about. The two of sat us in the living room and watched TV. Maa's absence and our swift reconciliation hung in the air. I was not sure I had completely forgiven Baba so I put him to the test.

'Baba? My friend Brahmi needs some money. Could we spare some?' I asked.

He stared at me for an odd ten seconds, and told me things were a little tight right now. Then he raised the volume of the TV, hoping it would fill our lives.

My last-ditch attempt to scrape enough money to help Brahmi entirely on my own and become her hero had failed. I tried and was unsuccessful in asking Sahil for the PowerBook. He had been getting quite good at coding and his face shrunk to a raisin when I asked. Rishab is another option but we are talking about a lot of money and a stupid idea, or rather the lack of one.

15 August 1999

I'm just back from Rishab's house and it hurts to write this.
My fingers are cut and bleeding from four different places and
I'm hurting not only because of them but also from the losses.

Brahmi had insisted we celebrate Independence Day the
way it was meant to be celebrated—by flying kites. Before long
we realized why. Brahmi was a kite-warrior if there's ever been
such a thing. She decimated Sahil, Rishab, Arundhati and me
with consummate ease, her *manja*, the thread used for flying
kites, cutting through our combined ranks like a hot knife
through butter. Sahil and Rishab had dressed in their finest
combinations of orange, white and green to impress Arundhati
whom they were meeting for the first time and, from what I
could gather, found attractive. The first few losses were put
down as fluke, the next few were attributed to Brahmi having
a good day, and the last few were spent grunting angrily.

It took us two hours and sixteen kites to accept Brahmi's
superiority.

'All this just to humiliate us?' asked Sahil.

'Why not?' said Brahmi.

Later we sat in Rishab's room and he showed us his
impressive VCR cassette collection. We watched the movie
Border on TV in tune with today's date and shouted in joy when
Suniel Shetty, Sunny Deol and Jackie Shroff won us the war.

'I thought you boys must smoke,' said Arundhati later.
'I have never seen three boys hang out on a terrace and not
smoke.'

'If my mom finds out, she will gut me!' said Rishab.

Arundhati laughed. 'You're right,' she said. 'He's cute.'

'You said that?' Rishab asked me.

'Brahmi did,' I said.

'Brahmi said that?' he said, his chest filling up with pride.

'Do you want to smoke?' asked Sahil. 'I can get a packet from the corner shop.'

'I don't mind,' said Arundhati

'Have you smoked before?' asked Brahmi.

'Umm . . . I am not a loser, of course I have. Have you?' asked Arundhati.

Brahmi shook her head.

A few minutes later, we were at Rishab's terrace again. We ran through a pack in an hour.

'What?' asked Arundhati when she saw Rishab gaping at her, smiling stupidly.

Rishab said, 'If you put that to your lips, it would be like you are kissing me.'

'Like the four of us just kissed each other?' asked Arundhati and put the cigarette to her lips, took a drag and passed it on to Brahmi.

Brahmi took a long, deliberate puff. The smoke dribbled out of her lips, her chest heaved, the burning cigarette dangled from her fingers carelessly. I took the cigarette from her before anyone could lay claim to the kiss that rested on the bud. On our way back home, Arundhati told me of her intention to date Rishab, which Brahmi wholly supported.

'You do know you have to ask him too, don't you?'

Arundhati laughed. 'What do you think he will say?'

Fair point.

22 August 1999

Maa held me for fifteen minutes and bawled like someone had died.

'My shona, my shona, what would I do without you? You're my everything! You told me you were eating but look how thin you have become!' she wailed, holding up my gangly arms. She threw an accusatory look at Baba who shrugged. She waved down a coolie. Before the coolie could reach us Baba had already picked up the suitcase.

'I'm not senile yet,' Baba said drily.

Maa–baba didn't talk at all during the taxi ride home. Maa kept her hands firmly wrapped around me, kissing me and ruffling my hair from time to time as if surprised I still existed. Our house soon began to be filled with the deliciously rich aromas of ilish cooked in mustard paste, and red mutton curry. Baba pretended like it was no big deal. We ate and watched TV like we always did. Like Dada was away at the college hostel and not in Bangalore, married to a Musalman woman who was carrying his child. While I completed my schoolwork, Maa scrubbed my room clean, reorganized my clothes and my books, washed my clothes, and changed the bedding.

We were making a new start.

In the evening, no one questioned me when I left the house to go to the temple. For the past week, Brahmi and I had been meeting in the evening to buy little knick-knacks she would need when she started her new life in Vedant's house. Both of us would steal a little from our family members' wallets and buy detergent one day, a deodorant roll-on stick another, or even packets of rajma and Maggi.

'I don't want to be a burden,' she would tell me.

Today we were scouting for undergarments, which was as embarrassing as it sounds. For the most part I loitered at least a hundred yards away from her when she entered a shop, most of which had posters of half-naked women stuck on their shopfronts, staring at me, labelling me a pervert for staring back. She laughed when I refused to carry the black polythene bags containing what to me was contraband.

'Are you happy?' she asked.

'That's a wide question.'

'With your parents' turnaround?'

'I'm not sure how I feel. I have seen the worst in them and it's hard just to overlook that.'

'Do you like idli–sambar?'

'Why?'

'Because I love idli and that's what we are going to have right now. But you have to dip the entire idli into the sambar because that's the only way to have it,' she said.

I was pretty full by the time I got back in time for dinner. I was asked innocuous questions about school, practical files, teachers, etc. The conversation veered while Maa–Baba washed the utensils and I hung around finding one pretext after another. They would fall silent every time they would see me around.

Maa said, 'We could call them here for a few days if you don't want to go. It's too much pressure for them. Zubeida's parents aren't reaching out to her. Leaving that poor girl to live alone. She gets so sick in the mornings. They haven't even found a maid yet.'

'I'm not letting that girl inside my house,' said Baba roughly.

'I am not losing my son,' snapped Maa.

Baba strode out of the kitchen and stood smoking in the balcony for a good hour.

When he came inside, Baba said, in the tone of a defeated man, 'Even if she does come here where will they stay?'

Baba's resolve to hate Dada was wearing thin.

'We will sleep in the living room. We can't make her sleep outside,' said Maa.

5 September 1999

I changed her bandages again today. We lied to Sahil and Rishab.

'It's a mathematics project we are working on. No, no one else is allowed in the team,' we told them.

We were in the basement and she took off her shirt and wore it from the front while I faced the other way. Unlike that day, there was no blanket hiding her. Pain trumped any shame for both of us. I saw her naked back with gnawing embarrassment and rage.

'Did it pain?' I asked when I was done. I turned away and she wore the shirt.

'Lesser than last time,' she said.

Her Tauji had noticed the missing money. Brahmi hadn't admitted to the theft and yet she got slapped around with belts. Years later I would look at these scars as wounds I helped heal. But she didn't seem bothered by it at all. She was just smiling morbidly.

'It's just a few more days,' she said.

'It was a few more days a few more days ago. Your parents aren't back yet?'

'No. I hope they don't come back before I go. It will only make things tougher,' she said.

'Won't they come looking for you?'

'They will. By the time they find me, they would understand,' she said.

'I will miss seeing you outside your window.'

'And I will miss you,' she said.

'You know what I was thinking yesterday? I was imagining a situation where Maa–Baba don't warm up to Dada and things only get worse. Then even I could run away from home and we could stay together.'

'What if I'm a really difficult person to live with?'

'It can't be more difficult than living without you.'

'Aren't you the sweetest?'

'No, I'm not. Okay, probably only to you because it's easy to be.'

'I will miss you, Raghu. I wish I hadn't had to leave.'

Later we jumped the school walls and took a bus to Delhi University. She had heard from someone about an old uncle who sat outside Miranda House and made magic Maggi. It wasn't far from the truth—a Pied Piper with masala noodles. We splurged on three plates of Maggi, travelled without tickets on the way back to school, and wondered if we were already addicted.

As time's passing, I find myself more in love with Brahmi, it's harder to see her go in the afternoon, tougher to not see her in the night, and impossible to survive without her.

Baba was home when I got back from school. He was poring over some papers and was on the landline, shouting. I didn't think of it much till Baba shifted to Bengali. Dada was on the other side of the phone. I went to my room and eavesdropped. Though tempers ran high, they weren't talking about Boudi but about money. Dada was called careless, a fool and a retard.

When he disconnected an hour later, Baba told me about the discrepancies in Dada's tax filings, and how an inquiry could have landed Dada in jail. I have no doubt about Baba's exaggerations.

Baba grumbled for an hour afterwards, marking out transactions on Dada's bank statements.

'Walking out of the house like he knows everything! Now see what he is doing. Making his father file his tax reports and his mother run around town scouring for doctors for his pregnant wife,' said Baba.

'You threw him out,' I said.

'Same thing,' said Baba and got back to Dada's papers.

Baba worked tirelessly through the afternoon till late in the night. He clutched on to the papers as if they were a raft still keeping him afloat in his relationship with Dada. He told Maa and me that he needed to talk to Dada again to get some clarifications. I wondered if he missed his voice.

12 September 1999

My exams are going well and yet it means nothing. I sit on the row adjacent to Brahmi's. In the last three exams she has been unusually fidgety. She used to write with three pens. Blue to write, black to underline and red to mark indents. I had picked up the habit from her. Now, she was using just one for her exams. Her question papers have an alarming number of circles for the ones she couldn't solve. Most of them easy pickings. After every exam, she would tear the question paper and throw it in the dustbin. I would fetch the papers from the dustbin, tape them together and estimate her marks. She wouldn't make it to even the top ten in class, not that it mattered any more.

I had decided I would put an end to this. She had to do well. It was her last set of exams after all.

It was mathematics. I took extra sheets thrice, two of which I didn't need. I stole glances at Brahmi's exam sheet which was sparsely filled. Instead of her god-like handwriting, the paper was filled with squiggles, scratched-out answers and big circles, as if her fingers had gone crooked overnight. With an eye on the clock, I copied the solutions of the toughest questions in the exam on to the two empty extra sheets in a tiny handwriting. On my way out to the washroom, I dropped the two sheets on Brahmi's table. She picked them up and read through hurriedly. She cancelled out her solutions and attached the two sheets to her exam sheet.

'You could have done that for me too,' complained Rishab after the exam. 'I'm definitely failing this one.'

'You sit too far,' I offered as an explanation.

Brahmi was too embarrassed to say anything. Later on, on the bus, she thanked me as if she was doing a chore.

'Something troubling you?'

'Don't help me in the next exam.'

'Whatever is happening isn't your fault.'

'I know it's not but I don't like being dependent. How will I enjoy the marks I get when I know I cheated?'

'My bad.'

'Don't feel bad. I would have done the same for you,' she said.

I felt bad and for which she held my hand and didn't let go for the rest of the bus ride. It helped.

When I got home, I saw the first chasm in Baba's resolve to not accept Dada back into the family. We went to Saraswati Vihar, a ten-minute drive from our house. It wasn't until we were in the flat with a property dealer and Baba was assiduously checking the taps and the hinges of the doors that I figured why we were there.

On our way back, I asked Baba, 'So Dada won't live with us?'

Baba shook his head. 'No.'

'But everyone in the colony already knows that Dada's married a Muslim so what's the difference where he stays?'

'Our house is too small.'

Baba drove on without answering any further questions. It wasn't the house, it was his heart which hadn't yet opened up to the possibility of a Muslim woman spreading a prayer mat in his living room.

I had refused to have any conversation with Dada till the time I was sure of what's going to be the new family dynamic. After the unfair meting out of punishment to me, I wanted to be sure of which side I wanted to be on. But today seemed like a good day to talk to him. I had expected an emotional, overwhelmed, crying Dada on the other side—like I was—but he was upbeat and boisterous.

'How's your girlfriend?'

'She's not my girlfriend.'

'What's she then?'

'I love her and she loves me,' I said.

'Aww, you're such a child.'

'Says the one who has an expertise in taking wrong decisions.'

'You're in love now, aren't you? Is that a decision you took, my genius brother?' he asked.

'Even decisions I take subconsciously are better than your conscious decisions,' I said tight-lipped.

Dada laughed and said, 'You're such a pain in the ass. I can't wait to see you.'

I laughed too. I couldn't wait to see him either.

My stellar mood took me to Brahmi's house. It was seven and I was ambling beneath her house waiting for nightfall when I noticed a group of labourers climbing down from the scaffolding on the building adjacent to Brahmi's. From where I stood I thought a carefully controlled jump could take me to Brahmi's ledge and from there to her window. For the next hour I stretched and lumbered up and wished my limbs were made of titanium. When I bounced the idea off Brahmi, she thought I had lost my mind and that I would break my neck and die. But with time her opposition crumbled and her eyes glinted with hope and possibility. I said a prayer and climbed up the scaffolding, taking Lord Hanuman's name on each step—like him, I would leap for love. It was harder than it looked and I was out of breath by the time it came for me to jump. She asked me to rethink the five-foot jump but it was too late for that. She knew it too. Catching my breath, I leapt,

I missed, and I hung shoulder down from the parapet, my legs dangling precariously.

Brahmi gasped and outstretched her hand quite uselessly. It took me all my might and more to pull myself up to the ledge. I climbed into her room, my T-shirt in tatters. The blood from the minor bruises had already started to clot. After she had whispered words of concern and we discussed in gestures how dangerous it was to sneak in like this, we became acutely aware of the silence and the darkness of the room. She lit a candle and asked me to be absolutely quiet. I could hear the clock ticking in the living room, I could see the fear on her face. There wasn't much to see in her threadbare room, which had just a bed and small cupboard but what I wouldn't give to be here with her, for this to be our little world. If one could be envious of inanimate objects I was of this room which held stories even she wouldn't remember now. The room knew what made her laugh when alone, what made her cry, the boys she loved, the boys she hated, the boys for whom she felt both; it knew how short days were and how long the nights, knew her desires and her fears, her peeves and her likes.

We knew how dangerous it was so we maintained a funereal silence. A little later, she kept her head on my shoulder and held my hand. We breathed softly. Our chests rose and fell at the same time. She wept softly and I found myself weeping in response. Dried of our tears, and too scared to use words, we stared at each other which was awkward at first, and then seemed like the most natural way to spend our life. I took in every detail of her face. A few days later, she would leave and I would no longer be able to see her every day.

I left after an hour.

18 September 1999

Things have been a little busy. The preparations to welcome Dada are in full swing. Baba has been working tirelessly to get the flat ready in time for Dada's arrival. He has maintained a serious, almost-angry countenance all through to prove he isn't happy with the proceedings. He walks out whenever Maa mentions Zubeida Boudi's name—who he still calls that Musalman girl—and then calls Dada ungrateful every time he offers to pay for incidentals. The frenzied activity at my house has helped me sneak out without being asked too many questions. Their rising concern and obsession around Dada would have rankled had I still been a child.

For the sixth day in a row I prepared myself to climb up and jump; it has become easier with time. I rubbed my hands and stretched and I looked up and saw Brahmi on the ledge. My first instinct was to run below the scaffolding and spread out my hands to break her fall, and I was still staring agape at her when she hopped, almost merrily, from the edge to the scaffolding. Of course, why shouldn't she? She was the athlete between the two of us. She clambered down easily.

'I could have come up,' I said.

'Don't worry, I'm not going to let my attention waiver from you.'

'I never said that.'

'But you thought it. I know because I did too,' she said. 'Now come.' She led me to Tauji's Bajaj Chetak whose key she had flicked and we climbed on. 'Hold me,' she said.

I rode pillion all the way to India Gate. Twice we came across police checkpoints and she dodged and sped through both. Her acute knowledge of the little lanes criss-crossing central Delhi left the policemen scratching their heads. She had taken me there for the kaala khatta chuski but we spent a few minutes gazing at the arched gate.

'It takes at least 82,000 men to die to have a memorial made after them,' said Brahmi later while sucking on her chuski. 'I can't believe you haven't been here.'

'I've been here only once, on a school trip. Not with family. Baba says the men whose names are scribbled served the British army and died for their cause in the First World War, so what's the point? He calls for a bigger India Gate with names of the men of Netaji's army or the Gandhians, even the revolutionaries.'

'And what do you think?' she asked.

'I love the lighting here.'

Our lips slowly turned beetroot red from the chuski and we argued about whose were redder.

'How are things at home?'

'It's like a room filled with LPG with the windows thrown open. I don't know what's going to happen if a match is struck.'

'Your Dada's lucky that they came around.'

'Dada always thought they would. Didn't he say Maa–Baba would regret not being there the day he got married?'

'Your Dada knows your Maa–Baba better than you do,' she said.

'That's quite shocking. I hadn't expected them to give in.'

'I know what you mean. My father's side of the family would have never accepted this. They disowned a cousin of mine who married a Dalit. When he had a child, my aunts in Delhi prophesized it would be an ugly, demonic baby. My aunts still calls her names even after so many years. No one visits them any more.'

'That's so not right,' I said, with a right conferred upon me by my Dada's marriage to someone outside our religion.

'My cousin converted to Buddhism. He had got tired of everyone referring to his wife as a lower-caste untouchable.'

I wanted to correct her, tell her that you never stop being a Hindu, or convert to Hinduism through a magic ritual. You're just born into this religion, this way of life, and it's always there with you, like a birthmark or a congenital defect, unlike Islam or Christianity. But, of course, like every organization, to sustain itself Hinduism adapted too and you could now convert to Hinduism or shed it like a snakeskin.

We finished our chuskis and walked hand in hand for an hour, after which she had to leave. She refuelled the scooter, drove us back and climbed to her room with the same ease.

At the breakfast table, I asked if Bengalis too have their versions of churis and chamars.

'Yes, we do,' Maa said. 'But all that doesn't matter any more. No one cares about caste except the politicians. For them every division is a vote bank.'

'So you will have no problem if someone in our family gets married to someone who's an SC, ST, a Dalit or something?'

Maa–Baba looked at me, horrified.

'We would mind,' grumbled Baba.

'Between a Muslim and a Dalit? Who would you choose?'

I was asked to finish my breakfast instead of asking them silly questions. Whatever division Maa was talking about is a vote bank for a reason. Because those divisions exist. At least in my house they do.

Now while I am writing this, I am thinking about Brahmi's niece and Dada's unborn child, children of unholy alliances.

If this were 1994, we would have known what the sex of the child was. Now it's illegal.

'It's because of the Haryanavis,' my maternal uncle had said a few years ago. 'They do these tests and if it's a girl, they go home and plunge knives into the wombs of their pregnant women and kill their daughters.'

I had asked Maa once, 'Do Bengalis do that too?'

'We are not brutes like the northerners.'

Dada had laughed and said, 'What about the Great Calcutta Killings of 1946?'

'That's ancient history,' Baba had butted in.

Dada had laughed again and said, 'You teach him about Ghor and Ghazni and Aurangzeb. That's not ancient history?'

'What had happened?' I asked.

'Thousands of Bengalis massacred each other. Men were cut up, burnt alive, women raped.'

Baba had argued, 'The Muslims did it. They wanted Pakistan. We didn't do anything.'

'We?'

'We! The Hindus. We never attack first. That's our weakness,' Baba had said.

25 September 1999

She had waited until late to tell me.

Like the past nights, we were roaming the streets on her
borrowed scooter. She drove past Tamarind Court where
earlier this year a model had been shot dead by a powerful
man, and past IIT Delhi and AIIMS, which were the only
two colleges worthy enough for the Gangulys. We came to
a stop at Nizamuddin railway station, where we ate fried
rice from a stall outside. Every night seemed endless till it
was time to leave. And the next night, eons away. Time's
plasticine, malleable; when love's in the equation, it's as
relative as Einstein theorized and was understandably lauded
for because every fool in love wants a scientist to back what
they feel.

'Vedant has found me a job,' she said when it was time
to leave.

'It had to happen,' I said more to myself than to her.

'Yes.'

'I will miss you, Raghu. I will miss this.'

'I will not miss bandaging you,' I said.

'I will not miss you threatening to murder my Tauji.'

'I'm not promising anything. Is that why you insisted to
pay for everything today?'

'I'm going to be a paid professional,' she said. 'It's the least
I can do.'

'When do you leave?'

'He will call me and tell me. He has asked me to be ready. His friends are staying over at his place and he wants them to leave before I come.'

'I will have to figure out buses to Gurgaon,' I said.

'That's something I wanted to tell you, Raghu. I don't want you to come there very often. You will have to concentrate on your studies. I wouldn't want you to take your academics lightly and I don't want to be guilty of that.'

'Oh please, don't overestimate your importance in my life. You're probably the tenth most important in the list,' I said.

'You're the first in mine.'

'And that's why you're going so far?'

'Raghu—'

'I'm sorry, I apologize. That was needless.'

'Come here,' she said.

She hugged me till her tears trickled down my shoulders.

'See, it's you who's crying,' I said. 'I'm absolutely fine. I will be totally fine without you. Like who are you? I'm not going to miss you at all. Not even a little bit.'

'Shut up,' she said and she laughed and cried some more. She left me wondering if I would see her again.

As I was writing this and trying not to cry like a baby, Maa knocked on the door. I looked at the watch. It was 3 a.m. I was prepared with what to say to her if she had found me sneaking out again. *I have friends, Maa, I need to see them. Everyone was there so why couldn't I be?* So I opened the door. She came and sat on the bed and stared at me for a good minute. Quite possibly to give me time to confess before she would begin laying out what I was accused of.

'I know you're getting older,' she said, her tone serious and full of regret. 'Dada and you think that we come in the way of your happiness and so we have stopped interfering in your lives. All we can do is what parents are required to do for their children. We know you go out every night and we don't know where you go, what you do with your friends, and we don't ask. We had decided not to say anything to you. But as your Maa–Baba, we worry. That much right we have as parents, don't we? Your Baba doesn't sleep till the time you come back home. We feel bad, we worry, but we think there's no point telling both of you what your boundaries are. You are free to do what you want. Times are changing. But there's one little request I have of you.'

'Yes, Maa?' I asked.

She opened her palm and there was little sachet in her hands. Rough Man Rider, the sachet said, on a graphic of a man riding a horse. It was a condom, not shampoo as I had suspected for a second.

'Maa. That's not mine,' I said.

'I found it in our dustbin outside,' she said. 'Raghu, you will lie now and I don't want to hear anything from you. All I wanted to tell you is that you're too young for this. I'm requesting you to concentrate on your studies.'

'Maa, I do!'

'Your practical files are shoddy, assignments are not up to the mark. Amarjeet ma'am says you don't attend all the classes because of your extracurricular activities.'

'You met my teacher?'

She got up to leave. 'Think about the girl who's doing these dirty things with you. What kind of a girl would she be? She's spoiling both you and her future.'

'Maa, I—'

'I am requesting you again, shona. Don't do these dirty things in my house,' she said and left.

One of these days, I'm going to slap Richa Mittal. Who else would have placed that condom? But full marks to her for finding the courage to go and buy one.

1 October 1999

Maa and I went to the railway station today to pick up Dada and Zubeida. Baba told us he had to oversee work at the Durga Puja Committee and hence couldn't come with us, which was a lie because Baba had bowed out of the committee a month ago. I had heard Maa–Baba talk. With a Musalman daughter-in-law at home he said it was embarrassing for him to be among his friends. Dada and Zubeida's train was late by three hours. Every hour the railway announcer would regret to tell us about the unavoidable delay. Maa and I played cards and drank tea and ate oily pakodas to pass the time. By the time Dada's train reached the platform my stomach was struggling to hold all that in.

Maa and I boarded the bogie and found Zubeida and Dada waiting with their suitcases. Zubeida Boudi smiled as she saw me. Her face had filled up and there was a visible bump beneath her burqa. I counted the weeks. About seven months to go. I searched for the pregnancy glow I had heard people talk about. Zubeida touched Maa's feet; Maa half-heartedly and unsuccessfully tried to stop her from bending. We took a prepaid taxi to Saraswati Vihar. Dada ruffled my hair and asked me about Brahmi. Luckily, Maa wasn't listening.

'Baba was busy,' said Maa in the taxi, looking at Zubeida with a rehearsed politeness, but looking at the bulge in her stomach with love. At the society gate, a man was waiting for us. Baba had instructed him to carry the luggage to their third-floor flat.

'It is nice,' said Zubeida to Maa as she looked around.

'We were looking for a two-bedroom but rents in this neighbourhood have gone through the roof. Then we found this,' said Maa.

'This is perfect,' said Dada.

'The fridge is stocked for two days. If you need anything else I will get it. You two rest now,' said Maa and turned to Dada and spoke in Bengali. 'Baba must be reaching home any time. I should leave now.'

'Isn't Baba going to come?' asked Zubeida.

There was a little silence, an infinitesimally small amount of time, as everyone absorbed Boudi calling Baba, Baba. I looked at Maa, and said a little prayer, beseeching god to make her see Mina in Boudi.

'He will. He's a little busy with work. You people rest. It's been a long journey,' said Maa hurriedly.

'Raghu, you can stay here and tell me what's happening in your life,' Dada said to me.

'I have homework,' I answered.

'Yes, he has,' said Maa. 'He has been roaming around quite a lot.'

Just as I was leaving, I saw Zubeida and Dada look at each other and smile.

'Did you see the baby bump?' asked Maa in the auto back home.

'I did.'

'It's like a little fruit right now, like a pineapple, my grandchild,' she said almost to herself. 'It's going to be a girl, I'm telling you.'

'Are you going to name her Mina?'

'No, of course not. I will name her Meenakshi.'

'You're so creative, Maa!' I said and saw that the sarcasm was lost on her.

Baba was already home when we got back. He had made tea for himself and left the kitchen drain blocked. Maa tried to unblock it with a plunger. When her hands started to tire she called me to help. Over the gurgling sounds of water in the drain, I heard Maa tell Baba that Dada had settled down, Zubeida seemed well, and that they seemed to like the flat.

'When will you go there?' asked Maa.

'I will when I feel like it,' said Baba and that was the end of the discussion.

3 October 1999

The way she said it, it seemed like the most natural thing to do.

'Of course we have to see them!'

So yesterday we went to meet Dada and Boudi at 1 a.m.

'You think they will be awake?' she asked.

As it turned out, they were awake and duly surprised to see us there. Brahmi and Boudi hugged each other as if they were friends from a lost time. They sat holding hands which felt weird because she was my Boudi, not hers. I felt strangely possessive about both Boudi and Brahmi, and oddly happy to see them mingle.

Dada expressed appreciation and anger at our behaviour. He gave me a token be-careful-the-nights-aren't-safe-in-Delhi lecture, and then asked me about all the places I had been to.

'What do you want?' asked Brahmi.

'We both want a girl,' she said. 'Do you want to eat something?'

'No, Bhabhi. You rest.'

'Hey, I'm not crippled, just pregnant,' said Boudi laughing. Brahmi laughed too.

Boudi offered to make tea and pakodas but Dada and Brahmi suggested we all go out and eat. Boudi joked that Dada was already sick of her cooking and insisted to cook himself every day. Which was strange, because Dada had not lifted a finger all these years in the Ganguly home.

Dada and Brahmi took a taxi, Brahmi and I drove alongside on Brahmi's scooter, and we went to an all-night kadhi–chawal place in Connaught Place. Dada was impressed to see how well I knew the city.

Dada and I ate like hungry wolves while Brahmi and Boudi talked non-stop. Seeing them get along so well sprouted the possibility of an alternate reality in my imagination. Brahmi could shift to Dada–Boudi's place, Dada could pay Brahmi's school fees for the next two years, and she could go to a college which would waive off her tuition fee on account of her being such a brilliant student. It was a win-win. Of course, there was the issue of Maa thinking Brahmi and I were having sex— which was absolutely ridiculous—and Brahmi not wanting to depend on anyone. I kept the imaginary scenarios to myself.

When it was time for us to leave, Boudi exacted a promise out of Brahmi to meet them soon. Brahmi nodded. Neither of us told her or Dada that she would be moving to Gurgaon sooner than later.

'You're such a stud,' Dada told me before leaving.

'And I?' asked Brahmi.

'You're responsible for making him one,' said Dada and waved us goodbye.

On the way back to her house on her scooter, she shouted over the wind, 'I love your Dada–Boudi.'

'They seemed more your Dada–Boudi than mine.'

We both fell quiet, letting the possibility of that future slowly sink in. I smiled and saw her smile in the rear-view mirror.

7 October 1999

It was a good day today, sort of unbelievable. After the long cold war between Dada and Baba, where neither of them wanted to visit each other's houses, Dada has softened his stand. He was home today. If I said it was all my doing, I might come across as pompous but there's no other way to say it: It was all my doing. Like a tactful negotiator I used all the tricks in the book. Persistent cajoling, emotional blackmail, beady eyes, and anger—I used all my arsenal. 'How different are you from Baba if you keep holed up here? He extended an olive branch, didn't he? It was Baba who found this house, got everything fixed, got sick with worry wondering if everything is okay, and you can't even come home? Boudi, why don't you tell him to come home? How will things get better if neither of them soften a little?'

Fake tears and real tears were at the precipice of my eyes and Dada gave up.

He came home. They sat together in front of the TV where a cricket match was on and Baba and Dada didn't even look at each other for the longest time. They weren't father and son but two men. Their icy stares at the television left me cold. It was only after Ganguly did well that the two senior Gangulys melted and smiled and then clapped.

'He should be the captain,' said Dada.

'Seeing a Bengali as captain, people will start respecting us again. He will restore our pride!' exclaimed Baba.

On the dinner table, Baba mostly steered clear of any conversation related to Boudi, except the accidental advice.

'Start spending less, save more; the little one has to have a good future.'

Maa and I went with Dada to his house. We carried casseroles of capsicum paneer and doi machh. Boudi insisted that Maa drink tea before she left. Maa stayed back because I knew by now that she had come to love Boudi's tea. Though she had dared not ask her about the recipe. Was it the tea leaves? Was it some masala? Maa kept her curiosity to herself, not wanting to give Boudi a lead on what was principally her domain—good chai. So imagine my surprise when Maa gave me a tight slap on my head when I called Boudi by the nickname I had thought for her—Sunni Boudi. Boudi had told me a few days back that she's a Sunni Muslim. Sunni. Sunni. Sunni. It coils funnily around the tongue, doesn't it? I have been calling her Sunni Boudi, Sunni Boudi for a week now. Boudi had no problem with me calling her that but apparently Maa did and I have to stop doing it. I had asked Boudi if she would rather be a Shia, another branch of Islam. She said she wouldn't. Had I been given a choice, I would rather be Shia. It sounds richer, like the sound of a formula car whizzing by. *Shia.* I have always wanted to be a Roy or a Chatterjee, regal surnames which spring to mind rich Bengali gentlemen with round spectacles and pocket watches.

Ganguly is too . . . clerk-like.

When we came back home, Baba asked me to call Brahmi back. Maa looked at me sharply.

'It's about some assignment,' I offered as an explanation.

When Maa–Baba retired for the night, I called Brahmi. She told me she would leave home the coming week.

11 October 1999

My head's bursting, my heart's bleeding and my fingers are failing me as I try to write this down. Let me tell you what happened today in a chronological order so as to make sense of it all.

Maa–Baba and I were quite surprised when Arundhati, Sahil and Rishab landed at my place, unannounced. Dressed in white kurta–pyjamas, the boys looked like little princes, and between them stood Arundhati, stately and resplendent in her blue-and-gold saree.

'Quick! Get ready. We are going out,' they echoed.

'Where?'

'A party, at my place,' said Rishab.

'For what?'

'That's a secret,' Arundhati answered.

I looked at Maa–Baba, who nodded. Maa helped me find my kurta and Baba ironed it. When I was all dressed up, Baba clicked a picture with his camera, and then one from Rishab's new digital camera.

'You can delete pictures and take new ones if you don't like them,' said Rishab.

'We know how digital cameras work,' said Arundhati.

'I was just—'

'Next you're going to tell us how cars work, is it?'

We all supported Arundhati's bullying of Rishab.

In the car to Rishab's house, they told me Brahmi was throwing herself a farewell party since she wasn't going to be a part of one in school. I felt slighted that Brahmi hadn't told

me about her wish to have one. I would have organized one
for her. Neither did I know when Brahmi told them about her
decision to leave school; she had categorically asked me to not
tell anyone, not even Dada–Boudi.

Brahmi was waiting at Rishab's house, looking wonderful
in a red-and-black saree. 'You look gorgeous,' she said and
stepped closer to me.

'So do you,' I said.

'When did you tell them?'

'They just know I'm shifting and doing my studies through
open school,' she whispered.

'What are you guys whispering? Let's click pictures!' said
Arundhati. 'Come here!'

Arundhati made me stand in between and linked her arm
around me. She exhorted Brahmi to do the same. My heart
fluttered and it shows in the picture that was clicked. Rishab's
parents met us and told us that the upper floor of the house
was ours and we were free to do anything except break the
showpieces. We all laughed and politely took their leave.

We huddled inside Rishab's room.

We sat and talked and smoked and coughed and laughed.
We made Arundhati sing for us and, by god, did she sing
beautifully. Later, Rishab played his mixtapes, and Sahil and
Arundhati—both fabulous dancers—showed off their moves.
Brahmi smiled all through. She looked happy. Then we took
turns to tell her how much we would miss her. The three hours
we spent at Rishab's passed in a flash. When it was time to
leave I volunteered to drop Brahmi home. She changed into her
regular home clothes and gave the saree she had borrowed from
Arundhati back to her. In the auto, she thanked me for coming,
told me she would miss this time and slept on my shoulder.

'We are here,' I said, tapping on her shoulder.

She woke up with a start.

'Can I walk you home?'

She nodded.

She froze ten yards from her house.

'No.'

This single ominous word escaped her lips.

Two adults, who I knew were her Tauji–Taiji, came charging at her. In a swift sequence of events which included a lot of cursing, shouting, slapping, her more than me, we were at her place. Their entire colony was watching—from their stairs, their windows, their balconies. She had been dragged by her hair, while I was given a more merciful treatment—they only pulled me by my hand. They pushed Brahmi into her room and locked it. Her Taiji was crying and her Tauji looked at me in angry silence.

'WHEN WILL THIS GIRL STOP TROUBLING US?' shouted her Taiji, pacing outside Brahmi's room.

I scouted the area for pointy objects, things I could jam into the carotid arteries of her Tauji–Taiji and break her out of there.

Her Taiji disappeared inside a room for a few minutes and then dragged out a big bag.

'She was planning to run away!' shouted her Taiji and pointed at me. 'Was she running away with you? Tell me or I will inform the police!'

Her Taiji passed a washing bat to him. Tauji kept it next to him.

I wanted to say, 'So what, and yes, she was planning to run away with me because I love her and who else would be more deserving of her', but the words died an early death in my throat.

'Is she running with you? What are you? Twelve? ANSWER MY QUESTION, YOU BASTARD.'

'Sixteen. I'm sixteen. Which twelve-year-old has a moustache,' I said and her Tauji charged at me and slapped me across my face.

Indignant, I told her, 'You slap me once more and you see what I do.'

At which point Tauji clenched the washing bat in his hand and pointed it at my face.

He said, 'Beta, you don't know who I am. It would be advisable if you tell us where you were taking her. Either you tell me or you tell the police.'

Who was he? Judging by the state of his house, he couldn't be a powerful businessman or politician who could legitimately use that phrase.

'Are you the police?' I asked him.

'I am an advocate at the Tis Hazari court. My friends in the police will make you disappear tomorrow and you won't even see it coming,' he said. 'If I want it, you won't see the light of day tomorrow, ladke. So open your mouth.' He patted my face with the bat. He said, 'Tell us where you were going with her?'

'Uncle, with all due respect, I am not talking to you. If you can please call her parents I will tell them everything.'

'Brahmi's parents?' asked her Taiji.

'Yes? Who else?'

'They are long dead,' said her Tauji.

'That's not funny, Uncle.'

'Oh, *bechara*, poor thing,' said her Taiji. 'He doesn't know. See? This girl is crazy!'

'What don't I know?' I asked, walking to the room they had locked Brahmi in, but her Tauji was swifter than what I'd expected and rammed me against the wall. He jammed the bat against my neck and pressed home.

'Look ladke, Brahmi's parents are long dead, it's been ten years,' he said and pointed to the picture on the wall, draped with a garland of dried flowers.

'But—'

'Our niece is crazy, that *saali*. For ten years she has gone around saying her parents are alive, her parents are alive, making up stories about them. She's made our lives hell. How much patience does she expect from us? Huh?' said her Taiji.

'But—'

The words died in my throat.

'WAS SHE RUNNING AWAY WITH YOU?' asked her Tauji and released the bat from my neck.

'No,' I spluttered.

'Don't know how many times we have taken her to the hospital for her bleeding wrists,' screamed her Taiji.

'But that can't be—'

'That's exactly how it is,' said her Tauji.

'But her parents are—'

Her Taiji continued, 'She just does it to trouble us! She of course knows they are dead! When she cries all night calling out to her Mumma–Papa, doesn't she know they are not alive? Then why in the morning she pretends that they are? Going around telling everyone that they are alive!'

'But—'

'She's an embarrassment,' said her Taiji. 'She should have died the same day her parents did. But no! She's still here, making everyone believe we are the villains in her life.'

'You hit her,' I muttered.

His Tauji let me go. 'Of course we hit her and we would do it again. What's she if not a burden to us? If she dies, we will be in trouble, if she doesn't then also people blame us for making the girl crazy.'

Her Taiji said, 'You want to run away with her? Do so! Rid us of her! She steals, she lies, and she doesn't let us sleep! We will do what is required of us. We will write a report that she's missing and then what happens will happen.'

'I was not running away with her,' I said.

'Then why this bag? Who the hell is she running away from?' grumbled her Tauji.

Vedant's name was at the tip of my tongue but I shrugged and told them I didn't know.

'Then who are you?'

'I'm like a brother to her,' I said, in more of a reflex.

They shoved me out despite my begging them to let me meet her. They told me she'd never be meeting anyone. She was going to live in that room, die in that room, and that's what was going to happen. I had tried to argue but Tauji had swung the bat and got me square on my face. My mouth filled with blood and a molar came loose. I waited beneath her window, strained my ears and my eyes for a sign and got nothing. As I walked the entirety of the way home, the pieces of the jigsaw fell into place. Her parents were dead, that was irrefutable. They weren't alive with shifting geographical locations. I had not once suspected her of lying.

The daze of mixed emotions has now left me. I don't feel angry that she lied to me about her parents, I don't feel left out and cheated that she loved me and told me all the stories behind her cutting herself but not the one that mattered. I don't feel cowardly I couldn't break her out of the house and run away with her. All I feel is overwhelming love. After all, I too had kept Sami alive in my head, in my behaviour, in the way I felt and interacted, in the way I lived and the way I loved, till I met Brahmi and everything changed.

Maa asked about the bruise and believed me when I told her that Sahil and I had gotten into a friendly scuffle.

17 November 1999

I have tried to rationalize my love for someone who might be a little—how do I put it politely—unhinged, by saying I have the capacity to love anyone, but it's not that. I know I just love her and I love her no matter what.

Maa–Baba's eyes were glued to the television. Thousands are dying as I'm writing this. Maa at one point lamented, 'Why! Why would something like this happen to the poor Oriyas?'

'Like the Punjabis?' I asked.

Maa nodded. 'Yes, like them.'

Baba chimed in, 'All thieves, every single one of them. That property dealer? He told us the kitchen was waterproofed. It drips every night now. He has the gall to say that we should look for another flat! Imagine! All of them are the same!'

'They don't have a coastline,' I argued.

I don't share Maa–Baba's sense of empathy. Who's them? Who's us? The definitions are fluid. For today, the Oriya people sinking in their watery graves are ours, Muslim or not. And that Punjabi property dealer who hadn't got the kitchen roof waterproofed is them. And Zubeida Boudi, a Muslim, is ours, her child is ours.

And whose is Brahmi? Who's going to cry for her if something happens to her? I have struggled to conjure up a future for Brahmi and me. But whatever it is, I will have my place in it. I have been checking on Brahmi every day. She still comes to the balcony every afternoon. She still looks like absolutely nothing's wrong with her life which explains a lot, now. Grief and she have been with each other for so long that suffering silently is second nature to her.

I have waved from beneath her window, written placards, thrown pebbles at her to catch her attention but nothing has worked. Yesterday, the watchman came running after me.

I got myself a buzz cut and returned today. And thank god, I did. I saw Vedant enter her house. I paced around outside, waiting for him to emerge with Brahmi. After a while, he emerged alone from the building.

Before I could reach Vedant, he drove off on his motorcycle.

Having had enough, I rang the bell to her house. Luckily, it was Brahmi who opened the door.

Before I could say anything, she said, 'Don't do anything stupid. I can help myself.'

Her name was called out.

Brahmi shouted back, 'SALESMAN!' and slammed the door on me.

'I love you,' I said but the she was long gone.

Now as I'm writing this I'm trying to recreate what had happened. Was she being hit? How sad was she? Did she have something on her mind? Does she still love me? Can I kill her Tauji–Taiji? How long will I have to wait to see her again?

19 November 1999

In the evening, we went to Boudi's house. Her bump is considerably larger now. Only yesterday, Maa helped Zubeida Boudi redo a stitching of her burqa. Maa's guessing it is going to be a boy from the size of her bump. It's surprising to see how irrational she can get despite her education. For the most part of the evening, Maa sat right next to Boudi, one hand firmly on her stomach as if she didn't trust her with the life growing inside of her.

'I have had three children, so I know,' said Maa. 'You should rest at this time, Mamoni. Work can wait but at this time you should concentrate on yourself.'

'She can't miss office now. She was just made the team leader. A holiday will set her back,' said Dada.

'That is such good news!' said Maa.

'Maa? Do you even know what it means?' Dada joked.

Maa frowned. 'I know that it means more money and respect, doesn't it, Mamoni?'

Zubeida Boudi nodded.

Maa–Baba had decided to call Zubeida, Mamoni, a common Bengali nickname which roughly translates to 'little girl'. 'Zubeida' was too . . . Muslim.

Maa continued, 'I won't ask you to not go to office but it is a risk. That's what I will say. Anything can happen. I have been working for so long now and everyone around me takes a holiday. If you don't want to it's okay but it's for the good of the baby.'

Boudi stole a glance at Dada. Saying no would have been rude, and I guess, saying okay wasn't what Dada and Boudi wanted.

To break the awkwardness Boudi said, 'We should all go to Ansal Plaza. My treat?'

'What's that?' asked Maa.

'It's a mall, Maa,' said Boudi.

'Ansal? Are they the same?' asked Maa looking at Dada. Dada nodded. 'No one is going there!' shrieked Maa. 'Not even you and Mamoni! Did you forget Uphaar?'

'That was more than two years ago,' said Dada.

'How does it matter how many years ago? People don't change. No one will go to Ansal Plaza.'

Two years ago, a fire had broken out at Uphaar, the cinema hall we were to go to that evening but changed plans at the last instant. Fifty-nine people choked to death. Dada had boycotted the place.

The next day, Maa–Baba went to Kali Baari and prayed for our good fortune. They donated a small gold set of Maa's to the gods.

Later, when Maa told Baba about Boudi's promotion, Baba said, 'So she's Anirban's boss now?'

'She still wants to go to office,' said Maa.

'You see, no matter what you do, she will never change. She has her claws in our son.'

'People don't change,' said Maa.

The conversation ended there.

While Maa came home, I stayed back at Dada's place from where I left for Brahmi's place to see if she would turn up at the window. Boudi said, 'Be careful, Raghu. If you need help, tell me.'

'Brahmi doesn't need help. She will take care of herself.'

'Then why are you so worried?' she asked.

'Because I need her.'

I left and like every day I stared at her window. And then something snapped and I found myself climbing the scaffolding faster than she or I had ever climbed. Within a minute I was at her closed window. I knocked lightly and there was no response. I whispered her name and it was futile. Learning from what I had seen in a movie, I wrapped my T-shirt around my hand and punched the glass which gave in. I let myself in. The room was empty. The bed—gone. The cupboard—gone. The candles lay strewn around. Her clothes weren't there. Neither were her books.

Brahmi didn't need me.

She had helped herself.

23 November 1999

Today's the fourth day with no news of Brahmi's whereabouts. Yesterday her Tauji had chased me out their apartment complex when I had asked him about Vedant.

To distract myself, I spent today evening in Dada's flat watching *Hip Hip Hurray*, a TV show set in DeNobili High School. It's fiction because schools like these don't exist. No one in the show knows how to tie a knot, or tuck in his or her shirt, and every skirt ends above the knee. The story is about eleventh and twelfth graders but none of us behave as audaciously as they do. The kids also look much older. And what kind of a name is DeNobili High School? Why couldn't their stories be more real? Like of a girl who misses her parents so much she pretends that they are alive? Like of a boy who misses that girl so much he feels like a hole has been punched where his heart should be?

Just after the show ended and before I left, I heard Dada and Boudi fight.

Maa–Baba often ask me how Boudi and Dada live, if Boudi is regular with her namaz, and if Dada lights incense sticks every day in the little temple Maa had tucked into one corner of their bedroom. Maa makes sure she's never in their house when it's time for Boudi's namaz. One time, I caught Maa cradling Boudi's prayer mat.

'What are doing with that?' I had asked her.

'Nothing, I was just . . . cleaning the house,' she had answered looking away.

To keep up with and to beat Boudi's religious fervour, Maa–Baba have taken to praying more often. It's not only on Tuesdays but Mondays and Fridays too that I have to go the temple. Arundhati doesn't mind. 'It's so calming,' she says. But it's not, and it's infuriating. My prayers for Brahmi have come to naught. Baba noticed my disinterest the day he came along. Tired and angry at Baba correcting my chants in front of the pundit and Arundhati, I had snapped, 'I am sure our gods know English and Hindi and Bengali.'

'And theirs don't understand anything other than Arabic?' Baba had retorted.

I asked Boudi the same. 'I was wondering why Arabic? Like he could have chosen a more popular language, no? Or is it the only language he knows?'

Boudi answered with the equanimity of a sage in her voice, 'That would be limiting of Allah to know just one language. He used Arabic because he thought it was apt for the revelation.'

'But why?'

'You don't question the word of Allah,' said Boudi.

'When you mean *you*, do you mean Muslims or do you mean *me* as well?'

'Where is all this coming from? Did Maa–Baba say anything?'

I shook my head.

She sighed and came and sat next to me. Boudi said, 'Hindus and Muslims have always found pretexts to cut each other to pieces. You see when the British left, we didn't kill our British oppressors who persecuted us, partitioned us, but we killed each other. We forgave the British immediately, but we will never forgive our own people. Like when Kashmir is no longer an issue, we will find a new reason to be at each other's throats and it might last another hundred years for all we know.'

'Will it ever end?'

'Not in our lifetimes, Raghu, not in our lifetimes. But things can change, right? Look at your Maa–Baba. They have accepted me in their little ways, have they not?'

'They have, I guess.'

'You still don't know where Brahmi is?' she asked. I shook my head. 'She will reach out. Don't worry.'

I am sure she will. But when?

30 November 1999

Dada's birthday has always been a dull affair. One-armed hugs. Paesh. Maangsho. Pulao. And that's it. No gifts. No big smiles. No hullabaloo. But today was different. A certain excitement had gripped the Ganguly household. The house was being wiped and dusted and swept clean. Two maids and Maa–Baba had turned the house upside down and were putting it back together.

'There's a puja in the evening. Pundits from Kali Baari are coming, it's for Anirban's birthday,' said Maa.

With Brahmi's abandonment of her school and me and our love, everything had been a little fuzzy. It's been eleven days now. I have checked the newspapers every day for any suicides in the Gurgaon area.

Thankfully Maa–Baba or even Dada haven't noticed the bereavement on my face for Maa's new obsession with Zubeida Boudi's pregnancy hardly gives her time, and during her spare time I'm usually outside Brahmi's house, looking for signs of life.

I took no part in the day's proceedings. Instead, I stared at the landline, willing it to ring, knowing full well she wouldn't call.

As our apartment slowly transformed into a temple, I left the haze of the agarbatti smoke behind and went looking for Arundhati, who had been looking for me as well.

'Boyfriend?' I asked as we walked around in the apartment's park.

'Yes. He asked me and I said yes. On the last day of the exams,' she said.

'Sahil knows?'

'Not yet,' said Arundhati. 'But Rishab is going to tell him today.'

Arundhati told me she was thankful to me for making me meet him. Quite frankly, I couldn't find it in my heart to be happy for them. How could they decide on pursuing a new relationship, fall in love, when a friend of theirs was going through what she was? I faked a smile and congratulated her and wished her the best of luck. They were not really my friends. They just filled the hours in my day.

It was still early evening when I was sent to Dada's house in order to fetch him and Boudi.

I rang the bell and waited. Through the rusted iron mesh of the gate, I saw Boudi's swollen red eyes staring back at me. Dada came and got the door while Boudi disappeared inside the bathroom to wash her face. She came out smiling. I was asked to watch television while Dada said he needed to talk to Boudi. Pumping the volume of the television to the maximum, I pinned my ears to the door to discern the nature of the assault that had reduced Boudi to tears.

'I can't wear this,' said Boudi, crying again.

'It's just for one day, Zubeida. Maa will be happy if you wear this. Everyone will be old and married in today's puja. No one's going to look at you, trust me. Why don't you look at it this way? Maa is finally accepting you! Her friends from the kitty and the colony will be there. It's her way of showing you that you're a part of our family.'

'Anirban, I can't!'

'It's just for an hour . . . Fine, do what you will do then,' mumbled Dada and stormed out.

In the car, on our way home, the tension was palpable. While Dada felt choked at the grief Maa would feel parading Boudi in front of her friends in all her glory, the little crinkle on Boudi's forehead told me about her consternation at her new family worshipping a statue with eight extra arms and another with an elephant head sitting quite unbelievably on a mouse.

Maa welcomed Boudi with open arms. Not a frown, not a wayward grimace.

The Ganguly house wasn't quiet in the two hours Boudi spent there smiling at everyone, bending down and touching people's feet, talking about their kids, her parents, her job and the little kid who was about to come. She talked with poise and grace, shifting from Hindi to broken Bengali to English with unmatched ease, a spitting image of Maa. She's beautiful, everyone said, some with love-laced malice. In a room full of jealous Hindu women who worshipped Surya, it was a Musalman woman who glowed like the sun itself. In hushed tones, they discussed the merits of the burqa. 'It blocks out the sun and gives these Musalman women a nice complexion and skin,' one said. 'They all come from Afghanistan, that's why,' another argued. 'But dark skin is more beautiful,' a third had her final say.

Baba scowled the entire evening. Maa steadfastly kept herself busy, laughing too loud, frowning too much, as if she were made of nerve endings, capable of feeling everything.

When the puja started, Maa chanted the mantras louder to compensate for Boudi's Muslim-ness. She chanted over the pundit's muted, indecipherable Sanskrit words. The blood red of her sindur, of her bindi, of the *alta* smeared on her ankles glowed through the loud chanting. It seeped out of her and into the women who too glowed with Hindu pride, with the fury and unpredictability of their gods, as if to overshadow the blackness of Boudi's burqa. Maa's half-closed eyes brimmed with anger and compassion and hate and love.

Arundhati and I sat together. She wore a red suit, in tune with the theme today, and looked to rush out the entire time she was here, waiting for Rishab.

After the pooja ended, women kissed their bunched-up fingers and then transferred their love to Boudi by touching her on the chin or her hands—osmosis?

Later we went to the temple and fed the hundred-odd beggars with watered-down potato curry and deep-fried puris. Maa must have kissed Dada at least a thousand times in the evening, trying to wheedle out of him compliments on how such a celebration was apt and also humanitarian. After Dada and Boudi left, I asked if my birthday would be celebrated like this.

'No. Dada had to be reminded this time. We don't want the child under her influence. He will grow up a Hindu,' said Maa and went back to cleaning the house.

A little later, she handed the garbage bag for me to put out.

3 December 1999

Fourteen days. That's how long it had been.

When I saw her today, I thought I was imagining her. But it was no mistake. She was blaring the screechy horn of her Tauji's Bajaj scooter. It was then that it struck me that I hadn't seen it parked below her house. She had taken it with her.

'Hi,' I said when she stopped near me.

We forgot how we used to greet each other so we shook hands like we were in business together.

'I don't have a phone,' she said, looking at me.

'I didn't ask if you had one.'

'Do you want to go somewhere?' she asked.

I climbed up, and sat as far back as possible. She drove us to Wimpy's.

'Will you not talk at all?' she asked.

'I have nothing to say. You're the one with a new life.'

'Fine, I will speak.'

She told me her employers were teaching her to talk in an American accent, and that once she finishes that, she would no longer be Brahmi but Becky. She talked in her accent which sounded like a parody of how they talk in English movies.

'I'm getting better,' she explained. 'You should see how good my colleagues are at this. The company knows we are lying about our certificates but no one cares,' she added in the same breath.

It was disconcerting as to how she had bunched herself up in 'we', how she had decided on the course of who she would be like. For the next hour or so, she said how lucky she was to have Vedant as a brother who was showing her the world and how we, Arundhati and I, were depriving ourselves of the wonders that the life beyond Pitampura, beyond Rohini, beyond Dhaula Kuan and South Extension held. Her eyes glinted, as did mine, hers with hope and mine with mad envy.

'Vedant spends lavishly,' she said. 'You two should come home sometime.'

'What's the point? It's not as if you're missing out on anything.'

'C'mon, Raghu.'

'Fine, fine, I'm sorry. But you can't expect me not to be grumpy.'

'I had to leave the way I did. You know that,' she said.

'What about Tauji–Taiji? They haven't come looking for you?'

'They don't know where I am but I called them, asked them to not look for me, or I will go to the police. Tell them about the assaults.'

'You would do that?' I asked.

'No, but they thought I would. That's why they couldn't even ask for the scooter.'

'As happy as I am to see you I know you're going to leave. You have been looking at the clock for the last fifteen minutes. So let's go.'

'Are you going to be okay?'

'As okay as I can be without seeing you for days on end.'

'Raghu.'

'I am not saying that to make you feel bad, which you probably are. But I had to say it to someone.'

'I know. I had to say something to you as well,' she said.

'What?'

'I love you.'

'I love you.'

She put on her helmet and sunglasses, which were a new addition, and we rode off towards my home. Maa–Baba had always told me sunglasses weaken the eyes and slowly rob one of his or her eyesight. I wonder if it will happen to her. Will she one day stop seeing my love?

'I will see you later?' she said after dropping me and kicking her scooter back to life.

I nodded.

She put it into gear and had only driven a few yards when I started to run after her scooter. I was on my knees, blinded and choked with dust when Brahmi noticed me in the rear-view mirror. She took a swift U-turn.

'Raghu? What were you doing? Why were you running?'

'Don't go.'

'What?'

'I can't bear to not see you. I look around in school for you and you're not there,' I said, the words streaming out of my mouth, unchecked.

'. . .'

'I'm sorry but I am doing badly in school. I need you there. Didn't you tell me the same? You needed me? Now where am I supposed to go without you?'

'. . .'

'Why don't you say something?'

'. . .'

'I can't call you. I can't see you. I don't have any secrets of ours to hide from Rishab and Sahil. You don't even care about Mina any more. Don't you think she misses you?'

'. . .'

'Why am I the only one talking? Why are you not saying anything?'

'. . .'

'I'm sorry. Did I say too much? I will not. You can go. I'm sorry to have stopped you.'

'. . .'

'I just wanted to tell you that I will be there if you need me.'

'. . .'

'Unlike you who just walked away.'

'. . .'

'Of course, you have your reasons.'

'. . .'

'And you don't need me. You have your brother to take care of you.'

'. . .'

'Bye. I love you. I'm sorry. I will just go now.'

She reached out for my hand and hugged me. We cried in tandem for a bit, which was liberating. Then she left without a promise of when she would be back to see me again. I couldn't bring myself to ask that one thing that was gnawing my insides—why does she lie to people about her parents?

11 December 1999

I don't want to be a whiner but eight days have passed and I haven't seen her or talked to her. How difficult can it be to pick up the phone at a PCO and call? If his brother spends so lavishly, I'm sure he can pay for a few odd phone calls. What if she has found someone among the people whom she called 'we'? Or am I thinking too much?

That one time Maa went to Madras for a teaching assignment, Maa–Baba used to talk just once for a few minutes every week. Dada and I have heard the stories scores of times, especially when the telephone bills are high.

'What's there to talk about every day?' Baba used to scoff. 'Maa and I used to get two minutes a week! So we chose to say things that were really important.'

This isn't much different. Just because local calls are cheap, and technology is where it is today, I can't afford to be spoilt.

So I've decided that starting today, I will try to be more interested in things Sahil has to say about coding or hacking or whatever he does with the PowerBook, and be more involved in the fights Rishab and Arundhati often find themselves in.

Charity begins at home, and so keeping that in mind, I volunteered to take Boudi for a scan at the nursing home. Dada was suitably impressed when he found out.

I wasn't allowed inside the scan room but later they showed me images of the baby who had grown to the size of a hardcover novel.

'During the scan, they make you listen to the heartbeat as well,' said Boudi. 'It beats faster than ours.'

'Don't you feel betrayed? The least a child you helped bring into this world can do is match your heartbeat.'

'You're missing her that much, haan?' asked Boudi.

'Wouldn't you miss your—hopefully—daughter when she is no longer inside you? From where you're responsible for everything about her, where when she suffers you suffers, to when suddenly strangers who don't know the pain you and your child jointly suffered mollycoddle her, love her, and she finds comfort in their arms, laughter and smiles, her memories of your womb a distant past? Won't you miss her then?'

'That's a really strange but deep analogy,' said Boudi slowly.

'I'm as surprised as you are.'

When I came back, Maa–Baba had a thousand questions about the visit. Dada had put a temporary ban on Maa–Baba visiting the nursing home with Boudi for their appalling behaviour in front of the doctor, after the doctor called Maa–Baba out on their blatantly superstitious beliefs regarding Boudi's pregnancy. They had fought with the doctor, called her incompetent, and the nursing home a fraudulent institution.

13 December 1999

Just like that time Maa–Baba had spent apart, another intermittent call came from Brahmi today. She called from the office landline and the call lasted less than three minutes. But three minutes is a lot I have heard Maa–Baba say, and you really can say the most important things to each other in those three minutes. And even though I didn't know when or whether she would call at all, I had prepared what I could say in those three minutes. Things that mattered, things we would remember telling each other years later.

I could have told her how Maa–Baba were furious to know that Boudi had chosen to travel to Bangalore for a day on work. How Maa had blocked the door and screamed, 'No, you won't go! You're not putting my grandchild at risk. I don't care what the doctor says. She's a fraud!'

How Dada had grumbled, 'Maa! Please, it's important, let her go. It's a meeting with the CEO!'

'I don't care if it's a meeting with god himself,' Maa had said and how Maa feigned fainting, and Dada rushed to her, made her lie down on the sofa, and Boudi fanned her with a magazine. Of how Baba rushed to Dada's house—hovered for a few moments outside the door —and then entered the house saying a prayer, and then took Maa's head into his lap and whispered her back to life, and then accused Dada for Maa's recent health problems.

I could have told Brahmi about my doubts about the genuineness of Maa's fainting episode, which I had expressed

217

to Baba, who had looked at me agape, insulted and then showed me the reports of Maa's health check-up.

'You think we are lying to you!' Baba had shouted and thrown a bunch of prescriptions at me.

Her blood pressure has shot up dangerously, and both of them are taking sleeping pills.

I didn't tell Brahmi that.

What I also didn't tell her is that Dada–Boudi had lied shamelessly to Maa–Baba afterwards. They told us that Boudi had cancelled the trip and I had believed them. But later that night when I dropped in unannounced to tell Dada about Maa's reports, her blood pressure and sleeping problem, Boudi was gone and so was her packed suitcase.

'She's going to return tomorrow afternoon. Just handle Maa–Baba till then,' Dada had said.

So I did that. I came back home and lied to Maa who looked pale but smiled thinking her son and daughter-in-law were stubborn but also pliable.

I didn't tell Brahmi all this, instead I told her I loved her, I missed her and that I could spend the rest of my life sitting next to the telephone waiting for her call.

She on the other hand wasted the first ten seconds in silence and then told me she loved me too. There was no joy in her voice. Unlike me, who had things to tell her, important things, she had nothing but a rough silence for me. She talked in an alien voice, formal, the one she reserved for teachers.

'Is something wrong?' I asked.

'Why would anything be wrong? Everything is perfect.'

'Is there something you want to say?'

There was a pause after which she said something absolutely meaningless, 'What's up?'

Why would anyone ask that question?

'Nothing. I'm talking to you.'

'Okay.'

'So nothing has happened that you might want to tell me about?'

'No, Raghu. What will happen? I work, I go back home and I sleep. Work's hectic and my sleep schedule is all topsy-turvy. I have to be up the entire night.'

'We used to be up the entire night,' I said.

'Yes.'

'And what else?' she asked.

I lost my patience here and asked her to get back to work. Without a word of protest, she said okay, and disconnected the call, not bothering to tell me when she would call next.

17 December 1999

As it has always been, secrets hardly remain hidden from Maa. So when today, Maa gruffly shook me out of my bed, asked me to put on my clothes and come with her, I knew something was up.

We left in a hurry and were at Dada–Boudi's place by seven-thirty. Maa rang the bell impatiently, and when there was no response, she turned and sprinted towards the bus stop, her chappals slapping furiously against her heels. Dada–Boudi were waiting for their office bus, chatting with their colleagues.

'Maa?' they both echoed seeing us there.

Maa held Boudi's hand and started to pull her away in full view of her co-workers.

'Maa? What are you doing?' asked Dada, embarrassed.

Maa chose not to answer and pulled her farther away from the bus stop.

Their office bus ground to a halt. Everyone's eyes were stuck to the pregnant woman being dragged away by her dishevelled mother-in-law. The conductor called out and slapped the side of the bus impatiently. Their colleagues boarded the bus and waited for Dada and Boudi. Dada motioned for them to leave, told them everything was fine, and then went running after Boudi and Maa.

'Maa, what's wrong!'

Maa spoke without slowing down, or releasing her iron grip on Boudi's hand, 'I know she went to Bangalore! All of you lied to me. Again!'

'Maa—'

'Shut up, Anirban. I don't mind both of you lying to me any more. What I do mind is you harming your child.'

Dada and Boudi had nothing to say.

Maa dragged Boudi and Dada to a Bengali Hindu doctor to get all the scans done again. Boudi's protests were squashed by Maa's harsh words and a constant stream of tears. She held Boudi's hand firmly all through as if Boudi would escape. The tightness on Maa's face only faded when all the scans came out normal. The doctor asked Boudi to take adequate rest and to not travel without her permission, which I suspect Maa would have asked her to say. Back home, Maa made Dada and Boudi sit in front of her for thirty minutes before she spoke.

'Both of you are old enough to understand what the loss of a child means.'

She stared at them, waiting for her words to register, got up and we left.

On the way back home, Maa told me, holding my hand as firmly as she had held Boudi's, 'I see what's happening with you. The girl has left you, hasn't she?'

'No.'

'Raghu, you're an innocent boy. You don't know the ways of the world. You think women are innocent but they are not. After all that she did with you, she left you. At the end of the day it's only family that sticks around with you, is it not?'

'Brahmi's not like that,' I said.

'I don't know her, you do. But remember, we are your parents. We will always be by your side. Who can say if your Boudi didn't go and meet her parents and her brothers? Family's always there for you. Didn't we take back Dada?'

Another day passed by without her call.

21 December 1999

It's been a month and a half since she ran away from her old life.

Her name has been struck off the school register for non-payment of fees and insufficient attendance. Shrikant Gupta sits where she used to sit, right next to me, smelling of sweat and kadipatta (curry leaves). Her doodles on the table have been drawn over by Shrikant, her roll number taken over by Chetna Jha. Kritika wears her lab coat and her place in the basketball team is now Mansi's.

Like slowly the markers of her existence are being wiped off.

Today was different.

When I came back home from the temple—which is a great place to sit quietly and visualize a different life—I found Brahmi's Tauji–Taiji sitting in the living room, sipping tea. Unlike the last time, the demeanour was calm, civilized even; neither of them was with a bat or an iron rod. I was asked to come and join them.

'They want to know where Brahmi is,' said Baba. 'Tell them.'

They waited for an answer, earnestness dripping from their eyes.

In a voice as dispassionate as I could muster, I told them, 'You beat her, you made her bleed, you locked her up in her room, and you drove her away. Even if I knew where she is why would I tell you?'

'Is that how you talk to elders?' grumbled Baba. 'Just tell them. They are worried.'

'She's with Vedant. That's all I know and thank god for that.'

Brahmi's Tauji looked at Baba for help.

'Look, Raghu, you are friends with Brahmi and we understand that. But imagine their plight. What must everyone in their colony be thinking about them? She has to come home,' said Baba.

All four adults in the room nodded in sympathetic affirmation. This was society. Four fully grown adults believing in and agreeing to something absolutely stupid.

'No, she doesn't. She's happy wherever she is. She has found new friends and a new family. She doesn't need your benevolence any more. Her past is in the past.'

'Raghu—'

'Please, Maa! You don't know how they are. They swung a bat on my face, knocked out a tooth, threatened that they would make me disappear. That's the kind of people they are.'

Her Tauji–Taiji stood up to leave.

'We didn't come here to be sounded off by your *badtameez*, ill-mannered, boy,' he grumbled.

'We are sorry,' said Baba. 'We don't know what's got into him.'

'We thought you would understand us,' said her Taiji. 'After all your son had run away too.'

Maa–Baba looked like they had been slapped.

'She's not coming home,' I said. 'If you want to keep up pretences, she can visit your house along with Vedant and me every two weeks for the society to see that the relationship still exists.'

They stared at me, nodded reluctantly, and left. The door hadn't even closed when Baba griped, 'The next time you embarrass us like this in front of guests, I'm going to smack you in the face. They didn't do anything wrong by hitting a girl like her.'

Maa added softly, 'Ask him about the condom.'

I turned and left, furious at Maa–Baba's endorsement of her Tauji–Taiji's behaviour. Later that night, I dreamt of Boudi's delivery and the newborn girl and Maa–Baba's hovering faces over the crib. Only that they looked like Brahmi's Tauji–Taiji. I woke up and now I can only hear myself say what I said to them. 'She doesn't need you. She has a new family. She has new friends.'

24 December 1999

She was leaning on her scooter, the helmet still on her head. That's how I found her. I felt like Maa. Tears dammed against the cornea, angry tears, tears that make you want to stride over and slap the person for going missing. How long can a person go missing for a relationship to be considered null and void? One month? Two months? Or is it an indefinite time? I'm asking because I need to know. If Brahmi goes missing for three years and comes back equally in love, what should be the ideal course of action? Of course, there will be some anger, frustration, arguments and counterarguments, but in the end all's well that ends well? Because time is relative, it stretches and contracts, and right now every day I spend staring at the phone is longer than a millennium.

But of course, till the time I was walking up to her scooter, the tears were in control and I was smiling because she was still my most favourite person in the world. She parked her scooter and ran towards me. She lunged at me and wrapped her arms around me in a desperate embrace. I thought she was taller and heavier.

'I'm sorry,' she muttered continuously in my ear till all my grouses washed away.

She drove us to Naivedyam, a south Indian restaurant, a fifteen-minute drive away, and insisted I order a lot of food. It was the treat of her first salary. While I ate she played around with her food, nibbling around the edges. I filled her in on the details of Boudi's pregnancy, about Maa–Baba's growing fear that Dada–Boudi will do something to harm the child, and Maa's spying on Boudi to see if she's still talking to her parents. She nodded most of the time, interested but not engaged. She had nothing to say, nothing to add. She was barely even there. So I turned the conversation to her.

'What about your friends? Did you make any?'

'I haven't had the time,' she said. 'I wasn't paying Vedant so I was doing all the housework after office.'

'There's something I wanted to tell you. About your Tauji—'

'I met them. They told me what they said.'

'You met them? Why?' I asked.

'To pay them.'

'Pay them what? Last respects?'

'Don't be like that, Raghu. I gave them half my salary.'

I felt sucker-punched. 'Why would you do that?'

'They've brought me up, fed me, clothed me and sent me to a school. This is the least I could do.'

'The least you could do was to report them to the police. Paying them half your salary is stupid.'

'Not for me.'

'Can I ask you about—'

'Please don't, Raghu.'

We turned to our food again. And now, it seemed she ate frantically just so she didn't have to talk to me. Things had changed between us. I could feel it, I could read it on her face, and I feel foolish to have held what seem now to be archaic ideas about love. I had held Brahmi's hand, I had embraced her, she had kept her head on my shoulder and cried and I had done the same but that didn't bind us for life, no matter how I wished it would. She could change as a person and so could I. And it was possible for us to like someone else. And it would be wrong for anyone to judge a person who finds himself or herself incapable of loving the person he or she once loved. The laughable rules might still apply to me—because what if it is possible that I would ever feel even a shred of what I feel for her—but they don't to anyone else. And having said that, I'm judging and cursing her for not being the same person who used to be in love with me. The look in her eyes was empty, her smiles fake, her hugs snug but cold, and even though only a table separated us, it was like we had never met.

I had lost Brahmi.

It was just a matter of time now before she would be sucked into her new world, her new life, and I would keep holding on to my defunct ideas and my incomplete love story. When she left for Gurgaon again she told me that she might come to see me the next day.

'Tomorrow . . .' she said.

I nodded. I had already started waiting.

25 December 1999

Six hours in the balcony earned me nothing but scorn from Maa–Baba.

I refused to accompany Maa to Boudi's doctors' visits—one to her own doctor and one to Maa's. Then I refused to join Maa–Baba and Dada–Boudi for dinner which wasn't devoid of drama either. Boudi wanted to cook, which didn't go down well with Maa for reasons I'm not sure of. Did she think it would loosen her grip on the family kitchen? Was it because of Boudi's religion? Or was it just concern over her pregnancy? At the end of it, Maa won, mothers always do, and cooked an elaborate fare which tasted like dirt.

I should stop waiting for Brahmi. What am I still doing in the balcony?

But there's someone who's waiting alongside me; only for her, I assume, it's a bit of a celebration. Richa Mittal. She's still there crouched at the corner of her balcony, like she has been since morning. By evening, her eyes filled up with love and despair and anger.

Just like mine.

Also, Merry Christmas.

26 December 1999

The day started off well. I was successfully weaning myself off her.

I waited for her only for three hours, after which I busied myself with homework and household chores. Maa came to me while I was struggling with a permutation–combination word problem and said, 'You're a strong boy, my shona.'

'I am,' I said.

And I was strong. There were chunks of time I wasn't thinking of her at all, till the time the phone rang in the afternoon and I rushed to get it, hoping it was her. The receiver almost fell from my hands before I could put it to my ear. No one spoke. I wondered if it was Brahmi who couldn't muster up the courage to talk to me after having left me in a lurch.

Dada–Boudi and Maa–Baba went to a Chinese restaurant in the evening.

'I need to be with Mina,' I told Maa and excused myself from the family dinner.

I dropped in at Didimaa's place, endured her screeching taunts about the devil in Boudi's womb and how my Maa, the demon, would carve it out, played with and fed Mina, and left for Brahmi's Tauji–Taiji's house. The labourers were pulling the scaffolding apart. If Brahmi was on the other side of the window it would have been impossible to reach her now. The distance, the jump, the fall—all of it would have been fatal.

Her Tauji–Taiji were surprised to see me but unlike other times they weren't baying for my blood. It seemed like the money they were getting from Brahmi had satiated them. They had probably assumed I was behind her visit to them last week.

'I just want to know the name of the company she works in,' I asked them.

There were surprised I didn't know.

I was not invited in. I was asked to wait and the door closed on my face. A few minutes later, they gave me a slip of paper with the company name, phone number and address on it.

'Tell her we miss her,' they said before I left.

From there I went to the closest PCO and dialled the number of the company. The receptionist asked me if I knew the person I was calling for.

'I know her,' I said.

The call was transferred to her desk. The phone rang but no one answered. I asked the receptionist to try again. She did it, with no effect.

'You should call after an hour. She is not at her desk.'

And so I waited outside the PCO, watching time go by. An hour later, I called her again. I was told the same thing.

'She's not at her desk. Why don't you call after an hour?'

So I waited, feeling stupid.

This time, she picked up.

'Hello?'

'Hello, Brahmi?'

'How did you get this number?'

'I found it in the directory. You were supposed to come see me?' I asked.

'I was swamped with work,' she said, her voice curt.

'It's okay. I have been really busy too. I don't think I would have had the time to meet you as well.'

'Did you call earlier too?' she asked.

'Yes, I did but never mind. I was just getting a little bored.'

'Is there something you wanted to talk about?'

'No,' I said. 'Not really. I just wanted to ask if you called me in the afternoon. There was a missed call and no one spoke.'

'It wasn't me.'

'That's what I thought,' I said.

'How's everyone?'

'Good,' I said. 'Listen, I need to go. I am really busy.'

'Fine, I will talk to you later then,' she said. 'Will you be home on New Year's?'

'I think so,' I said.

'I might come that side to see you.'

'Okay, the next minute is about to start. I should disconnect,' I said. 'Bye now.'

'Bye.'

We didn't need to say we loved each other.

What's wrecking my heart is not Brahmi's coldness towards me but her unwillingness to come clean and tell me that it's over, that she feels nothing for me. At least then I can start mourning and make a fresh start.

I just need to hear it from her.

1 January 2000

New Year's Eve came and went. All the nonsense around the change of the century and the millennium grated on me. What's the big deal? The last time the millennium changed, we found more religions, more pretexts to kill each other. And do you think those people would have still celebrated the year 1900 had they known they would suffer through two World Wars and countless genocides. It's hopeless and pathetic to celebrate the passage of time, to think the coming time will miraculously be better. It's the refuge of the impotent. Time, money, religion, society—everything we have collectively thought of and choose to believe in only hurts us. What power will money have, will time have, if we choose to stop believing in it. If we smash the clocks and burn our currencies. But love, that's not our invention. That's hardwired into us, to hurt us, to enthral us, to get us down to our knees. I waited for her till 11.59 and then at 12.00 I made a resolution to stop moping over Brahmi's prolonged absence, to scruff her out of my heart, not think endlessly about her, but at 12.01 all I could think of was to pick up the phone and call her, hear her voice, see her face, and maybe hug her again. I want to cry and bawl and run all the way to Brahmi, to be her knight in shining armour, have a job in a call centre, have a house and TV and whatever Vedant has. Why couldn't I be the hero for just fucking once?

I had still been struggling with these thoughts when Dada called home. Boudi had suddenly fallen sick. Maa–Baba and I rushed to the hospital, half dressed but wide awake. Most of all, it was Maa who was terrified beyond her wits.

She whispered in Baba's ears, 'What if something happens to Meenakshi?'

When they met Dada in the corridor, they asked first about the unborn child and then about Boudi, which was curious and disheartening.

'She's okay.'

'How did it happen?' asked Maa.

'She got hurt in the office.'

'And you're telling us now!' shouted Maa, inviting looks from the others around us.

'She didn't want to worry you. Anyway, the doctors did an ultrasound. Everything is in order. They are going to let her go in an hour,' said Dada.

We went to Dada's flat from the hospital. While Boudi rested on the sofa, the bulge in her stomach dangerously big, Dada and Maa fought, faces flushed, lips quivering.

'What's the need for her to go to office? How are the doctors still allowing this? And don't teach me about career. I have a career too. When it's time to rest, it's time to rest,' Maa addressed Dada as if Boudi wasn't in the room.

'If she wants to work, she will work, Maa. What will she do sitting in the house all day? She will get bored.'

'Bored! Just so she doesn't get bored she will put my grandchild at risk? No! Tell her she's not going to office tomorrow,' said Maa.

'Your Maa is correct. Enough has happened. It will be good if this house doesn't see any more misfortune,' said Baba.

'Nothing will happe—'

'*Chup kor to!* Shut up! How many kids have you had, huh? What do you know what can or cannot happen?' snapped Maa, invoking her right to win an argument like this. Our dead sister was helping Maa from even beyond the grave.

'Maa, I'm not getting into this. She will manage,' said Dada.

'I saw how she managed! I saw how the two of you managed! Great job! Should I clap for you two? Let's do that!' screamed Maa. She got up from her chair and turned to Boudi. 'In our families, it's the mother who takes care of her pregnant daughter. Since your family . . . that means I have to take care of you. I am asking you to stop going to office from tomorrow.'

Boudi looked blankly at Maa. 'Don't do what you did today. Tell me the minute something happens? Am I clear?'

She looked at Dada and said in Bengali, 'The next time she does something like this I'm going to slap her. Mind you.' She switched back and said, 'Both of you have done enough to hurt this family. Like your Baba said, I don't want another misfortune. You wouldn't be able to live down a dead child, Anirban. I'm telling you.'

As Maa–Baba turned away from them, Dada spoke, 'Maa. You can't keep talking to us like this.'

'What?'

'Maa, you keep taunting her. We are married now. She feels hurt when you say what you do.'

'What do you want me to say then? Praise? *Ei dekho!* Look here now! What great deed my son has done getting a Musalman girl home! Is that what you want me to say? We are doing everything to accept this situation. Please forgive us if we are not better parents to you. I hope in your next life you don't get us as your parents.'

'Maa—'

'I don't want to hear anything more. You're giving us a grandchild, that is *khub bhalo*. Very good. But we won't ever forget how you have hurt us, how you have disgraced us in public,' said Maa, now sniffling into her saree.

Before Dada could say anything, Baba ushered her out.

'I think you should listen to Maa,' I said. 'It's not too much she's asking for.'

Then I left.

3 January 2000

Today morning, I wanted to let it out, tell someone how disgracefully Dada had behaved with Maa–Baba, and so I rang Arundhati's bell. Who am I kidding? I had to fill the Brahmi-sized hole in my heart with anything I could get. It took her five minutes to get the door.

'You can't come in,' she said.

'Why? You have an exam?'

'No, Rishab is here,' she said and giggled.

'I needed to talk to you. It's im—'

'Raghu? Rishab, my boyfriend, is here.'

'So?'

'So! You have to go! I will talk to you later!' she said with a laugh and closed the door. I could hear her and her boyfriend, the boy I'd helped her meet, laugh from behind the door. I didn't even want to think about what was happening behind the door. Disappointed, I walked back to my room and wrote a long letter to Brahmi, not knowing how it would reach her. After a point, I realized the futility of it and tore it. She's gone. She doesn't care. Had she cared she would have called and explained her absence. Sometimes in the nights, I just put the phone receiver to my ear and pretend she's on the other side. I don't talk, obviously. I'm not a lunatic. But I imagine what it would be like to talk to her like that again. I miss her with every fibre of my being, no matter how much I try not to.

Today both Bhattacharya Uncle and Mittal Uncle were at home, telling Baba how inter-religion and inter-caste marriages are the ruin of mankind.

Mittal Uncle said, 'Do you think what's written in the ancient books is all dung? No? It means something. That's why the child in your daughter-in-law's stomach is giving so many problems. It's unholy.'

Bhattacharya Uncle was milder. 'Every race is different,' he said.

Later I was asked to fetch a mixer-grinder from Didimaa's house. I had planned a quick in and out but Mama wasn't home and I had to wait for him to come back. Didimaa welcomed me with a laugh that chilled me to my bones. She smelt my despair and kept asking me if the ruin of the Gangulys had come yet. She asked me to make her tea. I pretended to not hear her. The angrier she became the more it gladdened me.

I held on to my silence till she suddenly screamed, 'Yes! Yes! Laugh at the old woman! Why wouldn't you! Be happy, Raghu, celebrate, eat mangsho and paesh, because a dark time is upon you! A very dark time! You two brothers will never be happy. Never!'

I turned to look at her. Her glare bore into me.

'Ah! I'm right!' she continued in her evil prophetic tone. 'The brothers will never reconcile. Only death, only death will make you brothers again. Now, the kid looks at me! And why not? He's scared now. He's shaking in his bones. And why shouldn't he? There's a life at stake.'

I wondered who had told her about the scare a couple of days ago.

'Not to the child,' Didimaa screamed, waving her bony fingers at me. 'But to your Dada! What did you brothers think? Both of you will love and have a fulfilling life after how your Maa and you boys treated your Didimaa? No, no! I cursed you and your brother long back! Didn't your Maa tell you? I told that petni that both her sons will fall in love and die young! Both! And see, that's what happening . . . your elder brother married death itself! And you're going the same way. Falling in love, destroying yourself! Who can turn fate?'

'Fuck off, Didimaa,' I said.

I knew she didn't know what I had just said and maybe that's why I said it.

'Asking me to keep my mouth shut? Sure! Do that! But no one can stop what's happening. The beginning of your end is nigh. The girl in your life and the woman in his will take both of you to your graves! So go! Fall in love! And end the Ganguly bloodline once and for all! It's fate!' said Didimaa and started to scream and laugh.

I couldn't take it any more so I left. Had I stayed I would have smacked Didimaa. But now as I am writing this, her voice rings loudly in my ears.

6 January 2000

When I woke up, I found Dada smoking next to me on the balcony.

'You have been out for two hours,' he told me. 'Should we go inside?'

I nodded groggily.

Dada and I sat silently in front of each other for the good part of an hour. He didn't want an explanation for my ludicrous behaviour, which to him probably wasn't absurd at all. I had seen him during the time he thought his story had met with an untimely end and if anything he looked way worse than I do.

To cheer me up, or at least fill up my time, Dada–Boudi took me out to eat to Gola in Connaught Place. For the most part, they spoke, joked, laughed and hoped I would join in but I had nothing to say. Their smiles and their happiness irritated me.

'I don't want to talk in clichés,' said Boudi. 'But at least you can be happy that you felt something strong, something real. Not a lot of people can claim that now, can they?'

'I don't see how that's reassuring.'

Dada slapped my back and said, 'A few years down the line when you get over her, I will ask Zubeida to set you up with one of her cousins.'

'Preferably someone who's as religious as she is,' I said.

'Maa will be so happy,' said Boudi and laughed. 'She will love us!'

And then we all cracked up.

'I love Maa, though,' said Boudi.

'You don't have to lie. She has done nothing to deserve your love,' I said.

'No, I do, and she has done more than my parents did. I have no reason not to love her. I lost a home but I somewhat gained one in real terms. They did let go of their prejudices a little, didn't they?' she asked.

'I thought we were supposed to talk about my plight, not yours,' I said.

'Such an attention-seeker,' said Dada teasingly.

'Look who's talking. Everything has been about you these past months.'

'Envy, thy name is Raghu Ganguly.'

'Oh please, shut up. I didn't want to come out. I was doing very well with my broken heart,' I said.

Going out did take my mind off but now darkness awaits . . .

A while back, I called her office and she wasn't at her desk again. I had called just twice when the receptionist advised me to not call on the board so often or she would have to put the number on the block list.

9 January 2000

I had always thought there were only a few things in the world more humiliating than your teachers berating you in front of the entire class and complaining to your parents in a PTA meeting. And today, I was proven right when three teachers stood in front of Maa–Baba with my half-yearly answer sheets, pointing out the silly mistakes that riddled the papers.

'We didn't expect this out of him,' they echoed. 'He's dipped to the middle of the class from the top three.'

Maa–Baba felt as I did sitting there, the nerves in the necks pulsating in perfect synchronized rhythm. When the humiliation ended, Maa–Baba walked in perfect silence to the parking lot, their faces red, Baba's fist clenching–unclenching, Maa curling the end of her saree around her thumb till she cut off circulation.

'I forgot my purse in the class, get it,' said Maa.

I ran to the class, searched high and low for the purse, and couldn't find it. I ran back to the parking lot to find Maa–Baba and the car gone. I didn't have money so I walked my way home. It took me an hour and by the time I was home, Maa–Baba were done with lunch.

'You can go out and have some,' said Baba.

'I don't have money,' I said, pissed off at their cruel game.

And that's where I went wrong. They had me set up to say this exact line. They had planned their entire charade around this. Because at that very moment, they both turned to me and threw me volleys I had no intention to counter.

'If you don't clean up your act, you won't ever have any money,' said Baba.

'How can you get a 78 in mathematics? Chhee! 78! Why are you punishing us?' said Maa.

'Did you see how the other parents were looking at us? Like our son's an alcoholic or a drug addict!' said Baba.

'At least that would have been a better explanation. But a girl? A girl? Hey *bhogowan*! Oh god!'

'We should have known what to expect seeing how Anirban behaved.'

Then Maa added calmly, 'If don't want to study, just tell us. You can get a diploma and be a foreman at a construction site. I am asking you genuinely. As parents, we want to know what you want to do when you grow up. You can be a labourer, we don't mind, but don't make us spend unnecessarily.'

Baba said, 'Why didn't you take humanities? We wouldn't have said anything.'

I zoned out for a bit. At that point I marvelled at how indifferent I was. Two years ago the very same comments would have reduced me to tears, multiple times.

'Why are you now just looking at us and not saying anything?' asked Maa.

'Answer your Maa,' said Baba.

'I'm sorry,' I said. 'I will do well in the finals. Can I go study?'

As I was leaving the room, I heard Baba say, 'One boy stuck to a bad job because of a girl, the other won't even get to college because of one.'

'That girl from his school is a petni,' said Maa.

I stopped.

I couldn't take it any more. I turned around and charged at Maa, all sense of love melting away. I raised my hand and only stopped a few inches from her face. Baba swung his hand at me.

and I blocked his blow. He cowered away when I threatened to swing. They muttered and stammered and couldn't utter a straight word. I shouted at them to shut up once and for all. I told them that this was the last time they would say anything about Brahmi or Boudi or anyone, and that I, for one, will not tolerate any of their bullshit, and if they chose to continue this behaviour I will walk out of this house and never come back again . . .

NO.

I didn't do any of the above.

But standing there with my back towards them I thought it. It happened in my head. Then I walked to my room and now I am writing this.

11 January 2000

Everything that I wouldn't have imagined would ever happen has already happened so what happened today shouldn't have surprised me but it did. Maa had recruited Boudi to knock some sense into me.

'You need to study, Raghu,' she said in the taxi to the hospital for her doctor's visit.

'I have heard it all before, Boudi. I don't need a pep talk.'

'I believe you do,' she said.

'Not again. Two days—'

'You need to talk about this, not with me but someone else,' said Boudi.

I believed it was going to be Dada who was probably waiting for us at the hospital.

'We just crossed—'

'We are not going to the hospital. I don't have a doctor's visit today.'

'So where are we going?'

'To see Brahmi,' she said.

'What? Why? Did you talk to her?'

'No but we will. It will be nice if you tell me where she works so you can talk to her and figure this out,' she said.

At this point, I threw the biggest fit I can recall. The only thing I didn't do was jump out of the moving vehicle. An hour later, tired from the ranting and the complaining and the arguing about how it was futile, we were outside Brahmi's office in Gurgaon.

'It's going to be okay,' Boudi told me. 'Just talk to her. It's better to be certain about a few things. If she still loves you, let her tell you that. If she doesn't then you should start to move on. Either way, you have to talk to her about this.'

Boudi asked the receptionist to call Brahmi. The receptionist made the call and it went unanswered.

'Can you try again?' she asked.

The call was unanswered again.

'Did she come in today?' asked Boudi.

When the receptionist checked the register she found that Brahmi hadn't checked into office today. Boudi put on her brightest smile and asked her if she could tell her if Brahmi came the day before.

'She missed office a couple of days last week as well,' said the receptionist.

Boudi thanked the receptionist, and asked her if she could ask Brahmi to call on a number—she gave the number to Dada's office—and we left.

'She must be sick,' said Boudi on the way back home.

'Of course, Boudi. It's when you're sick you take staggered holidays. Not when you probably have a new boyfriend.'

'You can't assume that—'

'Brilliant plan though.'

We didn't talk for the rest of the drive home.

As I'm writing this I feel guilty for snapping at Boudi. But there was no need of doing what she did.

Up till an hour ago, there was no call on Dada's landline.

17 January 2000

Three days ago, Boudi was rushed to the hospital. It was a close shave.

I was kept away from most of the discussions but I heard the words 'bleeding' and 'placenta' and 'danger' and 'risk' and 'miscarriage'.

That's the reason Boudi was brought home today. Dada was sent to get her clothes and other belongings while Maa–Baba set about dutifully shifting things around in the house to make it more pregnancy-conducive. Dada seemed uncharacteristically happy about the whole thing, despite the sleepless nights he had spent in the hospital. Maa–Baba had stayed with him, running after doctors, pleading and praying. Despite my protestations that I wouldn't leave Boudi alone in the hospital I was made to go to school on both days.

'You're a child. You shouldn't be around here, shona,' said Maa.

While Boudi rested in Dada's room, Baba got freshly cut chicken for Maa to cook biryani.

'That's a little presumptuous. Just because she's Musal—'

I was made to shut up and go clean my room before Boudi woke up.

'What will she think about you? That we brought you up like this? And take a shower!' said Maa.

'Baba finished all the hot water,' I complained.

'He hadn't bathed in two days, shona. Wait then, I will warm up some water on the stove,' she said.

A couple of hours later, the house smelt like the inside of Nizam's, the legendary biryani outlet. Boudi had woken up. Dada was helping her to the living room when Maa saw them.

'What are you doing out of bed? Stay there! I will serve there only!' said Maa.

We spread newspapers on the bed, dragged the TV trolley to Dada's room and ate. Boudi couldn't eat much but she lavished praise on Maa's cooking. Maa blushed suitably. Dada and I joked quite uncomfortably about Maa's decision to cook biryani. We laughed and jibed like everything was normal. For a few brief moments I even stopped obsessing over Brahmi's absence, over her possible boyfriend.

'Both of you have gone through a lot,' said Maa. 'Take rest now.' Maa caressed Boudi's face and told her, 'Now that you are here I will take care of everything. If you need anything tell me.'

Smiles were exchanged and we left Dada and Boudi alone.

I helped Maa–Baba clear the plates. Dada had cheekily given me his Walkman and a list of sad songs to get over my Brahmi problem. I had been listening to them the entire day on loop, and doubting whether it was a good choice to do so. I couldn't hear Maa–Baba over the music at first. But then, I ran through side A and heard a bit of their conversation.

'Did Anirban tell you what had happened? How did the bleeding start?' asked Maa.

'Just that she was sleeping.'

'She told me she was in the kitchen. But I know what she was doing. She was praying, I'm telling you, that's what she was doing. She was reading the Quran, that's what she was doing. Can you imagine? Risking the baby for that!' Maa griped.

'Why would you expect anything different? Didn't you know what we were getting into?'

'My son now lies to me every day.'

'Is this why we brought him up?'

'I see her office papers lying around, I see bills of places they go to without telling us. They lie through their teeth about everything,' said Maa.

Baba shook his head and his shoulders drooped, more disappointed than angry. As if he knew his anger now meant nothing. Not only had he lost to his son, he had lost his wife to hate too.

'Did you notice those framed verses of the Quran she has put up everywhere?' asked Maa.

Baba said, 'It's your son's fault too. When was the last time he prayed at the temple you set up for him? Does he even light an incense stick?'

I stood there pretending I was to listening to my songs on the Walkman as Maa—Baba kept cursing their wretched luck.

'Look at how sweet she is right now. She has cast a spell on my son. What do you think she would do to our grandchild?' said Maa.

'What about the prayers the child hears five times a day?' asked Baba angrily. 'What do you think she is trying to do?'

'I won't let her pray near my grandchild. You just see! This girl thinks too much of herself! Took our son away, turned him against us . . . How much more do you think I will suffer? No, enough, this girl will see what I can do. I will not be helpless. I will bring up the child, you see. She can do all her career stuff for all I care.' Maa started to sob softly. 'You just see what I do.'

'Ei, hey,' said Baba. 'Talk softly and don't do anything stupid. All that you have done for the past few months will go down the drain.'

'I don't know how much longer I can take this. How long can I pretend that everything is okay? That I love Anirban the same! I don't! Which mother would? Why do you think Raghu is like this now? All because of that Anirban.'

Baba sighed deeply. 'Don't you think I feel like slapping him every day? Strutting around his wife everywhere.'

'How much long—'

Maa started to weep softly. Baba held Maa and said, 'Just wait till she delivers. Just a few more days. It's either this or our son lets our grandchild grow up as a Musalman.'

'Over my dead body. You see how I teach this girl a lesson once our grandchild is here,' said Maa.

'Hmmm . . .' said Baba. 'What about that other girl? Brahmi?'

'She has left him,' said Maa. 'Thank god for that. She wasn't even beautiful from what I hear, that shakchunni.'

Back in the room, I curled into a little ball when the pain became physical.

22 January 2000

I saw Brahmi today. It sounds innocuous if I put it like that. I waited for three mornings outside her office. It wasn't a decision based on reason. It was what my body, my heart and my mind yearned for. I struggle for words to describe what it was like. Maybe a little like burning, like everything was on fire, and only she could quell it. It sounds silly I know but that's the closest to how I felt.

Maa–Baba's brilliant acting rankles me. Their sweet behaviour is a lie. They never had had a change of heart. If anything, their hearts had only rotted further. Their concern wasn't how Dada will cope with a child, or how they'd lose their son if they didn't accept him, they were driven by the fear that their grandchild might be a Nazia or an Abdul.

Everything is a lie.

I was outside her office to know if 'Brahmi and I' too were a lie. If she too had lied to me about how she felt about our love.

'Raghu! What are you doing here?'

'Why are you surprised to see me? I dropped in a message a few days ago. To call on a number.'

'Oh yes, I have been meaning to call you but—'

'But you're too busy? Too much work? New friends? New boyfriend?'

'Why are you being like that?'

'If none of the things I just said are true then why haven't you come to visit me?'

'Do you want to have tea?' she asked, her voice losing the fake happiness she had mustered to talk to me.

My fury only multiplied on our walk to the nearby tea vendor.

'I don't drink tea,' I said.

'More for me?'

'I can't stay away from you.'

'Raghu—'

'Let me finish. It took me two hours to get here and I have been thinking a lot about what to say to you. I finally know what I have to do.'

'What you have to do about what?'

'About us,' I said.

'Raghu—'

'Brahmi, our story has to end now. It's the only way to go. I have thought about this long and hard. Clearly, you have a life here. You don't need me. And I can't keep waiting for you in school. You don't even have a phone from where to call.'

'Raghu—'

'Even if you do I will have to wait for your calls. It's not your fault. Don't look that sad. It breaks my heart. I realize what I feel for you is stronger than what you feel for me. And that's okay by me. You're you, you know. Like only the best possible girl ever, and I am me. Even I wasn't prepared for what I felt about you. I can't do this to me. I have to stop thinking about you.'

'So what do you suggest we do?' asked Brahmi.

'I want to stop waiting. I want to stop thinking of you. I want to stop being in love with you.'

Her silence was deafening.

I could hear my heart thump. Lup-dup. Lup-dup. She stared at me and her eyes said a thousand things, all of which had I had to translate would say she was in love with me.

'If that's what you want,' she said as if doing me a favour.

She didn't fight. She didn't question my decision. She just sat there and said it like it was on her mind as well.

She drank from both the cups. She cleared the bill. Even gave me some money. 'Go back in a taxi,' she said.

We walked to the taxi stand. Just before leaving, she said, 'You were wrong about one thing though.'

'What?'

'I needed you here. More than ever.'

I rode away in the taxi and came back home thinking of how else the conversation could have gone. But now all I am thinking about is the last words she said to me. There was something in her eyes, a sadness, and a cry for help that's haunting me. Maybe it's just my mind playing tricks on me, giving me pretexts to reach out to her again. 'I am fine,' she'd said as a consolation prize.

Like everything around me, what I said to her was a lie as well. I didn't want to stay away from her, I didn't want to stop loving her, I didn't want to stop thinking of her; it was not even close to what I wanted. All I wanted was for her to fight for me, stop me from going away, to love her and feel loved. That's all I really wanted. But I needed to know what she felt for me. And now I know it's not much.

Had she told me a lie before?

29 January 2000

I told Maa–Baba, Dada and Boudi, all of whom insisted on a party, that I didn't want to have one. They asked me if my friends weren't asking me for a treat.

'Of course, they are. But this time we aren't doing treats for anyone. I told them what we did for Dada's birthday, so now they want me to give away the money to a charity. I'm thinking Helpage India. What do you think?'

If they can lie so can I, and as convincingly.

Maa raised her hands in protestation. 'It's your first birthday after their marriage. You want it to be that boring? Okay fine, we will do whatever your Boudi picks. So Mamoni, tell us!'

We all looked at Boudi. I hoped with all my heart she wouldn't insist on a party. Won't it be sad? To be surrounded by non-existent friends and a family that I could hardly respect.

Seeing Boudi as the centre of all attention broke my heart. She felt important, loved, believed she was a part of this family. Luckily, she asked me to give away the money to Helpage India. Dada was disappointed in me, saying I was getting too blasé too early in my life. He fussed over me the entire day, goading me into going somewhere with Brahmi, Arundhati, anyone.

'It's depressing to see you sitting here on your birthday,' said Dada. 'I couldn't celebrate it the way I wanted to this time around so I thought I would live a little through yours but you're such a disappointment.'

'How does it matter, Dada? Just one year after another.'

'Oh, c'mon. Don't be this sad, okay?'

'Why would I be sad? Everything is just perfect, isn't it?' I asked.

Dada laughed. 'Yes it is, did you see how Maa asked Zubeida what she wanted? I never thought it would come to that.'

'We are fortunate to have such loving parents, aren't we?' I said, the sarcasm again lost on him.

'Sometimes I think that if all Maa–Baba wanted was a child to reconcile with my marriage I should have planned it that way. Do you look at Maa when she looks at Zubeida? Like she's got back our Mina,' said Dada.

I was confused whether to pity him or feel anger so I just nodded.

'Hey? I forgot to ask? What happened with Brahmi?'

'I broke up with her,' I said.

Dada started to laugh. He said, 'You broke up with her? You?'

'I don't know why it's funny.'

Dada put his arm around me and said, 'It's okay, Raghu. It happens.'

'Of course it does.'

Later in the evening Boudi had a severe coughing bout. Her doctor asked if we had a dog at home. We told him about Mina and the doctor advised not to have the dog inside the house until the delivery. Boudi is at a severe risk of developing allergies, he told us. When we came back, Maa made us all take long baths and scrubbed the house clean of Mina's fur.

'Didn't I tell you? Maa would do anything for Zubeida now. It's so cute,' said Dada, smiling.

I think this experiment has been great, writing to myself, but I think it will soon come to an end. And I know when to end this. Once I help Dada tide over the birth of his child, tell them about Maa–Baba, and settle them in the humdrum routine of raising a child. Earlier I thought I would do it the day of the birth but I think that would have been selfish and would be like stealing the child's thunder. I am sad, I'm not crazy. As I was writing this, I saw Richa on her balcony staring at the road. I snapped and shouted at her, 'NOW WHAT THE HELL ARE YOU STANDING THERE FOR?'

She said in a low tone, 'I'm not here for you,' and got up and left.

30 January 2000

This year it's a school holiday for Mahatma Gandhi's death anniversary. He died fifty-two years ago today. Nathuram Godse, a Hindu fanatic and a member of the Hindu Mahasabha and the RSS before that, fired at Gandhi, whom he blamed for helping in the partition of India.

'It's good that Godse killed him rather than a Muslim,' said Dada. 'Imagine the riots that would have caused.'

But I guess we do a good job at hiding that we dislike someone for our own gain. Like Maa–Baba, who have been fussing over Boudi like she is their child, or Brahmi who had loved me till the time she didn't. Had I not heard Maa–Baba that day in the kitchen I would have fallen for their charade as well. Had I not asked Brahmi to leave me, god knows how much longer she would have played out the charade of being in love with me. Brahmi hasn't reached out, which shows how devastated she is. Not even a courtesy call to ask if I'm doing well.

But the pain they have caused me would have been worse had I not known they were capable of lies, of betrayal. Brahmi had shown signs from the very beginning by lying to me about her parents, by hiding things about her past even though she told me she loved me, and the less we talk about Maa–Baba the better. It's like all these years some hateful creatures lived in a little shell buried inside Maa–Baba which broke forth and took over their minds and their hearts the minute Boudi walked into Dada's life.

Every time Maa holds Boudi, laughs at her quips, caresses her face, or is kind to her, my stomach churns. How many times did Brahmi tell me she loved me when she really didn't?

Maa, my beloved Maa, turns into an evil, conniving crone, like a shadow of Didimaa. It's in her blood, so why not. I don't want to say it. The word has a finality. You can't come back from it unless you use it frivolously. I have started to hate Maa. Even as I write this my hands tremble. But I'm sure this is what I feel inside.

HATE. It's as simple as that.

I hate her pretence, I hate her capacity to fake love and concern, I hate her machinations, and I hate her refusal to accept Boudi as a human. I hate that she thinks of the life inside Boudi as Dada's and Dada's alone. I hate that she smiles the same smile with me. I would pick Baba's rants, Maa's tears and Dada's rebellion over the stage performances of Maa–Baba any day. I would pick a splintered family than this excuse of one any day.

The choice to end this lies with me. I can tell Dada about the conversation I had overheard, ask him to take Boudi and go, make a life somewhere else, forget he had parents, bring up his child as an atheist . . . but I won't right now. I want to see what else Maa–Baba are capable of. So that when I abandon them I can tell them WHY in a list that runs endlessly. I want them to regret their decisions for the rest of their lives.

Moreover, if they could use Boudi to spawn their grandchild then why shouldn't Boudi use Maa's care that she so evidently needs during the pregnancy?

P.S. I haven't decided the building as of now. I will once the child is born.

14 February 2000

It's been days since I have talked to Rishab or Sahil or Arundhati. My attendance in school has been sketchy the past couple of months. I had made Maa–Baba realize that school was a waste of time and I needed more time at home to complete my IIT modules. Maa–Baba had promptly called the principal and eked out an arrangement. The principal had summarily objected but he knew that an IIT ranker in their alumni is just what they needed. My seniors were nincompoops and no one was expected to clear IIT. I was their shining light. I don't miss my school fellows at all. I don't miss Maa–Baba and Dada as they were. And of all the people I don't miss, it's Brahmi. I don't miss her voice, I don't miss her touch, I don't miss her presence—yes, I don't miss her at all. And why will I miss her? It's not as if I think she was a part of me. It's not as if the last few days of my life have been spent in abject despair, or as if I spent every waking minute reliving everything that we shared, everything that seemed real and true and everlasting, or as if I have mourned the loss of every possible future I have seen with her, or as if sometimes the pain is so hard to bear that I fiddle with the paper cutter.

So imagine my consternation when I found Brahmi waiting outside my school. Like a child running away from a swarm of bees I ran away from her. I ran and ran till I thought I would run out of solid ground to run on. But she was there too. Like a ghost.

'This is what you meant when you said you didn't want anything to do with me?' said Brahmi.

My heart thumped with a ferocity I had not felt before. Was it happiness? Was it sadness? Was it the exhaustion of running?

'Why are you here? I thought I had made it plenty clear that we shouldn't have to do anything with each other.'

'I just came here to see how you were doing.'

'What would happen to me? I'm fine,' I said.

'You don't look fine,' she said. 'Come, sit.'

'I don't want to sit. I want to go.'

'Don't throw a tantrum now. Come and sit here.'

She patted the pavement she sat on.

Begrudgingly, I did as asked. As much as it pained me to see her, I couldn't budge, like I was under her spell. She seemed to have become even more beautiful, if that was possible.

'You haven't been talking to anyone,' said Brahmi.

'Isn't that entirely my choice?'

'It is but they are your friends. You don't pick up their calls, you don't meet them, you don't even sit with them. Why?'

'I don't think of them as my friends.'

'Why not?'

'They don't matter.'

'That's—'

'I never had the need of making friends, Brahmi. And I don't want your advice. I think I was plenty clear that we shouldn't be in touch any more. So now I will get up and go home and you won't reach out to me.'

'But why, Raghu?'

'Because I don't see any reason why we should be in touch. You are not the person I was in love with and it's impossible for me to accept that. I will continue loving you till the time I can and it's unfair on both of us to be in an unrequited relationship. I know you don't feel the same way as you once did and that's fine. Just as that is your prerogative, this is mine.'

Brahmi sighed deeply and said, 'Raghu. There are things that are out of your hand. You can't do anything about it. The world's a shitty place and we have got to accept it. Maybe you're not meant to save me or I to save you.'

'I know that. But we were meant to suffer together, weren't we?' I asked.

'I don't think I can be there for you, Raghu.'

'Yes, I know,' I said and got up.

I walked away from her. A stupid, stupid, stupid part of me wanted her to come and stop me. So when I turned a corner, I hid to see if she was following me. She was still on the pavement, tossing pebbles, staring out in the distance. When the pebbles around her disappeared, she started to weep. At first softly and then her whole body shook. I wanted to run to her, hold her, ask what's troubling her but I chose to stand and watch for the next half an hour. Why should I be around to comfort her when she so brutally ripped herself out of my life?

And when has she ever opened up to me? She would talk in riddles and only make me sadder, if that's possible. She quietened after a while and then drove off on her scooter. I came back home.

Richa shouted from the balcony, 'Did you meet her?'

I waved my middle finger at her and what I assume was a celebratory look because of my break-up on her face. I have seen my seniors do that. Richa would have seen that too because she disappeared into her house.

It was late in the evening when Baba came home with an opened envelope addressed to me. It was without any stamps.

'Has the girl still not left you?' asked Maa.

'I have nothing to do with her.'

'You don't?' said Baba, mockingly. 'Then what should I do with this card?'

'Burn it,' I said.

Maa–Baba would have sensed the seriousness in my tone because they left the card on the table. Boudi picked it up.

'Why are the hearts cut out? Seems more like a break-up card,' she asked.

'I don't know,' I said and took the card from her.

Now as I'm looking at it the writing is Richa's, not Brahmi's. She seemed to have been heartbroken about me abusing her, or seeing Brahmi again. If only she would have known that there's nothing left between Brahmi and me.

21 February 2000

Boudi's heavily pregnant but with Maa–Baba fussing over her every little discomfort, it gives Dada a lot of time on his hands.

My retreat from the world of friends and frolic and going out has not been taken lightly by Dada. Apparently, Brahmi had reached out to Arundhati, Sahil and Rishab to involve me, talk to me, and make sure I was fine. It hadn't ended well for anyone. A couple of days ago, all three of them had landed at my place unannounced. I had only briefly recovered from a depressing bout of reminiscing about Brahmi so the last thing I had wanted was to see them—my last surviving tether to her. What really angered me on seeing them was that she could call them but not me!

I told them I didn't want to see them. They tried cracking stupid jokes, and suggest stupider things for me to do with them. Tired of their antics, I left the house and they came running after me.

Thrice I warned them to leave me alone, and yet they persisted. In my defence, I warned them suitably, so I am not solely responsible for what happened next. Rishab held my hand to stop me from walking away, and I wrested myself free, picked up a stone and swung it at him. He staggered back in shock and put his hand on his forehead. It came back red. Arundhati and Sahil shouted at me together. While Arundhati ran to tend to her boyfriend, Sahil charged at me, and received the same treatment. I got him in his ear and he fell down smack on the ground.

Arundhati shouted, 'You are mental! So is your girlfriend! YOU BOTH ARE CRAZY.'

I dropped the stone. 'She's not my anything,' I had said and walked away.

Maa–Baba and Dada–Boudi had heard of what I had done and Dada had been the entrusted with the responsibility of bringing me back to real life. Numerous times I have thought of telling him the truth about Maa–Baba, of my almost-firm plan of ending my life, but the thought of Meenakshi (possibly) has kept me from it. Dada has taken the task quite seriously. It started with him taking me to gaming arcades, which distracted me for a maximum of a couple of minutes.

'You know how you will heal?' he had said. 'By going everywhere you have been with her.'

'Sounds like the worst plan of all time.'

'You didn't let me complete. We will go and make better memories.'

'It keeps getting worse.'

I tried it just to make Dada stop talking and get busy thinking his idea was working. A short visit to Keventer's made me so depressed that the plan was aborted like many others that followed.

'I miss my old brother,' he often said.

'I miss everything about the old times, Dada. But that's not going to change anything, is it?'

'God, why are you so depressing?'

I wish I could tell him.

He took another line of approach—just dragging me along to wherever he went. He let me in on a big, happy secret after a lot of gushing and beating around the bush.

'I'm thinking of buying a new flat,' he said. 'Maa has been asking Zubeida and me to shift to their flat what with the kid coming. But you know how small that flat is, so I was thinking, why not shift to a bigger flat? I told Maa today I am moving into their flat.'

'Why—'

'Just listen. I'm hoping to close the deal before Zubeida delivers. After that I will surprise them with the new flat. What do you think?' he asked and stared at me for affirmation.

'That's stupid. You can't live with Maa–Baba,' I said.

'Why not? It will be fun. And it will be better for the child as well.'

None of my arguments held water. He was still going ahead with his stupid plan because he didn't know the truth. He dragged me to every building I had been to, that I had marked and checked the roofs of, and others I hadn't, and asked for my opinion of it. I rejected every one of them because I knew he wasn't going to stay in any of them after I told them what Maa–Baba really thought of them. But I let him have his moment for now. Why spoil what would be one of the most beautiful moments of his life?

He would walk around the empty flats, tell me where he would put what, which bed would be placed where, where the crib would go, how big the kitchen would be, how we would place the air conditioner if we bought one. His excitement was infectious and disgusting. It gave me a troubling insight on Dada, which crushed my heart. He had been more devastated than any of us after he had had to leave the house. His version of the future had all of us living together, even Didimaa and Mama, and dogs, in a big house overlooking a garden and little kids running around. Of course, what else could you expect out of someone appallingly optimistic? Dada has only chosen to see the good in people. Stupid as he is, he is even counting on Boudi's family eventually coming around and accepting him and the child. In his vision, we will be the epitome of Muslim–Hindu unity, both families living under one roof in the middle of Delhi. So naive of him.

Some time or the other, he would slip in a question about Brahmi. He would see the look on my face and not probe further.

A couple of days back, Richa Mittal bumped into me while I distributed prasad to the beggars outside the temple and said, 'I heard you are shifting.'

I wasn't even surprised this time.

She continued, 'Don't forget to tell her your address.'

'Are you referring to yourself as her?' I scoffed.

She glared at me and left.

Dada and I spent the entire day together. We had to pack up their house and shift everything they had into our flat.

He looked happy and I was repulsed by his foolish happiness. While he packed, he told me, 'Get into IIT Delhi. I don't want you to move out.'

'Why? Madras is much better,' I said to humour him.

'Your Boudi and I want you to stay with us. Four years is a long time and your nephew or niece would like you to be around. You wouldn't want to be away,' he said.

For the next few minutes, that thought did play on my mind. Would it be as easy to pull myself away from that little child and throw myself off a roof? Would it prevent me from doing it? Would it be another peg which I would be tethered to and destined to walk around in circles? And what would he or she think of me when she grows up knowing her or his uncle killed himself within weeks of his or her birth? Would that little child be worth the suffering that would come? And in that moment, it struck me that I was already expecting to derive my happiness from someone who hadn't even opened her or his eyes, who was still floating in amniotic fluid. I was like Maa–Baba, who had never stopped deriving their happiness out of us and when we failed to supply that, they turned against us like a virulent disease.

'I will think about it,' I said.

'What's there to think about? You will score well, I know. Just choose Delhi in counselling. Don't be a pain.'

'I told you I will think about it.'

Dada was clearly pissed because he didn't talk to me for an hour. On our way back I said, 'Dada?'

'What?' he asked irritably.

'I love you.'

'What a stupid thing to say to your brother,' he said and laughed at his own wisecrack.

I hope he remembers this.

It took us five trips between the two houses to shift everything. All the while I was thinking how long it would take Dada to shift out of the house. How much would he leave behind? How much would he take with him?

29 February 2000

It's a leap year.

Today's the day that comes once every four years.

But today it changes.

This day will come every day.

Dada died today.

I'm writing these words to make them sound real to me.

He didn't suffer, the doctors told us, the LPG blast would have been too quick, and too severe to be felt.

I disagree.

Between Dada's realization of the blue spark, and his heart coming to a stop, Dada would have felt everything. The second Dada would have switched the light on in that living room filled with LPG, and seen that spark billow into something more, he would have been filled with horror. Dada would have wondered how it could be, the fire, the din of the blast, and then the force crushing his body. In the first few microseconds, Dada would have taken it lightly, thought the flame would be little and brief, but in the very next moment he would have thought otherwise, his body floating, golden flames licking every part him. He would have felt the searing heat, he would have felt the skin melt off him, his organs would have singed, every tissue Maa gave Dada in her womb for nine months shrivelling, charring. Dada would have felt the unbearable physical pain of his body disintegrating. Fists clenched, jaws locked, vocal chords strained, he would have screamed. And then the pain would have become too much to bear. The brain would have cut off the pain synapses. And he would have looked inwards. Dada would have realized these were his last few seconds. His thoughts would have turned to Boudi and his child. A tear would have come to his eye, evaporating instantly in the heat. The entire life of his envisioned future would have passed in front of his eyes like a flip booklet. His heart would have grown heavy, he would have said a little prayer, he would have hoped for a miracle to see his baby grow up, to love her, to love Boudi, to live a life full of joy and sadness and success and disappointment. He would have made deals with god. 'Make me live, anyhow, crippled, burnt, half dead, but make me live,' he would have said. His bones would have cracked and melted under the heat. He would have thought of Maa–Baba, he would have thought of their sadness on his death, he would have imagined Maa going mad, Baba growing quiet, he would have thought, his body now getting charred, about all the things Maa–Baba forwent for his happiness. He would remember things he had long forgotten, coming to him in rushes of memories. Of the times when he was three or six or twelve or fourteen, of the days Maa–Baba were younger and capable of loving things other than their sons but chose to love them. His organs would have been shutting down by now, shredded apart by the vigour of the marching fire, and his thoughts would have turned to me, the stuck-up, strange brother, the brother whom he dearly loved from the first day he would have seen him, but who only looked at his Dada as a competitor for Maa–Baba's love and affection. With his heart slowing down, he would have managed a smile thinking that his brother would now get all the love from Maa–Baba since he would be . . .

With his heart now shutting down, his thoughts would have turned to Boudi, the feeling of being in love so irrevocably, of the feeling of it having happened to him, he would have muttered an apology for leaving her alone, a confession of his love would have escaped his lips just before the lights of his eyes would have gone out.

Darkness.

Dada left us.

5 March 2000

The last four days have been a haze, a toxic, strangling daze.

Every time I blink I wish this to be over, for this to be a substitute reality. It's hardly believable or fair.

Maa–Baba have been inconsolable. Maa has been to the hospital twice after fainting, her BP swaying wildly and dangerously, and every time she has wished she would die of it. Baba is mostly quiet, like me, trying to wrap his head around what happened, to make sense of it, to wait for things to go back to what they were before, to know if it's even true or it's an elaborate sham and Dada would come out of hiding and shout, 'Got you.'

Didimaa has been hysterical. The one day we saw her she started laughing, beating her chest, crying, all at once. To everyone's surprise, she got up from the wheelchair, and slapped Maa, and fell back on the ground. She was taken away. Maa had cried out, 'Why didn't she die instead?'

Relatives have been pouring in and out every day, trying to console Maa–Baba. Over the years, their envy of our relative prosperity has rankled them, but their grief over the death is real, their tears are real. It is not that they loved Dada as much but because they feel the loss. They have imagined losing someone close, they have put themselves in our shoes and then cried a little inside. They know what it feels like and they have been doing everything for Maa–Baba, Boudi and me. But even then, I know these distractions will end soon. Everyone will leave our house and slowly they will get absorbed in their own lives and they will forget about Dada, not miss his presence, not be able to feel the pain any longer till the time someone else dies. I don't resent them for it, it's just the way it is.

I wonder if Baba's doing what I'm doing in his silence. If he's lining up the perpetrators behind Dada's death. It was we who killed Dada, every one of us. If eye for an eye were an acceptable justice protocol, we should all have been shot in the head.

On the 29th of February, exactly five days ago, Boudi had asked for the charger of her PowerBook. Then she had changed her mind, saying that it wasn't really needed, like a dutiful daughter-in-law should.

But Maa said, 'No, no, Anirban will get it. You must get bored sitting at home and doing nothing.'

Had Boudi not asked for the charger, Dada would still have been amongst us, and how apt, killing the person you most love. Living for each other, dying for each other, that kind of thing. Absolutely romantic and absolutely revolting. Was she thinking that none of this would have happened had she not fallen in love with Dada? Had she not moved from Bangalore?

Had her parents accepted her, her pregnancy would have been their responsibility and not Dada's. She is quite clearly the culprit. I hope she knows that.

But then there's Maa, my lovely, lovely Maa, the mother of three children, of whom only one survives now and that too barely.

Had Maa not acted about how concerned she was about Boudi, Dada would have still been alive, counting days backwards to the birth of his first child. Had Maa not been acting to keep up the charade of the concerned mother-in-Law, Dada would have still been here. Does she care if Boudi is bored? No, she doesn't. If it were up to her, she could have put Boudi under sedatives for the entire duration of the pregnancy, deliver the child herself, taken the baby and raised her or him like a good Hindu Bengali citizen. She clearly murdered my Dada.

But why only her? My hands are stained too with Dada's blood.

Had I not judged Maa for her behaviour, had I not ruined my relationships with Rishab and Sahil and Brahmi, had I not been wallowing in my own pain, I would have gotten up, told everyone that I would get the charger instead of Dada, had gone to their old home, unlocked the door, switched on the lights, and waited for that little spark of the switch to ignite the room full of cooking gas and it would have been me instead of Dada. I wouldn't have minded that one bit. Who would have missed me? In the longer run, no one really.

But that's not even the worst part. The worst part is had I gone right then, the room wouldn't have filled up because it wasn't until two hours later that Dada reached the flat.

But Baba can't claim innocence either.

Baba and Dada had both gone to pick up the charger. Baba had chosen to stay down and smoke, something he rarely does. He had asked Dada to go on alone. I wonder what Baba feels, almost literally pushing Dada to his death? But had they both gone? How would that have ended? Does Baba think that if only he had more things to talk about with Dada, he would have gone up with him, and died with him? Or maybe he would have smelt the LPG, having had more years of experience of being in the kitchen?

Like me, Maa has been shifting blame. First it was mostly herself and then it was me.

'You should have gone instead! YOU!' Maa had screamed at me for an entire hour, the same sentence over and over again till she fainted.

Then it was Baba.

'Why did you leave him! Why!' she had bawled in Baba's arms for hours, hitting him, slapping him, till she had fallen asleep.

But now, I think she has finally found the person she would always blame Dada's accident on—Boudi. It's hard to see the malice that's fermenting behind the grief. But it's there and I fear the worst.

I miss you, Dada. I hate you for leaving us like this. I hate that we have ceremonies to do in your name. I hate that Baba behaves like there's peace in the afterlife and that it's god's will, that pujas and fasts will help. They won't. There's just death and that's it. There's nothing beyond it. Maa–Baba have each other in their grief, Dada, but where do I go? Rishab and Arundhati came to talk to me yesterday but I blame them for your death too so I didn't talk to them. Later when I went for a walk, I saw them sharing an ice cream. They were laughing and talking like nothing had happened. Why would I want to share my sadness with them? Didn't your death make them sad enough to not laugh? To not have an ice cream? To not be in love? And what do I say about Boudi? Irrationally I want to believe that there's an afterlife like Baba says, that you're looking down and watching over Boudi. Everyone has been crying, beating their chests, she has been mostly quiet. Her eyes are always bloodshot but no one has seen her cry. Her religion kept her away from you even in your death. Yesterday, I saw her bury a picture of you.

7 March 2000

The stream of relatives is unending. People I don't remember but who claim to have held me when I was little, women who say I vomited on them as a child, men who say I bullied them into giving me candies, are crawling like ants, turning our building into their nest. Their grieving process is already over. Sadder over Dada's death are the Mittals who have taken in many of our relatives, and so are the Bhattacharyas whose house is littered with Gangulys, Dattas, Mitras and Ghoshes and neither of the families have let out a groan. The relatives, like relatives ought to behave, have taken to complaining about food and water and comfort. To see them laugh, smile, discuss politics and food and how polluted Delhi's slowly becoming gets on my nerves and so I have taken to going on long walks.

On every walk, I bump into precisely what I run from. Someone who never mattered to me and vice versa; someone who sympathizes with the situation.

And today's highlight was Brahmi. Like last time, as I ought to do, I walked away from her but she caught up with me.

'You need to talk to me,' she said, her eyes tearing up.

'Oh, you're crying? Great.'

'You don't get to make fun of my sadness. I knew your Dada too.'

'Yes, for probably a few hours. A little less than me, don't you think? My Dada burned to death, not yours, so I can do whatever the hell I want to do.'

'I'm sorry. I . . . just wanted to see how you're doing.'

I stopped, turned towards her, and in the rudest, coldest tone, I told her, 'Fine. Here's my answer. I'm good. I'm sad but it will get better. When and how I'm not sure yet but it will. I accept your condolences. Is that enough? Now you can go wherever you came from.'

I turned away from her and started walking away. She didn't let up. She held my hand and stopped me. I wrested my hand free and shouted, 'WE ARE NOT HOLDING HANDS ANY MORE.'

She staggered a few steps back, surprised at my outburst.

'I want to be there for you.'

'Well, you can't! That ship has sailed!'

'Raghu, don't be like that. Talk to me.'

'Now I should talk to you? Now! When my Dada is dead? Is that what it took to make you talk to me?' I snapped.

'Raghu, you have to understand.'

'What the fuck do I understand? That you walked away the time I needed you the most? That all I wanted was for you to want to be with me? That you broke my heart into a million pieces? Where do I begin to start understanding you? Where?'

'From where we were friends and we could tell each other things,' she said.

'Tell each other? It was only me doing the talking, not you!' I said. 'You have only lied to me.'

'Raghu, you have to—'

'WHAT! WHAT! Understand? No, I won't understand! I won't damn understand. Do you hear me? I won't. No. And definitely not from you. You're just a lying, deceitful girl! You know what? You know what?'

'Don't—'

'You should be glad your parents are not around to see you!' I shouted.

In that moment, I didn't regret those words. The words broke her, which is exactly what they were intended to do. The tears started to pour. I watched her standing bolted to the ground, head hung low, staring at her feet, crying. I watched till I thought she should cry for her abandonment of me and then I went on my own way. In the temple, I prayed for forgiveness, not for the consequences of my action but for the action itself. I came back home, wanting to see her again, and every time I reminded myself of what she had done to me. I thought I was going absolutely crazy when in the night I saw her from my balcony, standing at a distance, eyes still teary. It had been at least three hours since our showdown. It didn't move me. It made me angry. So I stood there, calmly, smoked a cigarette and watched her cry for an hour before I was called in. The next time I was out in the balcony, she was gone.

I was asked to take bedding for our lovely relatives to the Mittals. Richa and I were making their beds when she said, 'Brahmi was there for three hours.'

'That's what you want to talk to me about? Not about how you're in love with me?'

Richa laughed derisively and said, 'I'm not but she is, even after what you said to her today.'

'I just want to make this bed and be done with it,' I said.

'It was not her first time,' she said.

Of all the times, this is when Richa decides she has a tongue, can form words, and give it velocity and meaning.

'She has been coming here for two months, probably more. Every other day, she's there.'

'You're crazier than I thought. That was months ago,' I said. 'We broke up.'

'I know that and yet she was here all this time, even after the relationship ended. The next time you call me crazy, I will

push a flowerpot on your head when you're in your balcony,'
said Richa.

'Why was she here? Are . . . Are you sure?' I asked.

She didn't choose to answer me and was called by her
mother. I ran to my balcony. No, she wasn't there.

Now that I'm writing this I think there are only two
reasons why she would do what Richa tells me she does.
Either she's in love with me. Which begs the question, why
would she let me lose her?

The second one is . . . if she has put a date on her death . . .
I need to see her.

10 March 2000

The official period of mourning has now ended.

Isn't it just great? The official period of mourning? So what are we supposed to do now? Stop remembering you, Dada? Now wouldn't that be convenient.

Because unlike Maa, Baba and I don't know how to deal with it. Only today, Maa went to the meat shop herself—for the first time in years—and got salami for all of us to eat. She made sandwiches for everyone for breakfast.

'We have been having bland food for so long that I thought we should have something special today,' she said.

Boudi just happened to check what salami went into the sandwich.

Maa said, 'It's pork.'

When she saw Boudi leave the table she nonchalantly said, 'I didn't think you were that devout.'

Later when Boudi cried, Maa cried with her, told her that she didn't know what came over her. Baba apologized to her as well, equally profusely, if not more.

'We just miss him. She doesn't know how to deal with his loss,' said Baba over and over again.

Boudi acted graceful enough to accept the apologies but stayed locked in her room, presumably praying. I wondered if she had any other choice. But later tonight, I heard Maa saying, 'The more I think about it, the more it seems right. Had she not come into his life . . .'

I can't sleep thinking of what else Maa might do. A little while earlier, Boudi came to my room. She sat next to me, quiet. Then she got up and left.

No matter what Maa says, I know it won't be the last time she does something like this, I can see past her lies and I can see past her truths. It's only going to get worse from here. She would need me now more than ever. At least till the time she delivers and the child tempers Maa–Baba's grief, distracts them from the hate they feel for Boudi.

My attempts to reach out to Brahmi have been in vain. She had not been going to the office, or at least that's what the receptionist told me, and I was told off when I asked for her residential address.

Desperate, I asked for proof of life, at which the receptionist told me, she had checked in with her boss all three days she had been missing from office. Which only brings me to the question, why is she missing?

I'm sweating now, hardly sleeping for the past few nights, and I cry and shout at intervals. Is this what they call a panic attack? When you feel like the walls are closing in on you?

13 March 2000

My labour bore fruit today. I was lucky to find Brahmi. Lucky is probably the wrong word to use. I have felt like taking my own life a lot of times but not someone else's. But now I do. If I'm going to die eventually why not murder someone and then go? It's not something I haven't done before. Sami's blood is already on my hands, how would it matter if there's one more to add to that list? Only this time it would be well-deserved. Ever since I have met Brahmi, my fingers are twitching to do it. I'm doing better though. No more sweating, just naked anger. Now I wondering if pure hatred is the cure to pure grief. Could be, right?

Brahmi was surprised to see me. She thought I was there to share my loss of Dada with her, so she asked, concerned, 'Raghu? What are you doing here?'

'I have been coming here for a week. Where have you been?'

'I wasn't well,' she said, clearly lying.

'Richa told me you have been coming to my house even after the break-up. I know it's true so don't refute it. Just tell me why?'

She looked at me for a minute. Her brain must have been processing a pretext, a lie she could come up with, and she failed for once.

'Ran out of lies? Tell me why were you there? You broke up with me, you wouldn't reach out to me and yet you would be there and watch me. Why?'

She had nothing to say.

'Sit here,' I said and she did. I took her hand into mine and asked her softly, 'Tell me? You can tell me. For once, please just tell me.'

She held her demeanour for a bit and then showed me her wrist which had up till now been covered with her full-sleeved shirt. All our meetings post her joining work clicked into place, and I realized she had never not worn full-sleeved shirts. There were clotted bandages. She had cut again.

'It's Vedant,' she said.

'Why?'

While I held her hand, she told me how she had found Vedant's hidden video camera in the bathroom after a couple of weeks.

'Nothing got recorded. I made sure I put the towel on it before bathing. He must have thought he was out of luck.'

'Why didn't you do anything? Tell anyone?'

She didn't choose to answer that. What could she have done? Where would she have gone?

'He got tired eventually. One day I found the lock broken to the bathroom. He walked in and acted like it was an accident. I was . . . naked. From that day I stopped bathing when he was awake,' said Brahmi. 'His patience wore thin. He came home drunk one day with his friend. The minute I saw them at the door, I knew what they wanted from me. I ran and locked myself in. I cut myself while they banged at the door. He probably thought I was sleeping.'

She sighed. My hands had started to shake so she held them tight.

'Then?'

'The next day he saw the cuts and stayed away. He didn't know why I had cut myself but he stayed off me. Probably got scared that I might kill myself in his apartment. It worked for a while. I would cut myself, behave normally the next day, and he would be freaked out, not wanting to push me in any way,' she said.

'It was dangerous.'

She looked at me as if to say the same thing. What else could she have done? Report to the police?

I wanted to ask her why she didn't tell me. I had the answer. Every time she would have cut herself, she would have thought she would go through the entire way the next time. She wouldn't have wanted to drag me along. The further I was away from her, the better. That's why she welcomed my break-up, why she didn't fight for our relationship. Because she knew it had to end at one point or the other.

'Then it stopped deterring him,' she said. 'He brushed past me, hovered around me, and touched me. The more he did, the deeper my cuts got.'

'Now?' I asked, wanting to scout him out and gouge out his eyes.

Brahmi wiped her tears. 'I must go back. It's late.'

'How do you sleep at night?' I asked.

'With my door locked and with a knife under my pillow.'

A helpless silence descended over us. We knew the eventuality of this, of how it would end. We both must have gone through everything she has gone through up till now, how unfair life had been to her, and how there's only one way to mercifully put this unpitying existence to an end.

'We will get past this,' I said to her, my words hollow.

'How?'

'I will save you,' I said, desperately.

'Will you? Like you're saving yourself?' she said, a tear streaking down her cheek. 'Don't you see it? We are doomed, the hopes we had clung to, gone, our own brothers deceived us. We can't run away from it. Don't I know what you're waiting for?'

'What?'

'For Boudi's child, are you not?' she asked. She got up, not getting a response. 'That's why, you should go your own way, as I should mine. We will only want to drag out the inevitable, hope that one of us will save the other. It will all eventually come to naught, Raghu.'

I held her hand.

'You still love me, don't you?' I asked.

'Of course I do.'

'Can I ask you for something? Can you wait for me?'

I told her of the visions I had had when I had just begun to know her—of the two of us with slashed wrists, fingers entwined, on the top of the building. I knew it was unfair for me to tell her to wait; Brahmi couldn't have lived in that house any more. There's only one other place she could have lived—in the flat where Dada died. The lease was for a year and Baba wasn't ready to let go of the apartment yet. The police and the landlord had been sufficiently paid in money and in tears to hold on to Dada's tomb. Grief is a powerful thing. We have all been there—Maa, Baba, Boudi and I. The kitchen and the living room is wrecked, blackened with soot, walls half-broken, the blood washed off, but the bedroom is surprisingly untouched. The flat has no running water or electricity but it's a house. Brahmi said she would have her bag ready tomorrow.

17 March 2000

Maa is like an evil hamster in the wheel. She finds ways to hurt Boudi and then cries and apologizes to her. Boudi who has no one else to cry with always forgives her. Sometimes she finds succour in me. Only yesterday, Maa found the marriage certificate of Boudi and Dada in the almirah and set fire to it. Boudi cried when she found out but Maa cried harder.

Every time I step out of the house, leaving Boudi behind, I feel guilty. But I have to.

For the last four days, Brahmi has been living in Dada's old flat. Vedant hasn't and I believe won't come looking for her because she had left him a threatening letter.

From a part of her savings she bought a little kerosene stove where she cooks all three meals, even snacks.

'If these are going to be my last few days, I'd rather live like a queen,' she said the first day when I pointed to the packets of chips and biscuits lying around.

'Quite a palace you have,' I had remarked.

And today she said, 'It is not far from it. It feels like home. I feel safe here.'

'Ironical,' I said.

'Because I have you here. I feel safe. I feel wanted. I feel loved. When you leave everything behind and come here and spend time with me, I feel nice. In love. Look at you blush,' she said.

I felt the same about her despite the memories this flat held. Dada's words came forth in my head, when he had suggested we go to the same places and create more memories to overwrite the old ones. That's what Brahmi was doing. Not overwriting them but at least filling the blanks with happy memories.

'Thank you,' she said, holding my hand.

'I am doing it as much for me as for you,' I told her.

And why not? Only yesterday, I told Maa–Baba I would stay at Rishab's place and went to Dada's house instead. We spent the entire night talking. It was light by the time we had wrested our old life back. The same little room, the darkness, the quietude and the candle between the two of us.

Unlike then, now we know time's running out so we don't hold back on words. We tell each other we love each other more freely, without feeling shy, we hold each other's hand more tightly, we clutch each other with more authority, exercise more control over each other. In the afternoons, we sneak out of the building and walk around parks like an old couple. We laugh and we joke and we wonder what lies on the other side of death.

She still hasn't told me how and why her parents died or why she hid it from me and I haven't probed. If these were going to be the last few days of our lives, I would rather spend them smiling. What scares me now is the time I'm not with Brahmi, when she's all alone in that blackened house, sitting in the darkness with just herself, waiting for me.

Like every morning I woke up early to maintain the charade that I was still going to school. Only today, I woke up a little too early and overheard Maa–Baba talk. Usually there's nothing more than silent sobs but today was different.

'Don't worry. She will have to do what we want her to do,' said Baba.

'Are you sure? Zubeida is not any other girl. She's wily. She trapped my son. She's smart. She can do anything,' said Maa.

'How long will she fight us? She will have to give up, won't she?' said Baba.

Then their voices fell silent.

I couldn't take their depraved fantasies and their evil machinations against Boudi so I left to see Brahmi. I don't know what happened in my absence but Boudi went into labour early. When I reached home, it was Arundhati who told me of it and Bhattacharya Uncle drove me to the hospital. It wasn't as much a hospital but a ramshackle nursing home. Boudi was still under sedatives when I got to the hospital; the operation had been a long one. I saw Maa–Baba cradling a little boy to whom I was suddenly an uncle. It might be totally in my head but the boy looked like Dada from his baby pictures. When I held him I felt a rush of dopamine, a happiness I had only felt with Brahmi. I might have even cried a little. Then they took the baby and put him in a little crib. Maa–Baba stared at the crib and sobbed in happiness. They named the baby Anirban. I rushed to see Brahmi to give her the news. She hugged me, kissed me twice on my cheek, and told me how happy she was for me.

'Is he cute?'

And for long, we talked about the baby. I didn't know a minute with the baby could have given me an hour of material to talk about. I left Brahmi to see Anirban Jr again. Boudi was still under the effect of sedatives and the baby was in the crib next to her.

Maa–Baba spent the entire night in the hospital—I kept going to and fro, between Brahmi and Anirban Jr—after which Baba and I went home to get a change of clothes for Boudi. But once we were home, Baba packed not one change but almost all of Boudi's clothes into a suitcase.

'You don't have to come to the hospital with me right now,' he said. 'We will come home with the baby.'

I nodded. When Baba left I went to see Brahmi, who expressed her desire to see the baby as well. 'Soon,' I told her. Sometime between all the baby talk, we would fall silent. We were both aware that the clock had started to tick. But neither of us mentioned it today. Today was a happy day. Till . . .

Baba had lied through his teeth. He came back home alone and without the suitcase. There was no Maa, there was no baby.

'Where's Boudi? Where's Anirban?'

'Maa's taken Anirban away. Boudi is not going to be living here.'

Baba told me, as dispassionately as he could, that they couldn't have allowed the boy to be raised by her, not after all that she had done. So they paid for her bills and left her there. Baba told me as if he was being benevolent, 'We have also deposited enough money in her account to last years.'

'For now, Maa has taken the child and gone to a relative's and Zubeida won't see the baby till she agrees to what we want.'

'Which relative?' I asked. 'What do you want? How the hell could you—'

It was answered by a resounding slap.

'You will go to jail for this,' I shouted.

'No, we won't!' Baba shouted back.

I tried to leave the house but I had forgotten how strong Baba is. He dragged me to my room and locked me inside.

'WHAT ARE YOU TRYING TO DO?' I shouted, my heart thumping out of my chest, disbelief and anger washing over me. How could Maa–Baba do this? What could they possibly want from Boudi? What kind of a monster rips a baby out of a new mother's arms? And for what! FOR WHAT! What family am I born into? How damaged are they? I banged the door to no avail, screaming till I lost my voice. I heard the bell ring a few times so I knew my voice had reached out to the Bhattacharyas and the Mittals. But Baba drove them away. Brahmi must be waiting for me.

Boudi must be waiting for me.

Crushed, I slumped against the door. That's when I heard a slight knocking from the other side of the door. It was Arundhati. I asked Arundhati to reach out to Brahmi, tell her about my house arrest. I skipped the details which would have made her uncomfortable. She, in turn, called Rishab who drove to Dada's house and told Brahmi that I wouldn't be coming any time soon. Rishab passed on the news to Arundhati, and questions of why I was locked up in my room, why was Brahmi was living in a squalid, wrecked apartment, and what the hell exactly was going on. I didn't have the strength or the inclination to say anything so I crawled away from the wall, into a little ball, and felt like dying.

I'm waiting for Baba to open the door.

21 March 2000

Boudi was at the door today. She bawled and cried. I am still locked inside but I could hear every word that was being said outside. Like I had imagined, Boudi threatened Baba and Bhattacharya Uncle, who had been enlisted to Maa–Baba's cause, with legal action. She couldn't form complete sentences. She would break down after every word. I now know what Maa–Baba had wanted from Boudi.

Baba gave Boudi a simple choice: rethink her faith, and they would be happy to let her back into their lives, to be a mother, to be their daughter-in-law, live with them as their own. Baba promised—in what was his grandest speech of all time—that she would be loved and cared for, everything that has happened will be relegated to a forgotten drawer, and they would start a new life together.

Baba wasn't just words. He had papers drawn up that said Boudi and Boudi alone, if and when she changes her religion, would be the sole heir to all that the Gangulys owned. Maa–Baba had put their money where their mouth was, they had committed their madness to paper, and they were convinced about going through with it. Baba broke down twice, like men do, while saying all that he had to say. In his endless impassioned speech he told Boudi that they never blamed her, only her religion and that unholy alliance, which has brought destruction to the Gangulys, and they can't let that affect their grandson, there was too much at stake. He invoked his love and despair for his dead son, swore on Dada's memories, and told Boudi that they would love her

more than they love themselves. Boudi had cried profusely all
through . . . muttering Anirban's name again and again and again.
The voices died down after a while. Boudi had gone.

In the afternoon, Baba unlatched the door to my room.
When I walked out, Baba was surprised to see the bat in one hand,
and a bag in the other. He came close and I swung. When the bat
was in the air, in those few seconds, I realized I felt nothing for
Maa–Baba. I hadn't pulled back on my swing, all my familial love
had drained out, nothing pulled me back. I was hitting a stranger,
or an enemy. Pure, distilled hatred. The tie had snapped. There
was no metaphorical umbilical cord between me and them.

I caught his arm. He staggered out of the way.

'What will Maa think?' he shouted.

'I don't care what you think!' I shouted back. 'Give Boudi
her baby back. He is her son!'

'We don't care! He is our grandchild, he is Anirban's son
and she's getting no one! NOT UNLESS SHE AGREES TO
WHAT WE SAY!' shouted Baba. 'If you want to leave, you
can leave! Go, do it! You haven't made us proud. Don't think
we don't know that you were there in his marriage to this . . .
girl! GO! GO, wherever you want to go.'

I stood there, my feet bolted to the ground. I thought I
would cry but the tears didn't come. Emptiness. I left with Baba
shouting his curses behind me. His words crashed against my
eardrums and didn't reach my brain. I didn't leave. I couldn't
do it. The face of that little child Anirban hovered in front of
me. I couldn't see Boudi being left alone. What would Dada
think of me? Would he not haunt me if life after death exists?
Baba called me a coward when I went back to my room, still
smarting from the assault. In the evening, I cried into Brahmi's
arms, who told me I was the exact opposite—brave.

'You need to stand by your Boudi,' she said.

We spent the night together, mostly silent.

23 March 2000

Baba and I haven't talked in two days. He walks about in the house like an evil warlord. Maybe he's sad, maybe he's unhinged now but I don't care. All I know is I'm ashamed that it was him who brought me to this world. My hope that Boudi would come back was dwindling. The phone was unhooked so I didn't know where Maa had taken Anirban. The more time went by, the more I got fidgety, wondering if he was even in the city any more. I couldn't go and see Brahmi, scared that Boudi might come when I'm not at home. It was in the evening, and Baba was watching the TV like nothing was wrong in the world while everything was, when there was a knock on the door. My ears were pricked and I ran to the door. Baba followed after.

I opened the door and there she was. Just as Didimaa had foreseen.

Boudi without her burqa. I gasped. She looked straight through me at Baba. Her eyes empty, like the soul had been sucked out of her. Baba opened the door wider, and welcomed her inside. Baba and Boudi looked at each other for the briefest second. Boudi walked inside.

Baba closed the door behind her.

'Call Maa,' she said. 'I'm ready to do what you say.'

She used the word Maa. She couldn't look up to see me.

'Boudi, you can't do that,' I said and Baba raised his hand to smack me and I readied myself to fend off that blow when Boudi shouted.

'Raghu! It's what I have decided.'

'You can't do this,' I said.

'It's not your decision to take,' she said.

'Shut up, Raghu,' said Baba.

'One more word, Baba, and I will not stop at just one blow.'

Baba's glowered at me in anger, probably wondering if I would go through with it. He knew I would.

'That's not the way to talk to your father,' said Boudi. 'Get out of the house if that's how you have to talk to him. Your Dada wouldn't have wanted to see you like this.'

'He wouldn't have wanted what you're doing either!'

'I DON'T WANT TO HEAR ANYTHING FROM YOU,' shouted Boudi with a dying screech. 'STAY QUIET OR GET LOST.' She looked at Baba and said politely, 'Ask Maa to come home.'

I looked at Boudi, at her dead eyes, at her pale skin. Maa–Baba had made her bow down, killed her spirit, did the worst that could have possibly happened to her. She looked . . . dead. Her child was all she wanted. No matter what I said, it wouldn't have changed things.

Baba dialled the number. While Baba talked to Maa in the other room, a single word escaped my lips.

'Why?' I asked.

'Does god even exist?' she answered.

'Did you—'

'My parents told me it was what I deserved.'

There was nothing else to say. Baba came and asked Boudi to talk to Maa. Baba put the phone on speaker. Boudi talked politely, and so did Maa, who even cried. I heard Anirban crying in the background. Boudi requested Maa to come back home, and Maa told Boudi how happy they were to be a family again.

There was nothing left for me there.

I packed a little bag, apologized for everything to Boudi, told Baba that I would never see him again, and left the house. While leaving, Baba shouted and reminded me that I was a coward. That I would stay at a friend's place for a few days and come back home with my tail between my legs. I looked at both Baba and Boudi, standing next to each other, and my heart broke. I looked at the house, the stairs, the nameplate, and took it all in for the last time.

I knew I was never coming back. Brahmi was waiting for me when I got there. It's time to do what we had always planned to.

Much time has gone by.

24 March 2000

I had wanted to jump off yesterday.

It's an irony, isn't it? The same building claiming the lives of two brothers. It's Brahmi who stopped me.

'Wouldn't you want to see your nephew Anirban once?' she asked.

So today morning, both she and I stood outside my house, the house I thought I had seen the last of, and waited for Maa to come home. It wasn't until late evening that a taxi stopped outside the house and Maa stepped out of the car with Anirban wrapped in a little white cloth. Baba and Boudi who were in the balcony rushed down to see Anirban. Boudi touched Maa's feet and then took her baby into her arms. The baby and she both cried. The Bhattacharyas and the Mittals too joined in, and they all baby-talked to Anirban, told Maa–Baba how cute he was. Then they all moved inside the building.

We were outside the house for another hour to see if they came to the balcony. When they didn't we turned to get back to the building.

Brahmi and I cleaned the bedroom the best we could. We threw out the garbage, folded out clothes, and packed our bags the best we could. The electric stove went to the watchman, the clothes to the nearby slum. It was late by the time we came back to the threadbare bedroom of Dada's flat. We walked around, taking it in for the last time, reminiscing about the odd week we spent there, the best of times, the worst of times.

Then we stepped out, locked the door and walked up to the terrace. The city was awake, lights twinkling, dinners being served, normal-relationship roles being performed. We sat there silently waiting for everyone to go to sleep.

We didn't say it but I knew we were thinking of the motion of events our deaths will unfold. This diary would be found for one. I hope Maa–Baba, Tauji–Taiji see how wrong they were; nothing will happen to Vedant in the longer run but it might give him a few sleepless nights at least. We held hands, waiting for the inevitable. When you're this close to death, your words assume an extraordinary power. We all remember and disseminate the last words of a dying man or woman. So we chose to keep quiet till Brahmi told me I should write the last diary entry. 'I don't want to let go of your hand,' I said.

'I have to write something for you,' she said.

I tore a page from my diary and gave it to her. For a long time she stared at it before she started to write. And then I got down to write the last words I will ever write.

'I love you, Brahmi. You're sitting in front of me and I want to tell you that I love you. You're smiling at me while I write this. Of course, you're going to read this in a while before we step over the ledge and I hope your last smile is because of me. Wouldn't that be a fitting end to our love story? I can thump my chest and claim our story is the greatest in the world. We loved, lived, and now will die together. Who can match up to that? I know, I know it's not a competition but we both love competition, don't we? So let's just say we win this one. You're so beautiful, I have to tell you this one more time. The world won't see more of you and it's a darn shame. To think I existed without you sounds absolutely impossible. You're blushing because I'm looking at you. You're asking me to look away. You're asking me to stop looking at you because you can't write otherwise. So I look away. I'm thinking of all the times we have spent together. Even in the darkest of times, you were the light I could always hold on to, and I'm thankful to you for that. Now you're getting up, walking towards me. In your hand is the letter you want to give me.'

'Read it once you're done writing,' you say and walk away from me and towards the ledge.

You're standing at the edge, stretching your hand out to me, waiting for me. Come, you're saying. You have stepped on the ledge, your hair blowing wildly. Hands outstretched, you have closed your eyes. You seem happy, lovely. Wait, I got to finish this and you have to read it. I should leave now. Close this book, read your letter and come to you. You're asking me to hold your hand. And now you're turning away from me. You are saying something but I can't hear you. It's too windy. You're crying now. Now you're smiling. I'm done. I love you, Brahmi. Now, give me a moment while I read your letter.

Hey Raghu,

I am at the ledge and you think what you're writing is the last of what you will ever write. You're thinking I will read it and smile and I am sure if I do I will smile but there's no time left for me. You are a lovely person. Raghu, you have the power to be happy and to make others happy, and you should be that person more often. You have the power to love, and the power to change, and you're a survivor unlike me. You're brave and I'm not. Didn't we always talk about how brave it is to die? No, it's not. It's brave to survive. to live the years god has given us. to hold close our happiness in the times of sorrow and to live on.

You can do that. I can't.

You have the capacity to live for others. Like this morning. didn't you agree in a second when I asked you if you wanted to see your nephew? You did because you have an unending capacity to love. to give, to live for others. And what kind of a person would I be if I snatch someone like you away from the world? Ask yourself what your answer would be if I had given you the option of staying in your Dada's flat. just you and I. scraping by. existing. You would have picked me and life. You would have done anything to keep happy. It's because you're a nice person. Raghu. You believe love overcomes all. the deepest of pains. the hardest of times. You gave me the best few. months of my life and I'm thankful for that. You were the only part of my life that was worth living for. Don't beat yourself up when I'm gone because it won't be your fault. I was always a goner. A bit crazy. mental. as my relatives always thought of me. I died the day my parents died. After that it was just a matter of time.

Now I think all I was waiting for was you. to fall in love with you. to have someone love me as selflessly as you do. you were god's consolation prize for my defeat in life.

You saw me differently, and I can't thank you enough for it. But I can't be with you, Raghu. I can't drag you into my sadness. So let me go. Look up and smile at me. Before I jump off this ledge, I want to look at you one last time. Don't try to run or talk. It's too late. Just look at me, smile at me, and don't be shocked. This is our last moment. I want us to smile. You're probably crying right now. That's okay. You will cry for a few days, mourn my absence, but you will get over it, Raghu. You deserve all the happiness in the world. You have a lot of time. You're not going to die today. You have a long, fulfilling life to live. You have to live. For my sake. And some day you will find someone who will love you more than I ever did, and that day you will thank me. Now it's time for me to go. When I jump, don't follow me, don't try to save me. Save yourself instead. If you have ever loved me, don't come after me. Now look up at me and smile. Don't cry, smile. Yes, that smile. That sunshine. That light, my love. It's my time to go. Bye, Raghu. I love you. I will always love you.

She jumped.